I0726813

THE WICKED WIFE

A MURDER IN MARIN MYSTERY – BOOK 2

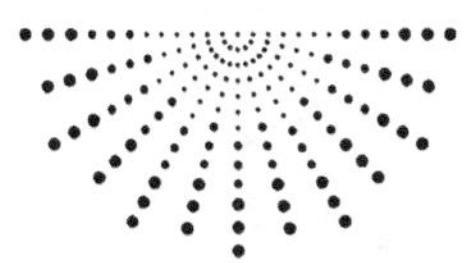

MARTIN BROWN

A BOOK BY

SIGNAL
PRESS

NOVELS IN THE MURDER IN MARIN SERIES

The Gossiping Gourmet

(Book 1)

The Wicked Wife

(Book 2)

The Phantom Photographer

(Book 3)

The Terrible Teacher

(Book 4)

The Horrible Husband

(Book 5)

Coming 2019

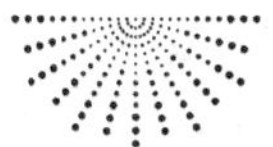

A few minutes after five o'clock on a Friday afternoon, near the end of another busy week, Rob Timmons, publisher of the Standard Community Newspapers, and Holly Cross, his production manager, were both surprised to hear the office's doorbell ring.

"Who the heck is that?" Holly snapped, more than ready to get out of the office and start her weekend.

"Whoever it is, I hope they're in and out of here in a hurry," Rob replied. "We're supposed to meet Eddie for drinks at Smitty's in less than thirty minutes."

"I better go take a look."

Holly rushed past Rob and looked down the steep staircase from the top floor landing of the two-story Victorian walk-up that housed the newspaper. "It's Sylvia Stokes. What do you suppose she wants?"

Sylvia, a tall, lean woman, who at sixty-four was approximately thirty years older than either Holly or Rob, was the community reporter for the Standard's Peninsula edition.

"Well, buzz her in," Rob replied. "Let's find out."

Hearing the buzzer, Sylvia pushed the door opened. Then,

gripping the aging wood banister, stepped energetically up the steep, dimly lit stairs.

"What's up?" Holly asked as Sylvia hurried past.

"Terrible news I'm afraid!" Sylvia replied ominously. "I was coming over the bridge, on my way home from the city, when I got a call from my husband, Jack. Oh, it's just so sad!"

"Well, don't keep us in the dark!" Holly prodded. Her appetite for hard news was exceeded only by her hunger for local gossip.

Rob sat down at his desk expecting to hear bad news.

"You both know the name William Adams, don't you?"

"Of course," Rob said. "He and his wife Fran are on the Forbes list of the world's wealthiest people. Highly successful venture capitalists. They live up near the top of Belvedere, on Golden Gate Avenue."

"Yes, exactly, well there's been a terrible accident."

"Oh my God!" Holly exclaimed breathlessly. "Are they dead?"

"No, not both—just Fran! She died in a skiing accident up at Heavenly, not far from their new home on Lake Tahoe."

"That's pretty sad," Rob said. "How old was she?"

"Fran and William were both the same age, fifty-five."

"Yikes! Any details on how the accident happened?" Holly asked.

"From what Jack heard from one of his friends over at Berkeley, Fran went missing yesterday near sunset when she went off course on a downhill run. The ski patrol didn't find her until noon today. She collided with a tree. Apparently, she died instantly. Jack told me it's called blunt force something."

"Blunt force trauma," Rob said softly. "In this case the result of a body in motion meeting an immovable object."

"Wow, that's so sad. I imagine they'll have a service for her either in Tiburon or Belvedere?" Holly asked.

"They were both members of the congregation Jack and I have been part of for years, St. Stephen's Episcopal Church in Belvedere. I assume that's where they'll hold the service."

"How well do you know them?" Rob asked.

"Jack and William met because both are active in a UC Berkeley alumni group, but we've never been close. As you can imagine, we travel in different circles, but we're certainly acquaintances, neighbors, even friends of a sort."

"They have any kids?" Holly asked.

"No. I suppose they never found the time to start a family. They invited us to a big twentieth-anniversary party they threw at their home. That was just four months ago," Sylvia said as she was again caught by the realization that lives can change in an instant. "They were both corporate attorneys who worked with high-tech companies and became investors in many of those firms. At the party, they explained that they had known each other for years but never found time to date. It was years after they met at law school that they decided to marry. They referred to it as part marriage, part merger. Everything in their lives, including romance, appeared to take a back seat to their work."

"Well, Holly and I have a standing date every Friday at five to meet our friend Eddie Austin over at Smitty's for an end-of-the-week cocktail. Would you care to join us?" Rob asked.

"No, I'd like that, but Jack and I have a dinner date with friends over in Tiburon at six. We should talk further about coverage of Fran's service. On the Peninsula, this is going to be a big story."

"Call my cell anytime over the weekend with developments, and text Holly when you have the date and time of the Adams service. I'll try to get our best community photographer, Michael Marks in Mill Valley, to go over to Belvedere for the service and shoot some photos to go along with your story. Poor William Adams must be devastated."

"I'm sure he is, Rob," Sylvia said as she got up to leave with both him and Holly.

Rob, stunned by the sad news, shook his head and said, "All the money in the world can never make up for a tragic loss like this."

Detective Eddie Austin was already into his first Guinness beer when Rob and Holly came into Smitty's, a favorite neighborhood dive bar on Sausalito's Caledonia Street. Located in the center of the only commercial streets that day tourists rarely visit, Smitty's was always quiet in the late afternoon. In four hours the music would be booming, and a group of locals would be celebrating the end of another work week. But at this time the three of them could have a drink or two in relative privacy and downshift from a demanding workweek into a hopefully restful weekend.

"Sorry we're a little late," Rob said, sitting down in one of the bar's aged dark maple wood mid-century captain's chairs. Tables and chairs were scattered haphazardly about the hardwood floor that on Friday and Saturday nights doubled as a dance floor. All three of them, as Sausalito natives, assumed little had changed inside Smitty's over the one hundred years of its history. That was undoubtedly part of its allure.

Holly waved to Gail, the only waitress on the floor at that hour.

"Hangar 1 martini, extra olives?" Gail said as she gave Holly a smile.

"You know me too well!"

"Only when it comes to your drink of choice, doll. Rob, a Guinness, right?"

Rob smiled and gave Gail a thumb's up.

"The end of another tough week I imagine?" Eddie asked as he took another sip of his beer.

"With four editions to get out, they're all tough weeks," Rob said as Holly nodded in agreement.

"Well, Rob, you were the genius who decided to add new local editions to the paper's original Sausalito-only coverage," Eddie pointed out.

"Yes, but if I had never expanded our circulation, I would not have been able to afford the services of the talented Holly Cross. Readership brings advertisers, and that's the only fuel that keeps our two-person business running. You cops can have a few slow months, and the landlord won't put you out on the street."

"True that. The business of law enforcement goes on regardless."

Holly stayed silent but nodded approvingly.

"You know, brains and beauty like Holly's don't come cheap," Rob said, raising his Guinness toward Holly in a toast.

"Does that mean I should be expecting a pay raise anytime soon, boss man?" Holly asked as she carefully tipped her nearly full martini glass in returning Rob's toast.

"Well, not in the immediate future, but as soon as our ad revenue picks up some more."

"That might be a while," Holly replied with a raised eyebrow.

"Exactly!"

"Okay you two," Eddie said with a smile and a shake of his head. "Speaking of local news, did you two hear about Fran Adams?"

"Just did from our community reporter with the Tiburon/Belvedere edition. Pretty sad," Rob replied.

"How did you hear about it, copper?" Holly asked.

"Heard it on the local news on the way over here. The reporter on KGO said the William and Fran Adams foundation last year gave over fifty million dollars to charitable causes around the Bay Area."

"Pretty incredible people," Rob said. "If Karin and I had their kind of money I would like to think we would be that generous."

"Before you start throwing money around, I hope I get that raise."

"Don't worry Holly; you'll be in for a piece of the pie," Rob said, giving Holly a wink and a smile as she looked down at a text on her phone.

"It's from Sylvia," Holly said. "She just heard from one of the deacons at St. Stephen's that Fran Adams' service will be eleven-thirty on Wednesday. They're going to have a brunch following the service. They're hoping for a big turnout from the congregation as a show of support for William."

"Wow!" Rob said. "I would imagine that's going to be one serious buffet."

"Are you thinking what I'm thinking, Rob?" Eddie asked.

"Should be one helluva a feed. Sure, why not?" Rob asked with a shrug. "I'll get into the office an hour early on Wednesday and leave an hour late on Tuesday night. That should keep us on schedule to get the Mill Valley edition out on time, and we'll do extended coverage of the Adams funeral for this coming week's Peninsula edition."

"You know," Holly said with a raised eyebrow as she bit into an olive and pulled it off the end of a long toothpick she had been using to stir her drink. "I have to start hanging out with a better group of people. A valued member of our community has died, and all you two can think about is the buffet following her funeral service."

Rob and Eddie looked at each other, shrugged, and then looked back at Holly.

"Our enjoying a world-class buffet will not change the sad event that happened, and what's the sense of putting out all that food if people are not going to eat it? And you know those society ladies all eat like birds, at least in public," Eddie said as Rob nodded in agreement.

"You know, Holly, you should come along," Eddie suggested.

"Why is that, Sherlock?"

"Well, you don't have to be a world-class detective to know that super-wealthy people often have super-wealthy friends."

"You think I should use a reception following a funeral as an opportunity to meet Mr. Right? I don't know, that seems a little creepy to me," Holly said as she began to consider the possibilities.

"Come on, maybe you'll meet Richie Rich, I mean Mr. Right, and you can leave my best friend Rob high and dry when you move into that deluxe apartment in the sky."

"I wouldn't mind meeting a millionaire," Holly said, beginning to wonder if she might indeed strike it rich.

"Millionaire?" Rob asked in a raised voice. "Billionaire! If you're going to leave me for a life of luxury, I want to see you sail out of Sausalito on one of those superyachts. You know, the kind that has their own helicopter pad."

"Of course, you'll miss the weekly grind at The Standard," Eddie cautioned, and Rob nodded in agreement.

"Trust me boys; with that kind of money, I'll learn to adjust."

CHAPTER TWO

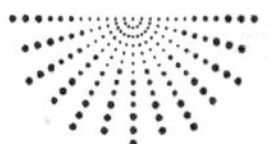

The front half of St. Stephen's Episcopal Church had already filled, and the back half was filling quickly when Holly, Rob, and Eddie entered and found Sylvia and Jack, who had saved them enough space to squeeze into their pew.

Both Rob and Eddie thought Holly looked terrific in a simple black dress she had purchased for the occasion.

"You came dressed to impress," Eddie whispered into Holly's ear just after they took their seats.

"I bought it last night, and I'm returning it to Nordstrom's tomorrow, so don't you and Rob get into a food fight at the reception and ruin my chances of getting a full refund."

"We'll be on our best behavior," Rob whispered into her other ear.

Reaching around Rob, Holly tapped Sylvia on the shoulder and asked, "Who are the people sitting alongside William Adams?"

"Those are William's parents, Fran's parents, and his longtime law partner, James Finch, and his wife, Jade. Behind them in the next pew are Fran's sister and brother, and William's two brothers. We met all of them at that big anniversary party."

The service was somber and relatively brief. James Finch

spoke about William and Fran's meeting at Berkeley Law, where he too had been a student. How they regularly put in sixty-hour-plus workweeks to establish successful practices and how they developed a passion for guiding new and promising talent in the growing field of high-tech.

"They gave far more to their community than they gave to themselves," Father Winslow Michaels intoned in a deep and somber voice. "Fran was someone who wanted to leave this world a better place. And those who know of her work in support of Bay Area schools, the homeless, senior outreach, and several of our programs here at St. Stephen's, know that she exceeded all her goals."

Forty-five minutes after it began, the mourners rose and mostly in silence followed one another into the church's spacious reception hall.

As they had anticipated, Eddie and Rob found an impressive buffet waiting for them.

"Now these, my friend," Eddie said, putting an arm around Rob's shoulder as they looked in wonder at the buffet table, "are the fixings for a sandwich worthy of the upper crust."

Rob, eyes wide, said, "I've got to have at least two."

"Not to mention trying those side dishes."

"I have a question: How do you guys eat so much and stay so slim?" Holly asked. "It makes me a little nuts."

"Twice weekly pick-up basketball games down at the old MLK School gym, that's how," Eddie answered. "You should come join us one night. We welcome ladies, but you have to be able to keep up."

"I'll pass. I see enough of Rob five days a week. Now if you'll excuse me, I have to go find a millionaire. Maybe at our wedding, I'll get the same caterers. I'd hate to disappoint you two."

"That's very sweet of you, Holly," Rob said with his mouth half full.

Eddie put his hand around her arm and pulled Holly close. "Remember, no mere millionaire. Go find yourself a billionaire."

"That's right, Holly," Rob said. "Stick to the game plan, Billionaire with a B."

"Well I'll try not to disappoint either of you," Holly said as she slinked away in a form-fitting black dress that said, "I'm grieving in style."

Less than an hour later, the three were walking back toward Rob's car for the ride home to Sausalito. Rob and Eddie were beyond satisfied, but Holly's search had fallen far short of her hopes.

"I met two handsome guys, apparently very wealthy, who were early investors in Google."

"Well that sounds promising," Eddie said.

"I thought so too until they mentioned they were happily married to each other."

"Ouch!" Rob said.

"Then I met another man, who made millions in the tech world and wasn't shy about telling me about his success. A bit of a brag, but I could have lived with that."

"Sounds like you caught a big one. You should have reeled him in and knocked the hapless soul over the head," Eddie suggested.

"I thought exactly that until he spoke of the thrill of shooting a lion on a recent safari in Nairobi. I can't go there. You want to go halfway around the world to kill Simba, and then mount his head on the wall in your den? Sorry boys, I'm all in on finding a millionaire, but you have to draw the line somewhere."

"So no luck finding lasting happiness among the bereaved?" Rob asked.

"No, smarty pants, it was a bust, but that wasn't the worst part.

One of William Adams' nephews ran into me and got chocolate cake on my dress. I doubt I'll be able to return it now."

"Well, if it's any comfort, I spoke to Adams for a bit," Eddie said. "He's fascinated by forensics. His grandfather was a chemist in San Francisco. He made many of the advances in the use of luminol, a substance that is used in forensics to this day. Pretty cool huh?"

"What does luminol do?" Holly asked.

"Spread luminol over a supposedly clean surface, and if blood had been there, it would cause it to glow under the proper light. It's been a critical help in criminal investigations countless times."

"I would have been happier if his grandfather had figured out how to get chocolate cake out of a two-hundred-and-fifty-dollar black dress."

"I don't know about luminol," Rob offered, "but you should show that dress to my bride. Between Micah and Alice, I think Karin has mastered the art of making every oops, including birthday party chocolate cake, disappear."

"Maybe you'll have better luck at the next billionaire's funeral you attend," Eddie offered.

"If Karin can't pull off a miracle, at least I'll have a second reason to wear this dress."

CHAPTER THREE

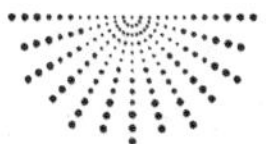

"I know you would like to write something about Fran," William Adams said privately to Sylvia near the end of the reception for his wife. "I want two or three weeks to hide from the rest of the world. I need time to think about what has happened. It's like my whole world came crashing down in a single moment."

"I wish there were something Jack and I could do, but I'm sure everyone you know feels the same."

"They do. Sadly, of course, there is nothing anyone can do. It's the one reality you're always aware of regardless of your financial successes. Right now, I simply need time."

Sylvia was the only reporter that William agreed to talk with about Fran's life. The Wall Street Journal, Bloomberg Business Week and others did obituaries on Fran, but in each case, the stories were about her business acumen. Fran had an uncanny gift for seeing the one high tech startup company out of a hundred that would be thriving five to ten years into the future.

The Adams' family portfolio grew faster than either he or Fran could have imagined. During Apple's turmoil, and then the decline and death of Steve Jobs, many investors headed for the exits. Fran argued that was their time to rush in. She bet substantially on a far brighter future for Apple, and her bet paid off. Together with substantial investments in Oracle, Google, and Salesforce.com to outperform expectations, she and William rode their combined talents and instincts to dizzying heights.

Even during lean times—bursting tech bubbles and recessionary economies—the Adams' family fortune continued its climb from the millions into the billions.

William, however, was disinterested in business stories about his wife's sudden and tragic death. The wound of her loss ran too deep. Although the law firm of Adams Finch and Adams had impressive accommodations in one of San Francisco's prestigious Mission Street office towers, William preferred working from home. Most days his mansion on Belvedere's Golden Gate Avenue was quiet as a tomb, with only his housekeeper, Mrs. Jackson, and his driver, Malcolm, present and available if needed.

Six weeks after Fran's service, William invited Sylvia to his home to discuss Fran's work and life.

Sylvia was excited and honored to have this opportunity. She alerted Rob, who in turn decided to make the interview his lead story in the next issue of *The Peninsula Standard*.

Sylvia spent an hour going over her questions and then another hour preparing herself for the interview. Outside of her two weekly columns, Belvedere Buzz and Tiburon Talk, it was rare for Sylvia to write a lead story. Between that and William entrusting her to share his insights into Fran's private life, she felt a bit uncertain when she rang the bell of the Adams mansion promptly at eleven.

Mrs. Jackson greeted her with a warm smile, pleased that her employer had invited a guest to the house. She seated her in a comfortable and impressive Massoud blue and white wingback chair. One of two that served as focal points of William's study, both chairs were positioned near a stately stone fireplace that had a fire already burning.

William entered the room a few minutes after Sylvia's arrival. He was comfortably dressed in dark slacks and a gray cashmere cardigan sweater over a white collared dress shirt.

"Sylvia," he said in a happy voice as she stood to greet him. "Sit please, did Mrs. Jackson offer you some coffee or something to eat?"

"She did. But Jack and I took a pledge last week: three meals a day and no food, tea, or coffee in-between. There are so many people in this community who keep themselves in great shape, biking, hiking, kayaking, that we have to do something that gives the appearance we're at least trying to stay fit."

"I've lost ten pounds since Fran's death. It's not hard to do when you have no appetite."

"You mentioned on the phone that you've been working from home and not going into the office."

"I'm sure I'll get back to my usual routine before long, but for now I'm content working out of the house. My partner, James Finch, has been with the firm almost as long as Fran and me, and I trust him completely to keep an eye on the operation. Right now if I went into the office, I'd find myself buried in sympathy cards and well-wishers, and that's not going to get my mind off what's happened."

"But you're alright talking about Fran for the profile piece I'd like to do?"

"Absolutely. Besides, I know Fran would want me to keep people focused on some of the local causes that Belvedere and Tiburon organizations like the Waterfront Preservation League have been working on for a long time. An article in the local paper is a good way for me to inform Pamela Botherton, Julia Hassie, and others, like Cynthia Buckley, that supporting community causes will remain a priority for me."

"That's wonderful. Let's start by talking about how you and Fran met at Berkeley Law."

"We were friends from the outset. We both came from middle-class families. Coincidentally Fran's parents were medical researchers, and my parents were chemists. In fact, my maternal grandfather was a rather well-known chemist in San Francisco. Both of us grew up with parents who worked hard and instilled that work ethic in us. In that sense, we were well suited for each other."

"As I understand, you knew each other for many years before deciding to marry."

William smiled, thinking back to an earlier time. "Fran and I would meet just about every Saturday for dinner or Sunday for a little free time and talk about our private lives, which were far less successful than our business lives. We were three years out of Berkeley when we made a pact."

"What pact?"

"If I failed to meet my soulmate over the next eight years, and she did as well, we would marry each other. Sounds like something out of a romantic comedy, doesn't it?"

"But you two must have been terrific friends to strike a bargain like that."

"We were! We had a great deal of respect and admiration for one another."

"Well, I'm guessing you both went without meeting your soulmate."

"More or less. A fling for me, a time or two of being smitten for her, but for both of us we knew no greater love than the drive for building our law practice, which in time became more of a venture capital practice. Those were exciting times both in San Francisco and Silicon Valley. There were bumps in the road like the time when the tech bubble burst in 2000, but through the years, with the right steps, our gains kept moving steadily upward."

"So after the eight years you had given each other, you got married?"

"We joked it was more like a merger."

"And you were married for twenty years."

"Twenty years and four months. That place we bought up near Heavenly was our twentieth wedding anniversary gift to one another. That didn't work out very well, did it?"

Sylvia looked down for a moment then said, "No, I suppose it didn't. But none of us know the future. And you did have a very successful, as you said, merger."

"Wildly successful," William said wistfully with a smile that vanished almost as quickly as it had appeared. "But Sylvia, what I'd like you to write about Fran was the great joy she found in philanthropy. She was so brilliant, and so hard working, that she could not fund one project or another without our net value rising to replace whatever wealth we gave away."

"How did you get started in philanthropy?"

"After you reach that tipping point and realize that you cannot spend the money you have accrued over a lifetime, perhaps several lifetimes, additional wealth is simply a way of keeping score. So while we worked hard, we wanted to see our money create new successes."

"So what did you do?"

"We began with the ancient wisdom that charity begins at home. Fran and I knew that our parents were beyond retirement age, but all four of them continued working. So I went to my parents and casually asked, 'What's your dream house?'

"They adored this stone mansion with a small adjacent vineyard less than a mile off the Silverado Trail up in Napa County. My mom and dad were speechless when Fran and I took them to lunch one day in St. Helena and then drove them to their new home.

"It took a few minutes for them to stop saying, 'You're teasing us.' But then they started to believe that this two-million-dollar home was theirs. They cried, then we cried, it was a fantastic experience."

"I guess you did the same for Fran's parents?"

"Absolutely. The very next weekend we took Eileen and Sandy and drove down to Carmel-by-the-Sea. For many years they had enjoyed an annual two-week getaway at this cottage they rented. Fran and I knew where it was because we had driven down a couple of times to have dinner with them and then spent the night near Pebble Beach. We found the owner of the cottage, made them an offer they could not refuse, and we gave two wonderful people a surprise they'll never forget."

"I can't imagine how overwhelmed your parents and Fran's parents must have been."

"No amount of money could have brought us greater joy than to make four such terrific people so happy. But let me add one more story. While Fran and I never took the time to start a family, we have several sweet, wonderful nephews and nieces. Our gifts to our parents happened at a time that the oldest one of these children was about to start applying to colleges. We brought our brothers and sisters together and explained our desire to underwrite the education of all their children, tuition, along with campus housing and expenses. All totaled these gifts represented a fraction of one percent of our net worth. I don't say that to be prideful. I'm amazed that many people with great wealth ignore the opportunities to give financial gifts that mean little to them monetarily, but mean something beyond words to others."

"And this is when you started to think about charity in a larger sense?"

"Absolutely. If you're blessed to earn a fabulous amount of money, it is an even greater blessing to see the joy that money can bring to the lives of others. Our giving in a bigger way started close to home, but it spread from Marin County to other parts of California, to America, and causes around the globe. No matter what your fortune you'll never be able to do all you'd like to do.

But to see how your money can change lives, improve lives, and actually save countless lives, is a feeling I could never adequately describe."

"William, that's just fantastic."

"I'll send you over some information on the charitable work Fran was involved in for background if you need it."

"Of course, that would be very helpful. Thank you so much for sharing all this."

"No, Sylvia, thank you for being here and listening. It's raised my spirits to talk to a friend about a woman I so admired."

CHAPTER FOUR

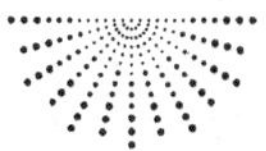

Two days after Sylvia's story appeared in *The Peninsula Standard* under the headline, "The Enduring Legacy of Fran Adams," William felt his spirits lift, and he returned to his San Francisco office.

He avoided the gentle requests of family, friends, and associates to join them for lunch, dinner, or cocktails. Instead, William did what both he and Fran were most accustomed to doing in the years they shared: starting work early and finishing late.

He remained utterly disinterested in hearing further words of sympathy or responding to inquiries regarding how he was getting along. Neither he nor Fran believed in sugarcoating reality. The simple truth was that Fran was gone. All the kind words and best wishes would not bring her back.

His work routine was his one relief from the emptiness that overwhelmed him. William focused on both the work of the law firm and the venture capital business. Two more bets that he and Fran had placed on emerging tech companies again exceeded expectations, but without Fran to share the news, keeping score of a billion here or a billion there was far less fun than it once was.

In those quiet times when he sat in his favorite wingback chair in front of his home study's ornate fireplace, he wondered if the pain of losing Fran would have been even greater if they had experienced a strong romantic attraction to each other.

That was one truth William chose to keep private.

❧

It was not until Fran was gone nearly a year that William's partner, James Finch, began his campaign to draw William back into San Francisco's vibrant social world.

There was no better place to start than the San Francisco Symphony's annual gala, the Black & White Ball. What James did not mention when he encouraged William to join him and his wife, Jade, was that he secretly hoped to introduce William to his fashion model superstar client, Willow Wisp.

The night of the gala, James looked through the massive gathering and saw William suddenly approaching from his left. Then, as though a sixth sense had moved him, he turned to his right and saw the alluring and statuesque Willow approaching.

James thought Willow had never looked more dazzling. He was only too happy to introduce the two of them.

Willow stepped closer to William and stretched out her hand for him to take as she flashed both a smile and her cornflower blue eyes.

William's heart paused and then leaped forward with lustful anticipation that sent a shudder down his spine. Her slender, beautifully shaped hand felt surprisingly natural in his. His eyes drank all of her in, and he instantly approved of what he saw. Willow's black and white gown had been designed specifically for her. It wrapped over her right shoulder, leaving her left shoulder exposed.

To William, she was a living work of art. The dazzling

diamond and emerald pendant that went around her neck only enhanced her beauty.

There was an awkward, electric moment between the two of them, in which they both laughed like children delighted to be meeting for the first time. The thought of her wearing nothing but that beautiful pendant flashed across William's mind. The idea embarrassed and thrilled him in equal measure.

As William was catching his breath, one of the several fashion designers in attendance squealed when he discovered Willow standing just a few feet from him.

He was very young and very thin. He wore a black and white puffy-sleeved pirate shirt, open almost to his navel.

Willow pulled her hand away from William's, but only after a small tug that made them both laugh awkwardly.

Noting their bashful exchange, the pirate cocked a brow and said, "I only want to borrow her for ten minutes. I promise to bring her right back."

William's eyes followed Willow until she vanished into the crowd. Then he turned to James and asked, "Who is she again? I'm certain I recognize her." How could he forget that striking face and those almond-shaped eyes? He asked himself.

"You pass her on your way in and out of the office every day."

"What do you mean I pass her every day?"

"Well, you pass her billboard," Finch reminded him.

"Good God! You mean she's that Willow girl—that client of yours who's become her own brand?"

"That's the one," James said approvingly. "She's done very well for herself."

"Well, she's certainly a stunner."

"I've wanted to introduce the two of you for months."

"You're not thinking of us as a couple?"

His studied silence provided William's answer.

"Are you insane?"

"Hold on, William. You're both, bright, intelligent, charming, successful—"

"But…I've got to be twenty years her senior!"

"A little more than that."

"God, she's young enough to be my daughter!"

"Who cares about your age difference?"

William frowned. "Apparently, I do!"

"You could use a little female companionship, and you could stand to have some fun for a change."

"That's one hell of a companion," William murmured, as his mind toyed with unimaginable possibilities.

"Why don't you go rescue her from that pirate who just stole her away? She might be needing a little adult companionship right now."

Just then Jade brushed past. After kissing William on the cheek, she dragged her husband off to meet mutual friends who had just arrived.

The large gala tent, which sat diagonally across from San Francisco's iconic city hall on Van Ness Avenue, had filled with hundreds of attendees. Willow was just one of many celebrities to cause a stir, none of whom were meant to eclipse the great maestro himself, Michael Tilson Thomas, who strolled triumphantly through the crowd, greeting celebrants and thanking them for their support of the orchestra's educational programs.

William was left in the middle of the noisy gathering to contemplate what he considered to be ridiculous, but wildly exciting thoughts.

Perhaps I'm a fool.

There was no denying the leap he felt in his heart when he touched Willow's hand. Perhaps he was being overly cautious. Why should he have the least regard for what others might think? Should that sudden burst of excitement he felt go unexplored?

Willow was something that Fran had never been. Fran was

reliable, brilliant, and substantial. Willow was a work of art sheathed in sparkling jewels wrapped in a stunning gown. What harm was there in following his instincts? William craved intimacy. Admittedly, he knew nothing about her, but when would he meet a more beautiful woman? Finally, he went off in search of her.

❀

Willow was given her first name at birth, but her last name, Bukowski, cried out for reinvention.

From the early days of her modeling career, which began in earnest just weeks after she completed four years at the private high school, Marin Academy, she was known only as Willow.

The work was nonstop, and the grueling schedule of modeling commitments was endless. Willow's visibility in the profession kept rising. Soon she caught the eye of French fashion designer Henri LeBon. It was then, at the age of twenty, that Willow's universe opened dramatically.

"She is my muse," LeBon declared imperiously whenever another model was suggested.

Soon Willow's slender, perfectly proportioned frame graced the pages of Vogue, InStyle, Paris Match, and Glamour. When she and her small circle found Willow looking fabulous on the back cover of Vanity Fair clothed in a soft, creamy fabric that clung perfectly to her, everyone knew she had arrived.

LeBon was so pleased with the sensation he had created that he busied himself in a new marketing venture, creating a signature scent for his muse. The ridiculously expensive perfume became an overnight sensation.

"Willow Wisp Will Haunt Your Every Dream," was the headline that adorned print ads, billboards, and window displays from Rodeo Drive to Piccadilly Circus, from Broadway to the

Champs-Elysees, and back home to San Francisco's Union Square.

Willow now belonged to the ages. The child Bukowski was subsumed by the carefully crafted marketing image of Willow Wisp.

Willow Bukowski, the Marin County girl who was often accused of seducing the boyfriend of every girl she disliked at Marin Academy, and taking other valuables that did not belong to her as well, was now an internationally recognized celebrity. Her name was often attached to a list of famous men in gossip magazines read around the globe. Leonardo DiCaprio was seen kissing her cheek at Cannes, Orlando Bloom casually had his arms wrapped around her waist as they played and shopped in London's Chelsea district. And through the watchful eye of a telephoto lens, she was seen tanned and gorgeous, in a two-piece swimsuit, lying serenely with her head resting on the lap of James Franco aboard a yacht off the island of Catalina.

Willow had her star athlete phase when she was frequently caught by ESPN's cameras blowing a kiss to her latest man of the hour, who had just helped his team, the Portland Trailblazers, secure a place in the NBA playoffs. But she quickly grew bored with basketball and traded her NBA power forward for a top-rated NFL quarterback.

After a series of passing flings with several of Hollywood's most sought-after leading men, and professional sports' highest-paid athletes, Willow was suddenly smitten with love for classical music. She settled upon the brilliant young conductor of the Vienna Philharmonic. Unfortunately for Willow, the Viennese maestro was more interested in Viktor Kozlov, the gifted Russian violinist who, to the conductor's disappointment, was far more interested in the intoxicating Ms. Wisp.

So began Willow's most passionate affair. She explained to her friends with an innocent smile, "He plays the violin, and I am undone."

Renowned for his sensitive yet forceful finger work, both on stage and off, the tempestuous soloist, known to classical music lovers as the "Magician of Moscow," began spending more of his time in San Francisco. There, he explained to a local music critic in his typically fractured English, "This most beautiful place. I enjoy much often staying here."

Kozlov's favorite view was from Willow's bedroom in a luxury high-rise condominium perched atop San Francisco's Nob Hill. While Kozlov looked out of windows offering incomparable vistas, Willow lovingly massaged his tired shoulders, arms, hands, and fingers that, in just the past month, had endeavored to please audiences from Sao Paulo to San Moritz.

James had come to know Willow while working as her attorney. As a thriving corporate entity, Willow quickly learned that expert legal representation was a necessity. James and his wife, a native of Hong Kong, invited Willow and Viktor to be their guests at the San Francisco Symphony's gala night. But, moments before their limousine was scheduled to pick them up, Kozlov got into a furious long-distance exchange with his agent over a contract for three appearances with the New York Philharmonic. Afterward, he announced, "I am too much upset for making party! Please forgive."

Already dressed and bejeweled, Willow was not keen on the idea of spending one more night at home with her dramatically dark lover. Instead, she headed out and was soon on her way to the gala.

A few days earlier, James mentioned to Willow that he would like her to meet his law partner.

"Why should I want to meet William Adams?" Willow asked coquettishly.

"Because he's unattached, and he's an incredibly wealthy man whose wife died last year."

"He doesn't look like the Monopoly Man, by any chance?" Willow asked suspiciously.

"Hardly! He's my age—mid-fifties—in splendid shape. Plays racquetball like he's going off to war."

"Sounds intriguing. And how wealthy is wealthy?"

"Billions—with a B."

Willow could feel her knees weaken at just the thought of such tremendous wealth.

The two were standing close to each other in James' richly appointed wood-paneled office; her lawyer, mentor, and one of her legion of former lovers brushed his lips against her bare right shoulder as he imagined taking her right there.

"Don't get any naughty thoughts, James; we agreed to keep our relationship strictly business going forward."

"That would be easier to do if I didn't find you so irresistible."

"Well, try darling, try. If I continue to tempt you, I might have to take my business elsewhere."

"You tease, but you would never do that. I've made you too much money."

"If making me money were the only criteria, then I would take Henri LeBon to bed with me every night of the year."

"I don't think you're his gender of choice."

"Dear Henri might surprise you."

"I'd rather not find out," James said with a smirk, while his eyes followed her delicate and tempting curves as she headed to his office door.

"Be a good girl to William if you meet him at the symphony's gala. I think you two would hit it off. I'm serious!"

Willow never gave the idea of meeting James' partner a second thought until Viktor's tantrum occurred just before their planned departure. She dismissed James' comments regarding William's wealth as one more example of his penchant for overstatement. But in the few quiet moments she had in the car heading south down Van Ness Avenue toward the gala, Willow thought it wise to quickly search Wikipedia on her iPhone to see if this man, William Adams, was someone she wanted to meet.

"Oh my God," she said softly to herself, as her driver negotiated yet another busy night on San Francisco's streets. Her heart skipped a beat when she realized that Adams was indeed on Forbes' list of the world's wealthiest individuals. Not only on the list but up near the top.

She was suddenly taken by the thought of how such great wealth would forever change her life. Her success and a series of wise investments had brought her millions, but his billions made her look like the forlorn flower girl she saw on the street corner as her limousine stopped for yet another red light.

For over ten years, her life had been photo shoots, personal appearances, Lear jets, gorgeous women, handsome men, and embarrassingly high earnings. But Willow was well aware that the shelf life of a top model is even less than that of a world-class athlete. As Oscar and Gloria Bukowski frequently told Willow as a child, "All good things must come to an end." She doubted most of her parents' advice, but not that bit of wisdom. William Adams' great fortune would undoubtedly outlive the lucrative but short-lived fame of Willow Wisp.

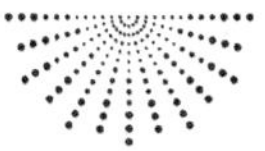

CHAPTER FIVE

Willow gave an innocent giggle when, over the noise of the gathering, William suggested, "Let's escape this madhouse and go someplace we can talk." Minutes later, they were in the backseat of William's town car, heading up Franklin Avenue on their way out of San Francisco.

"Mr. Adams, are you kidnapping me?" Willow asked, giving her best impression of an innocent young woman being swept away by this powerful, older gentleman.

"I won't lie. That's what I'd like to do." William knew he was behaving boldly, but an international superstar model, he reasoned, could not be all that innocent.

As their limousine climbed into the Marin headlands toward the Robin Williams Tunnel just north of the Golden Gate Bridge, they were treated to the nightly light show—of the San Francisco skyline, from the Bay Bridge to the Palace of Fine Arts, as hundreds of homes sparkled along the city's famous hills. As their limousine went down the steep Waldo Grade from where they could see a countless number of boats bobbing gently in the dark waters, they neared their exit, which leads to Mill Valley heading west or Tiburon and Belvedere heading east.

Having grown up a few miles from here, in the town of Larkspur, Willow knew the area well. It had been several years since she had been on this road that hugs the backwaters of Richardson Bay, which divides the Tiburon Peninsula from the houseboat- and yacht-lined shores of Sausalito.

Just after entering Tiburon's small downtown, Malcolm made a sharp right, heading over the short causeway into Belvedere. There he began a steady climb upward to Golden Gate Avenue. It was the longer of the two approaches to the Adams estate, but certainly the more scenic, offering views of Tiburon's boat harbor along with romantic views of San Francisco Bay. Although narrow and winding, Malcolm instinctively knew this was the route his employer would prefer on this particular night.

Small lights along a perfectly manicured lawn illuminated the driveway of William's stately home. As the car stopped in front of a massive glass door adorned with ornate ironwork, William was quite convinced that he must have, by now, impressed this young woman who had captured his eager attention.

W illow smiled as she stepped inside. She was immediately impressed with the mansion's two-story atrium, which surrounded a grand circular foyer with an Italian marble floor. A curving staircase, trimmed with mahogany accents, ascended to a second-floor balcony.

I could happily live here, Willow thought, as she imagined the spectacular parties she could host in this palatial estate.

William introduced Willow to a tired but smiling Mrs. Jackson as the woman who "countless women in the world would like to be."

"William, you're silly," Willow purred, as she took Mrs. Jackson's hand. The housekeeper offered to bring them a tea service, but William assured her they would both be fine.

Mrs. Jackson wished them both a pleasant evening and headed off to her downstairs bedroom, hoping she would never again see the flirtatious Miss Wisp.

William took Willow into the study. "It's my favorite room in this old place." As it was on any cold night, the fireplace grate, stacked with wood, was ready to be lit. This place is perfect, Willow thought.

She's utterly perfect, William thought, as he offered to make her a drink.

"Perhaps just a little sherry with water."

"Sounds terrific, I'll join you," William said as he headed over to a cabinet bar, hoping there was a bottle of sherry inside. There was, and William quickly poured their drinks. He sat back down just as the aged hickory wood in the fireplace began to crackle.

The pain and loneliness of the past year flashed through William's mind and seemed to stretch back an eternity. He pushed such thoughts away and reminded himself that he was in the presence of a beguiling woman. His turning sullen would surely ruin their evening.

As Willow sat back into the soft embrace of one of his two favorite chairs, both of which were positioned ideally to enjoy the fire's warmth, she graced William with a smile.

"You fascinate me! I want to know all about you," William said, determined not to be shy.

"Well, where should I begin?" Willow replied in the innocent manner she had long perfected when being interviewed by fashion and celebrity reporters.

"I got my very first modeling job at seventeen. One of my high school girlfriends dared me to go to a San Francisco modeling agency that was holding an open call for fresh new faces."

That was Willow's first lie. She didn't have any friends in high school. She had stolen far too many boyfriends for any of the girls who admired her during their freshman year to still be speaking with her by their junior year.

She then told of how she caught the eye of a top fashion photographer during her early months in the business.

"It was unbelievable," she related, in a story that had grown more polished over the past years. "He took me under his wing and polished my portfolio. He was a genius! An amazing photographer, very gay, and very brilliant."

William gave a warm, knowing smile, utterly unaware that this second part of her encapsulated biography contained several lies as well.

Yes, Michael Pierce was a top fashion photographer, but Willow plotted all that would occur in their relationship, beginning with how they met. In little time, Willow seduced him. She drained him not only of his creative energies but a long list of professional contacts as well—all of who helped her climb the ladder of success.

Willow reached the top rung with her seduction of Henri LeBon, a man who previously had been uninterested in taking a female lover.

Their liaison was intermittent and mutually beneficial. LeBon never objected to Willow's propensity for taking other lovers, like Viktor Kozlov. In turn, LeBon met many of his future lovers, such as the Viennese maestro spurned by Kozlov, through his relationship with Willow, whom he faithfully pronounced his muse.

Much of Willow Bukowski's actual story was left out, most importantly Willow's dalliances with William's partner, James Finch.

Finch was wise enough to know that Willow was a woman to be enjoyed whenever the rare opportunity presented itself, and discretion was a must both for her career and his marriage to a woman who grew uncomfortable whenever her husband was around any other attractive woman.

If there was a chance Willow became the next Mrs. Adams, James reasoned his opportunities to savor the delights of her mystical charms might increase. After all, why spend half a year traveling around the world promoting a bottle of perfume when you're married to one of the world's wealthiest people?

As for Willow, her motivation for taking James as one of her lovers was rooted in the occasional insider stock recommendations he would pass her way, all of which helped to grow her three-million-dollar nest egg: first to six, and then double again to twelve. James could have been disbarred and imprisoned, under the Federal rules regarding insider trading, for sharing some of his highly successful Silicon Valley clients' information. But, intoxicated by Willow's allure, James put his career, his partnership with William, and his marriage to Jade all at risk for those rare, brief encounters with an international supermodel.

Either the fire needed to be stoked again, or it should be allowed to burn out. Willow suggested it was late and she should be getting home. Part of William hoped that she would spend the night next to him in bed tightly wrapped in his embrace. But Willow, who read men far better than they could understand themselves, learned years ago that in the heat of passion a man loves the ferocity of a liberated woman, but in marriage, they desire a woman who picks lovers judiciously.

Thus far, in her relationships with men, Willow had all she could ever need, want, or imagine. But in William, she found a man who could serve a unique purpose in her life. Good fortune had put her in William's path because he was the man who would place her on a pedestal, adore her, and make her wealthy beyond imagination. All of which, Willow believed, she richly deserved.

But at this moment, she knew it was time to say goodnight.

CHAPTER SIX

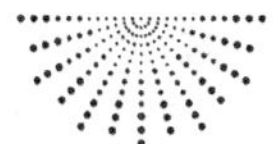

Willow returned from the Adams mansion well after midnight. Kozlov, who had exhausted himself pouting for much of the night, was fast asleep. The following morning, she awoke alone in her heart-shaped bed. Kozlov had slipped out quietly for a ten o'clock rehearsal at Berkeley's Zellerbach Hall, where he was preparing for a weekend performance of Tchaikovsky's Violin Concerto in D Major.

A text message on her private number from the front desk of her condominium informed her that twenty-four long-stemmed yellow roses had just arrived for her.

"Is there a card with them?" she texted back.

"Yes ma'am," the building's concierge replied.

"Well tell me what it says, silly!"

"'The beauty of these roses pale in comparison to you!'"

"And is there a name?"

"It just says, William."

Not only was Willow delighted with the flowers, she was especially pleased that William was paying attention when, during their fireside chat, she told him that her favorite color was yellow. Taking note of her likes and dislikes was a promising sign.

For the next hour, Willow relaxed in a warm tub, enjoying the gentle fragrance of lavender bath salts while contemplating her next move.

Following her bath, and after a long and well-practiced routine of head to toe moisturizing, Willow noticed a text message from William suggesting dinner on Saturday night. Given the fact that this was Friday, it was evident to Willow that William was already in full pursuit.

Before replying she thought: Should she be available on such short notice? Willow had planned to go to Viktor's performance in Berkeley, so she texted back, "I have a commitment, but I will try to reschedule. Let me check with my secretary and get back to you in a couple of hours."

She had no intention of passing up a dinner invitation from William Adams, but she waited for two hours before texting back: "I've cleared my calendar." She teasingly added, "What have you planned, Mr. Adams?"

William's plan was worthy of his extraordinary wealth. He would pick Willow up by limousine, take her to a private jetport just south of San Francisco, and fly her to San Diego for a catered dinner on a yacht in which he owned a timeshare, although he had not used it in two years. Fortunately, it was available on very short notice.

After dinner in the yacht's impressive dining room, they could decide to share the craft's private master bedroom, sleep in separate accommodations, or return late that night to San Francisco. Great wealth, he had learned, allows for a variety of options. William knew this was ridiculously extravagant, but what better way to impress a woman he could not get off his mind?

When William shared with Willow part but not all of his plans, she strongly suspected that her billionaire had sincere intentions regarding their future.

The only anticipated bump in Willow's day would be sharing with Viktor the disappointing news that she would not be attending his Saturday night performance. She explained that she was appearing at "a private engagement" and that it might require her being out of town for the balance of the weekend.

It was not at all surprising to her that Kozlov was furious when she broke the news. He hurriedly made plans to have his driver take him to the suite booked for his use at the Claremont Hotel near the Berkeley campus.

"You will much miss me, for I will not be back!" With that, he stormed out of Willow's bedroom, slamming the door behind him.

All of which was fine with Willow, who had begun entertaining happy fantasies of being a billionaire's wife.

On the ride to the jetport, William plied Willow with pink champagne as he promised her a memorable evening. She had never before contemplated a long-term relationship with a man so many years her senior, but given William's wealth, she was more than willing to expand her horizons. He didn't have the fire, the power, or the dashing good looks of Viktor—or for that matter, any one of her twenty- or thirty-something athletes and assorted celebrities—but he had something that was perhaps more attractive. Above and beyond his incredible wealth, there was a calm dignity about William that Willow found charming.

After a seventy-five-minute flight, the limousine waiting on the tarmac at San Diego International had them dockside ten minutes after they touched down. The captain and her staff graciously welcomed the couple as they stepped aboard the

Romantique, a 125-foot, Italian-built luxury craft featuring a full sundeck, beautifully appointed staterooms, and a mahogany-lined formal dining room. This forty-million-dollar pleasure craft came complete with a private screening room.

Within the circles she traveled, Willow had seen her share of private jets and comfortable yachts. She recognized, however, that for a first date, this was quite remarkable.

William was a perfect gentleman. Throughout dinner, he played the charming host as they enjoyed an expertly prepared and presented meal. After a light dessert, they went to the yacht's rear deck and sat in two comfortable outdoor chairs that looked out on a calm moonlit sea and the distant lights of the seaside community of La Jolla, located a few miles north of San Diego.

William was so desperately in need of affection that he was tempted to pour his heart out to Willow in the quiet moments they shared. Although words escaped him, he responded to his desire to hold her close. There could never be a better time than this, William reasoned. So he leaned over and kissed Willow softly and tenderly on the lips.

She rose from her chair. Taking his hand, she gently pulled William up out of his chair and into her embrace.

William looked desperately into her eyes and kissed her deeply.

After a lingering embrace, Willow said, "It's a little late for flying home tonight, don't you think?"

"You're right."

"I didn't think to bring a nightgown," Willow said with feigned innocence.

"That's all right; I promise to keep you warm."

William did not have the brute force of Willow's usual lovers. But she was pleased to bring romance back into his life. What she did not know was that raw passion like this was something William had never experienced.

After breakfast on the sundeck, they held hands and looked

out on a soft blue sky. Both were feeling satisfied with the night they had shared.

William and Willow concluded that their twenty-four-hour getaway had accomplished both their goals; he to hold her in his arms and experience her; she to discover that she may one day become the second Mrs. William Adams.

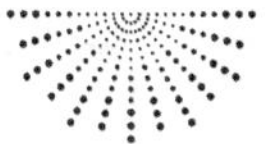

CHAPTER SEVEN

Two days after her night aboard the Romantique, Willow gave Kozlov his notice of termination.

She waited until the restless Russian had left California to begin rehearsals for a weekend appearance with the Cleveland Orchestra before having her assistant contact his assistant to arrange for his things to be moved out of her condominium. Anticipating an angry call in response, Willow had Kozlov's cell number forwarded to her assistant, who explained over his tangled and shouted insults that, "Miss Wisp has chosen to go in another direction."

Kozlov, Willow had decided, was part of a period of her life she now thought of as "Wistful Willow." This new creation was someone she called "Wiser Willow," a more mature woman ready to face the challenges of her thirties and beyond.

Willow quickly resolved that every aspect of her life needed to be reinvented, and there was no better man to have at her side at this time than the brilliantly successful William Adams.

William's attributes were strikingly dissimilar to the parade of tabloid cover men who had previously filled her life. First, and most obvious, his financial assets gave him an air of relaxed authority that Willow found intoxicating.

In fact, except for such giants as Warren Buffet, Bill Gates, and Jeff Bezos, or those of vast inherited wealth like the Waltons, the Mars, and the Bettencourts, there were only a handful of wealthier individuals than her "dear, sweet, William."

Beyond his enormous wealth, Willow disciplined herself to remember that there was also his brilliance, kindness, and considerable charm.

"There is so much more to William than just his wealth," Willow professed to her small circle. "He is far more substantial than any man I have dated! A real name in the world of both law and venture capital. Not just a shooting star. My Mr. Adams will be around long after all these athletes and celebrities have been forgotten."

More importantly, stars and athletes so often find ridiculous ways to burn through most, if not all, of their wealth. Not her William. His fortune, to her endless amazement, was so great that not even she could imagine ways of spending it all.

To those who insisted she was suffering from a father complex, she quickly dismissed the suggestion with a laugh. "If you knew my father, you would never say that."

Henri, in particular, took a jaundiced view of her new relationship. "It's no more than a passing fling," he sniffed.

Then again, he knew the great love Willow had for money. And when he did a Wikipedia search of William Adams, it dawned on him that he might lose his muse to the one love more lasting than beauty or fame: wealth.

William was uncomfortable describing his relationship with Willow to anyone. But when cornered, he merely explained, "I'm just having some fun for a change."

His small clique of Belvedere golfing buddies, who met for lunch two Mondays a month at the Corinthian Yacht Club at the base of Tiburon's Beach Road, teased him about online and in-print tabloid reports of his involvement with the famous international model. His answer was casually dismissive. "Since when do you believe anything you read in gossip columns?"

James and others were equally curious. In all cases, William consistently downplayed the relationship. "Believe me; this is more gossip than fact. More smoke than fire. I don't deny that I'm very fond of the girl—God only knows she's a great beauty—but I'm not running off and marrying a woman half my age."

Being continually pressed about his romance bothered William. For all their wealth, William and Fran were able to live a life of relative seclusion. He often thought about that on mornings he left Willow's condominium on Russian Hill and wondered if some enterprising photographer might be lying in wait for him, or whenever he sent Malcolm to San Francisco so that Willow might spend the night with him in Belvedere.

As they cuddled in bed one Saturday morning, they realized that neither of them had any other commitments for the rest of the day. They came to the mutual conclusion that they were perfectly content just being in each other's company.

"I've never known a man like you," Willow purred.

"I've never known a woman like you—and I've never felt like this in my life," William replied.

They hurried to dress so that they could take a long walk, winding down through the hills of Belvedere and out along the waterfront. They walked over the short causeway into Tiburon, passing the small, colorful shops along Ark Row that, in less than two hours, would be busy with tourists visiting from San Francisco.

William wore an old baseball cap, sunglasses, and a turned-up collar, hoping to avoid local acquaintances. Willow wore a broad-brimmed sun hat and sunglasses, in the hope of not being recognized by one of her more aggressive Project Runway fans.

Strolling along Tiburon's waterfront park, they sat for a short time on one of the benches that directly faced the Golden Gate Bridge. East of the bridge was a perfect panoramic view of the San Francisco waterfront. With Willow comfortably tucked into the crook of William's arm, they listened to the waters of the bay slapping at the riprap along the shoreline just a few feet away.

In this state of relaxed comfort, William began to consider Willow as a partner in his life. The difference in their ages and interests, he reasoned, were not insurmountable given the rapport that obviously existed between them.

Willow sensed their closeness at that moment as well. She was tempted to say something but decided to be a bit more cautious, concerned that he would somehow find the gap in their ages, social, and professional lives insurmountable.

Perhaps he's just having fun, and this is nothing more than a fling, Willow worried. But her fears subsided when she reminded herself that what they had was indeed more than a fling.

She began to consider in earnest the steps that would help her transition from Willow Wisp to Mrs. Willow Adams. It had all been great fun, she thought, but the time had come to close this deal or to move on.

Not every woman Willow's age had the ambition to seize every opportunity for advancement. Her success was based as much on instinct as on beauty.

On a long flight to London for an event promoting her signature perfume, Willow sat as the lone passenger on a private jet provided by Harrods Department Store. It gave her the undistracted time to consider how she could complete William Adams' transition from loving admirer to adoring husband.

First, she considered the life of Fran Adams. It was apparent that William still missed her. It was equally evident that Willow wasn't Fran's intellectual equal. She considered herself to be intuitively bright. While Marin Academy is an excellent preparatory school, Willow had never stepped foot onto a college campus except to do a photo shoot or make a personal appearance. Fran, on the other hand, had earned a doctorate in law from a prestigious university.

Second, Willow was comfortably secure in the belief that Fran was far from her equal as a lover. All men, whether they admit this to themselves or not, are proud to be in the company of a woman other men desire. Considered one of the world's top ten models, Willow was confident in the arena of physical pleasures and exquisite beauty; the second point, undoubtedly, went to her.

Third, Willow knew she had to integrate herself into William's social circle, and eventually his professional sphere, beyond James Finch. No union between them would ever be complete if she failed to become a presence in William's life beyond the bedroom.

Fourth, Willow thought it wise to give William a real taste of the world of high fashion. She was scheduled to be a guest on an upcoming Project Runway special from Paris. Why not invite William to spend a night or two in her domain? Let him meet LeBon and some of his play pals, and he'd understand why she is more than ready to step away from this life. Better still, this would allow William to be her knight in shining armor riding in and rescuing her from this vain, petty, and mean-spirited business.

By the time her Lear jet lightly touched the tarmac at London City Airport and glided quietly to its remote location where a limousine driver and a Customs and Immigration officer waited to greet her, Willow had outlined her design for the future. If her plans went well, months from now Willow would begin her transition from the world of supermodels to the more exciting world of the super-rich.

Three days later, back in San Francisco, Willow called William with a question: "How about dinner at my place? I'd love to cook for you."

The chance to see a side of Willow he had never seen before was an offer William could not refuse.

Yes, she knew which cupboards held the pots and pans. And in the case of an emergency, the housekeeper had taught her how to turn the knobs on the La Cornue Grand Palais Range that was the centerpiece of her penthouse's kitchen. All that was left to do was to send her driver to pick up two dinners from her favorite Mission District restaurant, Lo Linda. The manager, Louis Zapata, was accustomed to this drill and boxed her dishes individually, with a note that provided a link to online photographs showing the best presentation methods for when the meal was ready to be served.

By the time William arrived, she had presented it all as her own creation.

There's something about perfectly prepared medallions of beef that brings out the beast in nearly every man. William was no exception. He wasn't sure if it was the light jazz playing on the Bose sound system, the candlelight, or the excellent meal. Perhaps, the marvelous Pinot Noir wine she poured or the featured attraction, a stunningly beautiful woman he had begun to think of as a living work of art. But it all combined to lift William to dizzying heights that he had never before experienced.

As Willow had hoped, that one night marked a breakthrough in their relationship. Afterward, William never shied away from leaning in to kiss her, regardless of whether the location was private or public.

Before Willow went to London, William was smitten with her. Soon after her return, he was genuinely in love.

"Why not?" William asked James as they both looked out from a fortieth-floor conference room window with views of the financial district and the blue waters of San Francisco Bay beyond. "I've earned a life of my own. I thought the rest of my years would be with Fran. But God had other plans. I've spent too much time thinking about what others might think of me being involved with a younger woman. I've decided to set all those concerns aside."

James nodded in agreement, feeling more than slightly jealous as he imagined having afternoon play dates of his own with Willow.

"You should do what you think is right," James insisted. "What are people going to do, call her a gold digger? I've managed her business affairs for the last five years. Willow is worth twelve million dollars, and her fame and wealth are growing. She could spend the rest of her life comfortably if she married you or a hapless poet." As he put one hand on William's shoulder, he added, "I do think she loves you for you."

"I keep wondering if people will say I'm a fool?" William said with almost painful shyness.

"We've been attorneys long enough to know that there are people who can and will say anything. Some will be confused, some will think you're crazy, and some will be happy for you. Speaking for myself, I'll be insanely jealous."

"Why? Jade is an exceptional and beautiful woman!"

"She's not an internationally recognized supermodel."

"Only a few women in the world are."

"William, you are one lucky guy," James said as he gave his partner a congratulatory slap on the back.

As William patted her dry after their shared shower, Willow thought that step one of her plan had gone exceptionally well. After enjoying one another in a marble shower the size of a small bedroom, William led her back to bed, where they both quickly fell into a deep sleep.

Willow awoke early to find him softly kissing her slender shoulders. However, he was dressed and ready to leave for work. "Good morning, darling," she said.

"I thought it would be fun if we had a little party next Saturday at my place," he said in a casual tone. "No more than thirty or forty people. I want some of my friends and neighbors to meet you. Are you available?"

Willow sat straight up in bed. "Why, of course, darling! That would be fun. I hope they like me."

He placed his arms around her waist and pulled her in close. The sheet that had been covering her fell and exposed her bare body down to her narrow hips.

William thought of her as a rare, exotic creature. Nevertheless, he kissed her forcefully.

As he stood, he looked at her silently in loving admiration. He smiled and said, "They had better like you, or it's time for me to find some new friends."

Willow silently congratulated herself, confident that the second piece of her plan had just fallen into place. And how easy it had been! Without any subtle hints, William had suggested arranging an introduction to his circle. She was indeed becoming an essential part of this fantastically wealthy man's life.

For the first time, Willow felt confident that her goal of becoming the second Mrs. William Adams was moving within her grasp.

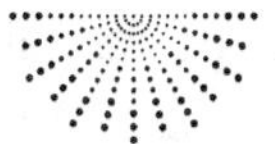

CHAPTER EIGHT

"Pick up, Rob! Sylvia Stokes needs to speak to you," Holly shouted from her office.

"Sylvia, what have you got for me?" Rob said in his usual busy, clipped tone. With four different local editions to put out every week, both he and Holly had little time for anything other than work.

Having followed the celebrity magazine gossip of recent weeks concerning William and Willow, Holly was dying to know if Sylvia had any inside news on Marin's most talked-about couple. She did her best to overhear Rob's part of the conversation.

"What have I got?" Sylvia asked with a raised voiced. "Just the biggest social story of the year, Rob. I've gotten an invitation for Jack and me to attend a reception for Willow Wisp at William Adams' mansion Saturday afternoon!"

"Great," Rob responded. He'd take Sylvia's word for it that this was a big deal. Until a few days earlier, when Karin had shown him a gossip item in the Independent, the county's only daily newspaper, he had no idea that a person named Willow Wisp existed.

"There is an actual person named Willow Wisp?" Rob had asked. "I don't believe you!"

Awed by her husband's apparent ignorance of all things celebrity related, Karin shook her head. "She's a famous model with her own perfume line and…"

Rob replied with a distant stare and a soft, "Oh."

The Independent's blurb written by its society editor, Sally White, was short and to the point. Karin read it aloud to Rob, in spite of his apparent disinterest. "Belvedere billionaire William Adams has been seen out and about in recent weeks in the company of Marin County native and international superstar model, Willow Wisp. Rumors are flying among Marin's smart set that the two of them are an item, with William and Willow sightings in many of San Francisco's top restaurants and nightspots."

Now that Willow was also on Sylvia's radar, Rob's competitive nature kicked in. "I'm glad you got invited. So, what do you need from me?"

"The Tiburon/Belvedere edition comes out on Friday, but the gathering is on Saturday! I can't report on something that hasn't happened! I'm worried that Sally White will cover it in the Independent's Sunday edition."

Rob only needed a moment to think before replying. "For this Friday do a short background piece on Willow—superstar model, glamorous life, career, et cetera—and mention the anticipation surrounding Saturday's party. Then get a few quotes from some of your socially connected gal pals over there about the upcoming event, and tease the reader promising complete coverage of the party in next week's column."

"Wonderful, Rob! Will do!"

"And one other thing Sylvia: avoid being at all critical of these two or their party."

"I wouldn't dream of it, Rob!"

"Good, because if those two get married, and it's Marin's social event of the year, perhaps the whole Bay Area for all I know, then you want to be on that invitation list. Your real value is to be on the inside covering this for all of us who won't get an invitation." He paused then added, "Better yet, ingratiate yourself to Willow. Being new to town, she'll appreciate your friendship, and you'll appreciate being first in line for the stories those two will likely generate in the months and years to come. If that happens, Sally White will be following your column to know what's going on."

"As always, Rob, you've been so helpful."

"That's what I'm here for," he said, and then clicked off.

Later, when Holly brought Rob the page proofs for the Sausalito edition, she seemed a bit down. "I was right when I said it wouldn't be long before some conniving woman got her claws into William Adams."

"You're just sore because you're not that conniving woman."

"You bet I am. In fact, if Adams had wanted to throw me over for that emaciated hussy, I would have happily stepped out of the picture for a mere million dollars. Make that two million, with inflation and all."

"You think Adams would have thrown you over for that, what's her name? Willow Branch?"

"God, you are a Neanderthal! Not Branch, Wisp."

Rob shrugged. "Branch, Twig, Wisp, whatever."

"I think it would be fun to go to that party. It never hurts to rub elbows with the rich and famous."

"Call Sylvia and see if you can tag along. Maybe Adams will dump Wisp and start chasing you."

"He wouldn't have to do much chasing; I have a soft spot for anyone on Forbes' list of the world's wealthiest. To me, even the oldest man on that list doesn't look a day over eighty."

"That's my Holly—one eye on romance, one eye on the bottom line."

"Even without romance, a million here and a million there can buy a gal a whole lot of happiness."

Everyone in Tiburon and Belvedere had an opinion about Willow and William as a couple, even though none had met the celebrity model. Someone famous enough to have graced the cover of People, who lent her name and image to the best-selling perfume in New York, London, Paris, and Hong Kong, was bound to generate local excitement and interest.

Willow and William were the most discussed topic at either one of the Peninsula's two yacht clubs—the San Francisco in Belvedere, and the Corinthian in Tiburon—and at the local social societies, houses of worship, and the monthly meetings of the Belvedere Waterfront Preservation League. Obviously, this was a story that demanded the continuing attention of Sylvia and her column.

Sylvia got busy gathering quotes, beginning with one of the grand dames of local society: Pamela Botherton, the wife of Marin County Superior Court judge, Peter Botherton.

Pamela took a few moments to collect her thoughts. Two nights before she had asked her husband, "What in the world is William Adams doing with that Willow Wisp woman?"

Peter, who thought that William Adams' social life was none of his concern, shrugged and then mumbled, "Having a good time I imagine."

Pamela was annoyed, but not at all surprised. Throughout the social calendar year, she dragged her aging husband from one event to another. His lack of interest was unchanged, regardless of the attendees. He only stirred if a fellow member of the bar was in attendance, and the conversation turned to the outcome of something like the property dispute in the case of Wilkes versus the Town of Tiburon. Otherwise, he mostly hid in the shadows, attending to matters through his iPhone in spite of his wife's endless complaints that he spent "more time with that phone than you do with me!"

Sylvia's requested interview finally gave Pamela the perfect moment to air her views. Tilting her head back and pausing thoughtfully she began, "Well, Sylvia, off the record, of course, I find it all a bit disturbing. Could there be an odder match than William Adams and this ridiculous Willow Wisp? William and Fran were pillars of this community, very active in the BWPL and other worthy causes. I can't imagine what poor Fran would have thought of all this. She had such an engaging intellect. This Wisp girl is just as vacuous as that ridiculous name of hers. She might be a fashion icon, but I can't imagine that she's anything more than an arm charm to William, and I shudder to think what else might transpire between the two of them."

Pamela's casual dismissal of Willow and William's relationship gave Sylvia nothing she could use for her column. After an awkward silence, Sylvia gently prodded Pamela, "So, could I say that you're looking forward to seeing Willow and William as a couple for the very first time?"

Pamela took a few moments to consider this created quote and then nodded with a dismissive wave of her hand: "Yes, Sylvia, that would be fine."

With the three other women at the top of Peninsula society's food chain—Cynthia Buckley, Vivian Green, and Julia Hassie— Sylvia's interviews unfolded similarly: "Outrageous! Imprudent! Questionable!"

All their comments, with permission, were reimagined as "Exciting! Intriguing! Refreshing!"

Sylvia had known all four of the women to have occasionally sharp tongues and cold hearts, but even she was surprised by the level of social distaste that William and Willow had unknowingly stirred.

Sylvia cobbled together her story. Of all the columns she had created for *The Peninsula Standard*, she had never worked so hard to accomplish what she delicately explained to Jack as "softening the truth."

Following Rob's advice about making the item about the Adams-Wisp party include a mix of local comments and information regarding two very different careers, Sylvia went online to research Willow's decade-long rise from young runway model to fashion icon.

"Jack, this young woman has had an incredible career! Do you know she was bright enough to get into Marin Academy on a full scholarship? Her father, Oscar, is an accountant and works for the California Department of Transportation. Her mother, Gloria, is a teacher at St. Patrick School and works part-time at the church's thrift shop. They live near the school in Larkspur. That's where Willow grew up. Talk about local kid makes good! That should be the angle of my story. What do you think, Jack?"

Getting no response, Sylvia got up from the kitchen table and walked into the living room. To her disappointment, her husband had fallen asleep in his leather recliner with the Giants baseball game muted on TV, and a copy of University Horizons magazine spread across his chest.

Despite all of Willow's accomplishments, Sylvia concluded that her social standing in Belvedere would hover somewhere between loathed and ignored.

Perhaps all she needed was a trusted friend. After all, Sylvia reasoned, you can't blame someone for falling in love with a man as charming, brilliant, and successful as William Adams.

And if Willow was a gold digger, as suggested by Botherton and her clique, she obviously brought to her relationship with William great wealth of her own.

When finished, Sylvia was pleased with her effort. Let these society women come bearing smiling faces and hidden daggers, she thought. I'll extend the hand of friendship to someone who is going to need all the friends she can get.

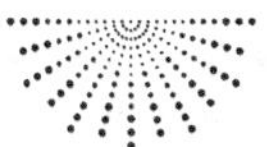

CHAPTER NINE

Before she called, Holly invented a story about fact-checking one of Sylvia's recent columns.

"I've got a reader who sent in a letter, signed, 'Tiburon Fan.' No return address. So obviously this could be from anyone. The writer asked whether your item in Tiburon Talk on Mr. and Mrs. Madison's fiftieth wedding anniversary party was not, in fact, their fortieth. Should I add a correction notice at the bottom of your next column?"

"Oh no," Sylvia responded quickly. "I was at the party. It was indeed their fiftieth. In fact, there was a big five-oh right there on the cake."

"Okay, no need for a correction then." Holly quickly followed with the real purpose of her call. "You did a great job on your Belvedere Buzz column this week. It was the perfect lead-up to the Adams-Wisp party."

"Oh, thank you for that, Holly!" Sylvia said, pleased to get any feedback from either her or Rob.

"In fact, I'm meeting a friend for lunch tomorrow over in Tiburon, and I was going to ask if you wanted to meet for a cocktail, or coffee, afterward. But then I remembered that you had the party at the Adams house."

"Oh, darn! That would have been fun. Say, I heard through the grapevine that their invitation list has grown from forty to nearly a hundred. I don't think one or two more at this point is going to make any real difference. Why don't you join me, as a member of the press? The party starts at three."

"Wow! I'd love that! Thanks for including me."

"Meet Jack and me at our house, and we'll ride up there together. This should be fun!"

Moments after her call, Holly told Rob that she was attending the party at William Adams' house for his meet Willow event.

"How did you con Sylvia into that?"

"The old 'fact checking' call."

"I wish I had a few bucks for every time you've pulled that routine. What's the big deal anyway? I never thought of you as star-struck."

"I live in a one-bedroom apartment on Caledonia Street in the heart of sleepy Sausalito," she explained. "If I can get myself invited to a party thrown by one of the world's wealthiest men to introduce his fabulously rich and famous girlfriend, I'm so there!"

"Don't count on their handing out bottles of Willow Wisp perfume as party favors."

"Maybe I'll get lucky, and they are. My Christmas list is pretty long, and you know better than most, this Santa has to get by on a pretty tight budget."

"This is where my late uncle Steve would have said, 'You're some piece of work.'"

"Boss man, a girl's got to do what a girl's got to do."

❀

In a dramatic departure from so many of her public appearances, Willow decided she'd strike a different pose for this all-important event: humble, down-to-earth Marin County girl, rather than an international, high-fashion icon.

On the morning of the event, Willow's hair stylist and makeup artist arrived at her penthouse at ten o'clock to begin her preparation. Willow's direction to both of them was to create a look that would be "natural, but stunning."

It was a demanding role for her to play: dressing down while dressing up. The day before, Willow thought and rethought her outfit. Finally, she settled on a bright orange Valentino lace sheath. It was sleeveless and knee-length with a jewel neckline and pencil skirt.

Four hours later, she was both low-key and picture perfect. No matter what William's friends might think of their relationship, no one, particularly no man, would come away feeling anything less than, "William Adams is a very fortunate man!"

While she prepared, William sent to her iPhone the first three paragraphs of Sylvia Stokes' column, "The Belvedere Buzz." Naturally, Willow was pleased to see what Sylvia had written:

"Peninsula Society on Saturday will welcome for the first time the international celebrity supermodel Willow Wisp, believed to be the world's second most photographed woman, behind the Duchess of Cambridge.

"The party at the fabulous Golden Gate Avenue home of William Adams, one of San Francisco's top attorneys and one of the world's wealthiest individuals, is to welcome Ms. Wisp, the woman he happily refers to as, 'The bright light of my life.'

"Many of the Peninsula's social stars will be in attendance, including the Bothertons, the Buckleys, the Greens, and the Hassies."

After listing the quotes she coaxed from those local luminaries, Sylvia concluded with a brief recap of Willow's meteoric rise from Larkspur native to pop culture icon; followed by a promise to readers for "much more on this exciting event in next week's column."

After Willow pronounced herself satisfied with the work of her hair stylist and makeup artist, she dismissed them and listened to a phone message from her occasionally insane but always irresistible Russian violinist, Viktor Kozlov. His brief message, in his usual tortured English, pleaded with her, "Most lost not having you! Please to call, must soon speak!"

Absentmindedly, she stared at her iPhone. For all of his quirks, there was no doubt she missed Viktor's powerful and magical touch. She had often imagined being the muse that brought him worldwide acclaim.

"Play me," she whispered in his ear whenever she longed to feel his strong fingers pressing down upon her.

"You like, no?" he asked as their two slender bodies wrapped their way around each other.

"Oh, yes. I like, maestro," Willow responded passionately, demanding yet another solo performance.

The thought of all those beautiful moments brought her anxious index finger to the verge of pressing her phone's callback option. Her intention, she told herself, was to explain why their relationship must remain permanently in the past.

But the breathless sound of his voice as he pleaded, "Must see you, world most empty without you," melted her intention to keep far away from Kozlov.

"I'm rushing out. I'm already late for a personal appearance. Where are you?"

"Coming in plane for San Francisco, two days I will be there."

Against her better instinct, she agreed to call Kozlov on Monday.

"This most excellent will count many minutes until we are sides with each other."

The memory of Kozlov's touch was still on her mind as William's driver brought her to the front gate of the Adams estate, where a team of valets for parking the cars of arriving guests was already in place.

The guests began arriving shortly after four on a picture-perfect afternoon.

William, tanned with dark hair streaked with wisps of silver, clad in a soft yellow cashmere sweater atop cream-colored linen pants, looked successful and distinguished. His strikingly attractive companion looked as though she had stepped off the pages of Vanity Fair.

Together they greeted their guests and conveyed the impression they both desired: William and Willow were the perfect couple.

The Adams mansion, on one of Belvedere's highest points, had an expansive third-floor sundeck, which was perfect for receptions. It had spectacular views of the entire San Francisco skyline, from the dome atop the Palace of Fine Arts to the peak of the Transamerica Pyramid looking down on North Beach, China-town, and the financial district, continuing across the iconic Bay Bridge and beyond to the golden hills of the East Bay.

Sylvia reasoned that it would be less noticeable that she turned her "plus one" invitation into a plus two if she came a little late, so she, Jack, and Holly arrived after most of the guests were already enjoying an assortment of hors-d'oeuvres and the music of a four-piece ensemble playing light jazz. A gentle breeze was just strong enough to cool the warm afternoon sun.

Finally sighting Willow, Holly observed her from afar. As she glided comfortably through the gathering, it was apparent that she was accustomed to being followed by dozens of sets of eyes. Sometimes, she leaned casually on the arm of William, but just as often she confidently struck out on her own, each time introducing herself as if the guests had no idea who she was.

As impressed as Holly and Sylvia were with Willow's natural grace, it irritated Pamela Botherton and Julia Hassie. The two huddled near an alcove that led back to a spacious family room.

Accustomed to being the center of attention at most Peninsula gatherings, they were irritated by the positive reaction Willow was receiving. Worst of all was her grace, charm, and undeniable beauty.

"I can't imagine what William Adams sees in her," Pamela said in a low growl.

"I suspect he's more in lust than in love," Julia responded as Pamela nodded approvingly. "I think he's making a fool of himself, flitting around with a woman who is half his age!"

"Men can be such fools, Julia; particularly the rich ones. Someday she's going to walk away with a nice piece of the Adams estate."

"I understand she's worth millions on her own."

"Perhaps," Pamela sniffed. "But I'll bet the family jewels she has her eye on trading her millions for his billions."

"I'm sorry that we haven't yet had the chance to meet," Willow said as she walked up behind Pamela and Julia.

Both the women giggled nervously over the thought that Willow overheard a portion of their conversation.

Pamela steadied herself and quickly put on her brightest smile. "Don't give it any thought my dear! You're busy meeting so many new people that I'm sure it's all a bit overwhelming."

Try doing six appearances a day with handlers pushing and pulling you in different directions, and you'll know what it feels like to be overwhelmed, Willow thought, hiding her feelings behind a gracious smile. "We should do tea one day, and get to know each other better," Willow said, confident that these two stars of Peninsula society would require careful observation.

"Oh, we'd enjoy that!" Pamela and Julia said in unison.

"I'll have my person contact your people, and we'll get something on our calendars," Willow suggested, knowing that it was highly unlikely that either of these two women had personal secretaries.

In her life as a celebrity, Willow had honed an uncanny sense of those who thought kindly of her, and those who loathed her. That expertly tuned radar indicated to her that Pamela and Julia tilted toward loathing.

Sylvia stood at the opposite end of the expansive sun deck. She was quick to observe the interplay between the three women. "How many women at her age, or any age, could move with such poise, grace, and dignity?" she murmured to Jack.

Given Jack's years of work in the University of California's financial system, she knew he was no stranger to great wealth. Despite the opulence of his surroundings, the tentative half-smile plastered on his face was proof that he was thoroughly disinterested. Sylvia shrugged and put her husband's lack of interest aside. She was more determined than ever to do as Rob suggested and get close to Willow.

Sylvia's goal was within reach when Willow took hold of both of her hands as if she was greeting a long lost friend. "Thank you so much, Sylvia, for your kind words in yesterday's *Peninsula Standard*."

Delighted in learning that Willow knew who she was and appreciated what she had written, Sylvia responded brightly, "Oh, it was my pleasure! I was pleased to have the chance to include it in this week's column. In fact, I'm doing a follow-up next week."

"I don't think that William is used to receiving all this attention," Willow leaned in closer and said in a conspiratorial manner. "For all his success, he's a remarkably private man."

Sylvia smiled. "Well, attention comes with the territory if you're fortunate enough to date a celebrity."

"Oh, I'd hardly call myself a celebrity. As you get to know me better, you'll see I'm just a Marin girl at heart who looks forward every year to the county fair."

"You're a beautiful young woman with great poise, charm, and intelligence," Sylvia said with the certainty of a loving aunt. "You make your breaks in life. I'm sure you worked hard for everything you've accomplished."

"You're too kind, Sylvia," Willow said, as she gave the local society scribe a gentle kiss on the cheek.

At that moment, Holly came up alongside the two of them. Taking Sylvia's arm, Holly smiled innocently at Willow.

Sylvia took the cue. "Willow, let me introduce Holly Cross, my dear friend, who is the production manager for all of the Standard newspapers."

Willow smiled. "Delighted to meet you, Holly."

"You're my favorite perfume," Holly gushed.

Willow laughed. "I always love hearing that. In fact, if you both have your cards on you, I'll have my assistant send you each a bottle."

Sylvia's polite entreaty—"Oh, you shouldn't bother"—was drowned out by Holly's excitement: "Oh my God, I'd love that!"

As the three of them laughed, Willow declared, "Sylvia, you have to be a little more like Holly. When you have a chance to get something you want, you should go for it. I know I do!"

At that moment, the three of them formed a bond.

Willow knew women like Botherton and Hassie would do what they could to make her life unpleasant, but Sylvia's positive coverage in the local community newspaper should help dampen whatever negative gossip those two chose to spread.

Sensing an opportunity, Willow pushed ahead. "In fact, after I make a quick trip to Paris for a Project Runway special, why don't the three of us get together for lunch? I'd like to discuss how I can get more involved with some of the local charities. I know it's important to William that we do what we can to help our community, and I think the three of us together can come up with some good deeds that need doing."

To end on a high note, Willow kissed each one of them on the cheek and promised to be in touch.

Jack may have been content to stay at a distance, but that didn't stop him from closely following their interaction. As Willow strolled off, Jack walked over. "I think you two have a new best friend."

"I wouldn't go that far," Sylvia responded.

"I would!" Holly exclaimed. "She wants some good local press, and I want some ridiculously expensive perfume at a steep discount. I'm sure we could work something out. If we play our cards right, she can make our Christmas shopping a whole lot easier."

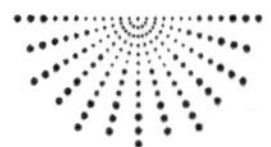

CHAPTER TEN

Soon after the last of their reception guests departed, William took Willow's hand and declared, "The party was a total success. Don't you agree dear?"

"I enjoyed every moment," Willow responded with a relaxed smile.

"Everyone adored you, and I think they're looking forward to seeing you again."

"I enjoyed meeting everyone, but I must say Pamela Botherton and Julia Hassie seemed to have their noses a bit out of joint."

"Pamela has made a nuisance of herself for years. She and that pal of hers, Julia, and the rest of their socialite posse would presume you're not quite right for me. I'm too old, you're too young, and whatever else they can add to the mix. They're just two jealous old goats who think no one has a place in Peninsula society without their approval. Don't pay them any attention. I invited them because Fran served on several local charitable groups with one or both of them. She found them tiresome, but always felt that we should be involved and supportive of the entire community."

"At least I have one big fan in Belvedere society, Sylvia Stokes.

In fact, she brought along the paper's production manager, Holly Cross, and she was also a sweetie."

"Sylvia has a good heart. When Fran died, she was the only reporter I felt comfortable sitting down with to talk about Fran's life and charitable work. You know, Sylvia's husband is a finance guy with the UC system. It would be fun to get to know them a little better. I'd like to consider getting more involved with the University of California on a philanthropic level. It 'd be interesting to hear from someone on the inside how they're doing with their investment portfolio. When you give to an organization, it's nice to know they can grow your money, rather than just spend it."

Willow nodded. "I'd like that; I noticed Jack keeps to himself. But I would imagine that most financial planners tend to be quiet people. But Sylvia and Holly are sweethearts. I think I'll be seeing more of them."

Back home, Willow prepared for a morning flight taking her to a one-day event at the Beverly Center in Los Angeles. She reflected on the success of the afternoon. Willow thought she had been well received. She was glad that James Finch and his wife had not been there. Becoming an essential part of William's life, she certainly didn't need Finch hanging about, expecting sexual favors in exchange for stock tips and financial help that she soon, hopefully, would no longer need.

Steps one and two of her plan now accomplished, it was time for step three: giving William an insider's taste of a celebrity model's life and how he might be able to rescue her from this glamorous but demanding life.

After that, Willow hoped William's proposal would come in a matter of weeks. It could not happen soon enough, Willow thought as she dabbed generous amounts of an anti-aging cream on her face, neck, and hands. It was a formula prepared especially for her private use. As with all such beauty products, she had doubts as to its actual value.

Willow gave a weary sigh as she put on a light cotton night-gown, slipped between soft, inviting sheets, and placed a comfortable silk mask over her eyes. In the darkness, her first thoughts were of Viktor's strong fingers wandering over her neck and shoulders as he kissed her endlessly.

A flash of annoyance pushed Viktor from her thoughts. What am I thinking? Seeing Viktor would never be worth the risk! She scolded herself in silence.

As a lover, William was not qualified to carry Viktor's bow. But as a life partner, he had far more to offer. As age thirty approached, Willow thought it wise to give further thought to her essential needs rather than brief, but spectacular, moments of passion.

Willow drifted off to sleep dreaming happily of a life filled with opulent homes, grand and exotic trips, and dazzling jewels. She was close enough to feel the thrill of William Adams' immense fortune. She would be a fool to let that slip from her hands now.

The next morning, on her way to the airport, Willow made two calls. One to William to tell him how grateful she was for the party; the second to Viktor to reassert her original decision that their relationship had come to an end.

"But this cannot, must not be! I can be a secret lover like Czarinas had in the time before Bolsheviks!" Viktor insisted.

Once again, Willow thought of hitting the red disconnect circle on her iPhone's display, but each time she paused. Images of Viktor's flat, toned abs, his carefully defined chest, and broad, tanned shoulders, kept teasing her. His perfect features were minus the lines that appeared around William's eyes. Viktor exuded the power of youth, whereas William had the faint, but distinct, hints of physical decline.

Finally, Willow could not resist. As if in a trance, she uttered one word, "When?"

"Tomorrow, yes?"

"What time?"

"Three! No, two! Must rehearse."

"Where?"

"Four Seasons. Come to Penthouse. I wait here for you."

W illow spent her in-flight time, heading down to Los Angeles and her return back north, considering her options.

The thought of being disloyal to William by reigniting her trysts with Viktor was of little concern. A far greater concern was the potentially disastrous consequence of William learning she had been unfaithful. Willow knew she was treading a thin line, but the specter of Viktor's insatiable passion haunted her every thought.

She awoke the next day at eleven, wondering what she should wear to her rendezvous with the maestro.

She settled for an outfit that was both alluring and discreet: black leather pants, a black silk blouse covered by a black-and-white trench coat. She shoved her hair into a black leather newsboy cap. Her disguise was complete with an oversized pair of dark sunglasses.

For fear of being recognized, the last thing she wanted to do was stop at the hotel's front desk, so she texted her lover for his room number and the elevator code to allow it to stop at the penthouse level.

Viktor answered the door clothed only in a silk robe. He had ordered champagne and caviar, which he planned to charge to a generous expense account provided by the company that had brought him to the city to record Tchaikovsky's Violin Concerto in D Major, accompanied by the San Francisco Symphony.

Willow and Viktor exchanged silent nods and then passionately tore into each other. Neither of them had ever been more desperate to be with one another. Never had Viktor's lovemaking been such an intoxicating blend of tenderness and ferocity.

Afterward, as she lay spent in his strong arms, her mind wandered back to those particular words: "He plays the violin, and I am undone."

That evening, Willow resisted William's offer of dinner, fearing that he would want more than just a meal and would somehow sense that she had spent the afternoon in the arms of another man.

"I don't know why darling, but I've had this frightful headache all day long…"

William, disappointed, told her to rest and promised to call early the next day to see if she was feeling better.

"Alright," Willow responded sweetly, "but not before ten."

CHAPTER ELEVEN

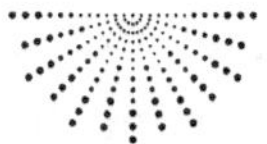

Holly came into Smitty's on Friday evening carrying a copy of the just-released Tiburon/Belvedere edition that featured Sylvia's column, which was devoted solely to the Adams event.

While the men enjoyed their Guinness beers, Holly sipped on her martini. "I don't know if either of you gentlemen noticed, but I was prominently mentioned in the society column of today's edition of *The Peninsula Standard.*"

"Oh, darn! I haven't had the chance to get my copy yet. The society page is always the first thing I turn to," Eddie said while rolling his eyes.

"I only read it because I read every damn word of every damn paper I put out. A lesson I learned last year after the death of the gossiping gourmet," Rob said.

"Okay," Eddie said. "So, read me your news. Not every day of the year one of us commoners makes it onto the society page."

"Then, for Eddie's sake," Holly said as she snapped open the paper, turned to the inside back page, and began reading. "'Belvedere's William Adams introduced Peninsula Society last

Saturday afternoon to the new woman in his life: international celebrity model, Willow Wisp. Ms. Wisp, who looked stunning in a flame-hued lace Valentino sheath, was enthusiastically greeted by over a hundred guests at the afternoon event held at the dazzling Adams estate on Golden Gate Avenue. *The Peninsula Standard* was represented by both this reporter and its senior editorial staff director, Holly Cross—'"

"Hold it right there," Eddie interrupted. "Besides its illustrious editor, I thought The Standard only has a staff of one."

"Well, yes, if you're going to be uncreative in your approach to our system-wide staffing policies."

"Huh?" Eddie replied with a cocked brow.

"If you look at the big picture," Holly continued, "we have part-time staff in news bureaus throughout central and southern Marin."

"You mean your collection of aging community volunteer writers, correct?"

"Well, yes, if you want to put a harsh light on this group of gifted contributors!"

Despite enjoying the verbal jousting between his two best friends, Rob felt the need to interject, "Let her finish! This is the most fun she's had since the days of Sausalito's dear departed chef."

"Okay," Eddie conceded. "Please continue, Senior Editorial Potentate, or whatever your job title is this week."

"Thank you!" Holly nodded and gave the paper a proper shake. "Now, where was I? Let's see, oh yes…'Together, Adams and Wisp will be at the top of everyone's party list. He is an internationally renowned attorney and investor, and as most are aware, on Forbes' list of wealthiest people in the world. And thanks to the incredible success of her perfume, 'Willow Wisp,' the Marin County native from Larkspur is recognized in fashion capitals around the globe.'"

"Holly, unless you're mentioned again, I think I've heard enough. This society ya-ya is not my thing," Eddie grumbled. "Now, if someone bangs one of these beautiful people over the head, and buries their body in a ditch off the 101, give me a call. Otherwise, it all sounds like yadda, yadda, yadda to me. Anyway, since when are you into all this silliness?"

Before Holly could answer, Rob offered, "Since she started scheming to get free perfume for every woman on her Christmas list from the enchanting Miss Wisp."

"So, you're conning her," Eddie suggested.

Holly lifted her chin and sniffed indignantly. "I wouldn't say that."

"Of course you wouldn't. That's why you've got friends like Rob and me—to say it for you."

"Listen, you two! Those gift bottles—which, by the way, run over a hundred dollars a pop—make lovely Christmas and birthday gifts, and I've got a big family! If I can knock a few people off my shopping list, it's like money in the bank. Not to mention, at the cost of that perfume it makes me look like a very generous soul."

"Now, that's more like our Holly—working all the angles," Eddie said, as Rob nodded approvingly. "Holly, be honest; what are those two, the billionaire and the glamour puss, doing together?" Eddie asked.

She shrugged. "I think they need each other. Adams' wife died, and he's ready to move on. I suppose to him, Willow looks like a good choice. She's bright and charming. Most of all, she's an incredibly attractive woman. I guess you could say she's the ultimate arm charm."

"So, what does she see in him?" Rob asked. "Karin tells me that he's nearly double her age."

"My first thought was she's eyeing some huge dollar signs," Holly admitted. "But Sylvia thinks—and I can see why—that she's got plenty of money of her own. I mean, let's face it, she's a regular on Project Runway, she models at major couture shows, and she does a lot of top fashion magazine covers. Even if she's getting a tiny percentage of Willow Wisp perfume sales, that would still be an awful lot of money! Retailers can't keep the stuff in stock."

"Being the detective in our little threesome, I think there's got to be something more to it than that."

"Like what?" Rob asked.

"I'm not sure. But just like firefighters believe that where there is smoke you'll find fire, police believe that where there are significant amounts of money, there's great potential for mischief."

"Do you think Willow's interest in Adams is just about his money?" Holly asked.

"That's my guess," Eddie said as he leaned in. "I asked Sharon about her. Willow has also dated some of the best-paid sports stars, not to mention a fair number of Hollywood actors. If she were into mere millions, I would think she would have sunk her claws into one of those guys. Instead, she dumps handsome, well-paid celebrities for an older guy, who lives the glamorous life of a corporate attorney and high-tech guru? I'm just not buying that! My bet is she finds his incredible wealth wildly attractive."

"Wow," Rob said, shaking his head. "There are people in this world who need that much money?"

"It takes all types, buddy-boy. Work my job for a year, and you'll see what I mean. There are people in this world who can never get enough. I suspect the lovely Willow Wisp is one of them."

"Speaking of money, would one of you boys mind picking up my drinks tonight? The job of senior editorial staff director doesn't pay as much as people might think."

"You know, you're worth more than I can afford to pay," Rob said. "If Willow Wisp becomes Willow Adams, you should see if she's interested in buying a chain of community newspapers. If she thinks she has a glamorous life now, wait until she gets an exclusive on Tiburon's plans to update the town's sewer lines."

"I'm sure she'd be thrilled. But for now, I'll focus on getting a few more promotional perfume bottles. I'm a gal with simple needs."

CHAPTER TWELVE

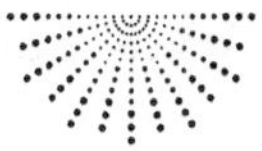

Their busy schedules left Viktor and Willow no other time to rendezvous before she flew off to Paris for a series of personal appearances and the taping of a new segment of Project Runway.

Halfway through her trip, William arrived, joining her at the Georges Cinq. When he knocked on the door of her room a little before five in the evening, he was holding two dozen long-stemmed yellow roses.

Willow put her arms around him and kissed him passionately.

"I was thinking of going out to dinner, but if you prefer we can stay in," William suggested.

"Oh no, we have to go out! We have dinner reservations at Epicure at eight o'clock. LeBon and the new love of his life, Jacques Allard, are meeting us there. Allard is a famous jewelry designer, and he makes the most beautiful pieces! Then we're all going over to the Latin Quarter, to have late night cocktails at Le Six."

"Sounds wonderful, sweetheart. Maybe I should jump into the shower and freshen up after that long flight."

"Go ahead, darling. It's a fantastic shower, so take your time and enjoy."

William stood under a steady stream of hot water, hoping to restore a little energy to his travel-weary body. Even though he had a comfortable first class seat, the strain of a long work day, followed by a late San Francisco departure time, a nine-hour time change, and a ten-hour flight for a three o'clock arrival time in Paris, made him feel fifteen years older. Nevertheless, William was determined not to play the role of the aging traveler. He stood under that shower until, finally, his weariness faded, and a sense of vitality returned.

By the time he stepped back into the bedroom of their two-room suite, Willow was dressed and ready for a night out.

"You look fabulous," William said with as much enthusiasm as he could muster. But as he reached over to kiss her, Willow pushed back. "Not now, darling! You're still damp from your shower; you'll make a mess of my hair and makeup."

"You're right, sweetheart." He sighed. "I've just missed you."

"Later tonight darling, alright?" Willow said, as she smiled, kissed him on the cheek, and sent him off to get dressed.

William thought the meal at Epicure was superb. He was less enthralled, however, with LeBon and Allard, or Henri and Jacques, as they insisted on being called.

Willow tried to include William in the conversation, which drifted from French to English and back again. William tried his best to keep up. But between the rich food, the bilingual gymnastics, a glass of wine, and his befuddled body clock, he found himself falling further behind.

In spite of his valiant effort, when it was time to get the check, he insisted on staying to pay but told the three of them to cab over to the Left Bank while he went back to the hotel for some much-needed sleep.

Watching the three of them leave, William felt more like Willow's father sending her off for the evening than a lover anticipating her return. For the first time, William seriously considered if he could ignore the gap in their ages.

William thought about this as he strolled along the Avenue Matignon, turning onto the Champs-Elysees at Franklin D. Roosevelt. For just a moment, given the street's name, the late president came to mind. FDR was not more than seven years older than William when he died of a massive stroke. Could his trying to keep up with Willow do to William what twelve years in the White House did to Roosevelt? That was a sobering thought.

In the cab on the way over to the nightclub in the heart of St. Germaine, LeBon and Allard teased Willow about her billionaire boyfriend. Now that William was no longer around, LeBon made a more significant effort to speak English to the one woman who piqued his sexual interests. "He is very kind and indeed very wealthy. But Mon Dieu, my dear! I cannot see how he will ever make you happy."

Willow smiled but didn't say a word.

"I think what will make you very happy is all that money, mais oui?" he insisted with that knowing smile that irked Willow in a way only LeBon could.

"I'm not getting any younger, Henri. And besides, William is a wonderful man," Willow said emphatically.

That led to LeBon and Allard exchanging asides in French faster than Willow could follow. She was annoyed, even agitated, but calmed herself with the thought that soon she would be well settled with a personal fortune that LeBon could only possess in his wildest fantasies.

She made what every member of her entourage agreed was an early exit from the nightclub where they had gathered.

"A wretched headache," was her stated reason.

Fifteen minutes later, she slipped into bed next to William, who was in a deep and much needed sleep.

The next morning at breakfast, William apologized for his exhaustion the previous night.

Willow insisted that it was she who should apologize. "It was thoughtless of me to plan such a busy schedule after you had an all but sleepless night during that long flight."

"No, it wasn't thoughtless of you. I've never slept well on planes, no matter how comfortable the accommodation. It's the endless whining of those engines, I suppose."

"It couldn't be much worse than listening to LeBon whine about his schedule. People in the fashion world are mostly vain and self-centered, and frankly, it can be exhausting being around them."

"I'm sure it's not all the glamour and excitement most people imagine."

Willow nodded in agreement and then fabricated a Eureka moment. "I have an idea, darling. I'm free after today, and I don't have any other commitments for a few days after that. We should take off and go anywhere in Europe you'd like—just the two of us."

"Anywhere?" William said with an uncertain smile.

"Anywhere!"

"Okay. Let's take a quick flight up to Amsterdam."

"Absolutely," Willow said enthusiastically. "What made you think of Amsterdam?"

"When I finished my undergraduate degree at Berkeley, I wanted to get away for a while. So my dad said, 'take off for a month or two and backpack around Europe.' I had been here before with my parents, but never on my own. So I took his advice. After a couple of lonely weeks in Madrid and London, I landed in Amsterdam and fell in with a bunch of kids—all early twenty-somethings. I spent four weeks there. In that time, I made up for some of the partying I hadn't done while studying to pass the exam to enter law school. I got so plastered one night that I fell asleep with some of my pals in a park near the Rijksmuseum and the Van Gogh. I woke up the following morning being poked by a police officer telling me to get moving. Me, William Adams, sleeping on a park bench! It's one of my favorite memories."

The thought of William spending his night in a city park made Willow laugh. "Well, let's do it. But if it's okay with you, we should get a room. I don't think paparazzi capturing photos of us sleeping on a park bench would help the sales of my perfume."

Willow spent a busy day and night completing her commitments for Project Runway and doing a signing of Willow Wisp perfume gift boxes at Printemps, one of Europe's oldest and grandest department stores.

Meanwhile, William made plans for a three-day getaway to Amsterdam. Just the thought of this brief adventure lifted his spirits. He could not recall a time when he felt a greater need to connect with memories of his youth. If Willow had not suggested that they change their plans, none of this would have happened.

He was equally relieved not to be spending another night with LeBon and Allard. He winced at the thought of what their entire clique would be like as he realized for the first time that Willow's seemingly magical world was a lot less glamorous than he had previously thought.

Amsterdam was perfect.

When they stepped into their suite at the Hotel Conservatorium to find accommodations even more impressive than those they had left at the Georges Cinq, Willow said, "I guess you decided against sleeping in the park?"

"I might feel like a twenty-something in your company, but I'm a little old to go without a bed and a pillow."

They enjoyed long walks along the picturesque canals and through the city's grand plazas, all the while dodging the crowds of local bicyclists. They marveled at the works of Dutch greats, Rembrandt, Vermeer, Hals, and others. And spent hours thrilled by the world's most complete collection of Van Gogh's work.

For three days and two nights, William had a permanent smile on his face. He took Willow on a complete tour of his "Amsterdam misadventures," from a walk through the seedy Red Light District to the open space of the Museumplein where he spent a night under the stars. She snuggled in close to him as they sat at a coffee shop adjacent to the Bloemenmarkt, Amsterdam's famous flower market, and William further reminisced about his time as a young man at play.

Willow "confessed" that she was relieved to be away from "LeBon and all the insanity of the fashion world." William thought she needed a man who would protect her from the continuous pressure of celebrity life.

She took care, however, to explain that she wished to remain active in the promotion of Willow Wisp Perfume. Without the occasional trip to New York, London, Paris, Tokyo, or a dozen other spots around the globe, how would she be able to rendezvous with Kozlov? Belvedere was certainly too small a fishbowl for them to play together unnoticed.

As they headed back to Amsterdam's Schiphol Airport for their flight to San Francisco, William was reveling in their brief visit. He took one last look as their limousine moved through the city's light morning traffic and concluded that all people are just as young as they think.

As long as Willow was at his side, William could not imagine growing old.

❦

William popped the question in less time than Willow had dared hope. Particularly noteworthy, the ring was unexpectedly generous given her extraordinarily high expectations.

"This is insane!" Willow said as tears came on cue to her eyes.

"Nothing is too beautiful for my perfect flower," William replied, using an endearment that since their time in Amsterdam had entered into their lovemaking. Willow disliked this new pet name, but she kept that to herself, at least for now.

The happy couple kissed as they sat nestled close to each other, enjoying a warm fire on a chilly evening at the home William and Fran had purchased in Lake Tahoe.

Willow jumped up and ran to the mirror to admire from a variety of angles her new pink pear-cut diamond engagement ring. She placed her left hand on her right shoulder and struck a variety of poses. Later, after William had fallen asleep, Willow did an online search hoping to tease out the approximate cost of this fabulous new bobble. She found a similar diamond in a ring given by Enrique Iglesias to his tennis star bride-to-be, Anna Kournikova. That ring had a stated value of over 2.5 million dollars—nearly twenty percent of Willow's total worth, but a tiny fraction of William's fortune. Should she have expected something more? Perhaps a few carats larger?

Willow banished the thought. This was a lovely gesture on the part of her future husband, and in time, she was sure, he would buy her many more fabulous pieces. As she learned in the growth of her career, practicing patience was essential to long-term success.

❦

Willow's love affair with the world's most exquisite jewelry began when she attended the Bulgari exhibit at San Francisco's DeYoung Museum. She went back three times to visit the same exhibition, disguised each time behind dark glasses and various hats. She was not there to be disturbed by fans, but rather to enjoy the dazzling emeralds, rubies, sapphires, pearls, and diamonds in elegant silver and gold settings.

Listening intently to the exhibit's audio guide, Willow learned the history of Sotirio Bulgari, a Greek immigrant who opened his first shop in Rome in 1884, choosing to follow a different path than the Parisian school of jewelry design.

"Where the French followed a tradition of creating delicate pieces, Bulgari's works were massive by comparison," the exhibition's audio guide explained. "By the 1920s the house of Bulgari had become known for a distinct style that designers and customers recognized and valued. In the 1950s, when Italian design for everything from clothes to furniture to automobiles became popular around the globe, the unique approach of Bulgari to fine jewelry became an international sensation. Before long, stars like Grace Kelly, Audrey Hepburn, and Marilyn Monroe were all photographed wearing their most beautiful Bulgari creations."

The exhibit's highlight was Elizabeth Taylor's stunning collection. If Willow had any hope of accumulating nearly as impressive a collection of jewels at 21st century prices, her wealth of twelve million dollars fell far short of what she needed. Several of the exhibit's pieces were valued individually at over a million dollars. In fact, nine months after Taylor's death in March 2011, her entire collection was auctioned off for one hundred and sixteen million dollars at Christie's auction house in New York. Many of the pieces that brought winning bids of five million dollars or more were gifts from Richard Burton to the woman he married once in 1964, divorced in 1974, then remarried in 1975, and divorced one year later.

Willow recognized it would take the wealth of a billionaire to drape her in these exquisite gems, which to her were the essence of lasting beauty. William's twelve-carat diamond engagement ring was lovely, but to Willow, it was a mere starter piece.

Willow knew that in time her beauty would fade. Her collection of magnificent jewels, however, would be ageless.

CHAPTER THIRTEEN

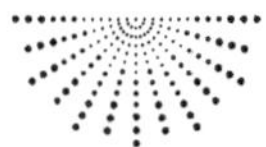

In Sylvia's upcoming Belvedere Buzz column, she planned to feature a photograph from People magazine that captured William and Willow at play in Amsterdam. As she studied the photo, she paused to consider what precisely a billion dollars represented in today's world. On the Forbes list of the world's wealthiest three hundred individuals, Adams was number thirty-eight, with a fortune of twenty-four billion dollars. Just above him, a Brazilian beer king. Below him was a German supermarket tycoon.

Truly rarefied air.

To her surprise, better-known billionaires like Bezos, Gates, Musk, and "the sage of Omaha," Warren Buffett, were vastly outnumbered by names she had never heard.

"I suppose that would be true of William Adams as well," Sylvia murmured to herself. "Jack, is that true?" she asked, in the hope of diverting her husband's attention from the financial papers he was busy reviewing.

"Is what true, dear?" he asked barely above a whisper.

"That most people don't know the name William Adams, even though he's one of the world's wealthiest people!"

"Certainly, I think that would be true. Of course, if he keeps getting photographed by paparazzi on the hunt for Willow, that's going to change quickly."

"But don't you think it's fascinating that he's involved with a very wealthy woman as well?"

"Not really. Wealth has a way of attracting wealth. But don't think for a moment they are close to being in the same financial bracket. I'm certain Willow has nowhere near the wealth of William Adams."

Sylvia winced. Jack's officious tone around all things financial frequently irritated her. "Oh, I think she's very wealthy in her own right," she countered.

"Just how rich, dear?" Jack asked with a raised eyebrow.

"Well…I'm not certain, but I think she has a considerable amount of money!"

"Let me see what I can find out. I'm sure there are countless articles about Willow online."

Jack started typing away furiously on his laptop. He was someone who could find quickly any obscure fact on the Internet, particularly if the information began with a dollar sign.

"Okay," Jack said less than five minutes later. "Ballpark, I'd say she's worth twelve million, perhaps a bit more."

"There, I was right! You see? She has a fortune of her own."

"Well, yes and no," Jack said with a short laugh. "In sheer numbers, she's a pauper compared to William Adams."

"Impossible!" Sylvia said with her voice going up an octave.

Jack took a pad and pencil and started writing down numbers. At the top of the page was a one followed by nine zeroes. At the bottom was the lowly number ten. Using his pencil as a pointer, as he sat next to Sylvia he said, "You see, dear, one million is to one billion what one thousand is to one million."

"Jack, what does that mean?"

"It means that Willow's total worth of twelve million to William's twenty-four billion is the equivalent of someone with twelve thousand in the bank marrying an individual worth twenty-four million. Therefore, her twelve million is only a tiny fraction of William Adams' stated worth."

"But…how could that be? Twelve million dollars is a large amount of money!"

"It is, but while people throw around a figure like a billion dollars very casually these days, they forget, or never realized, just how big a number one billion represents. Here's one simple example: one billion minutes ago, the Roman Empire was at its peak."

"In other words, Willow might only be interested in William Adams' fortune?" Sylvia asked, bewildered by the thought that someone so successful and wealthy could covet such enormous wealth.

"Tough to say. Setting those comparisons aside, unless you're careless with your money, twelve million dollars invested conservatively in, say, US Treasury bills—and there is no more conservative investment—should provide you with a comfortable life, and leave a respectable estate as well. But if you're someone who hates the idea of flying in anything less than a private jet, and you can't imagine living in a home that is less than a mansion with a view of the Golden Gate Bridge or atop a Manhattan residential skyscraper, you can go through twelve million in a flash."

"I never thought of it like that," Sylvia murmured. "But it certainly is true that there are the rich, and then there are the super-rich."

"I know it's all a bit unimaginable if you're one of the ninety-nine point ninety-nine percent of us common folk, but here's a simple rule: All wealth is relative. The average wage earner making a ten-dollar charitable donation is the equivalent to Willow giving a thousand dollars, or Adams donating two million. Each of them is donating an equivalent amount in terms of their total net worth. That's why all non-profits, including my employers at the UC System, appreciate the support of mere mortals, but they work hard to cultivate the wealthiest among us.

One major donor can be worth the contributions of a thousand or more modest donations."

"If he asks her to marry him," Sylvia said, thinking aloud, "I presume he'll expect Willow to sign a prenuptial agreement."

"I would think so. He doesn't have children, but any family—nephews, nieces, siblings, not to mention Fran's side of the family—or a foundation, or private charities he wants to give a portion of his wealth to, he'll need to define the boundaries of what she gets. Regardless of whether they are still married, or divorced, at the time of his death."

"It's all a lot more complicated than when we got married!"

Jack nodded. "We had it easy. I was making fourteen thousand a year in my first accounting job, and I think you were making about the same. Poor marrying poor doesn't require a roomful of attorneys ironing out the details."

"It does make life a lot simpler, doesn't it?" Sylvia said with a weary smile.

"That it does. But I'd happily trade our thousands for her millions—or even better, his billions. We can always have lawyers slug out the details. After all, we'd have the money to pay them and still have plenty left over."

CHAPTER FOURTEEN

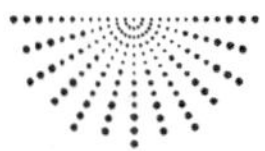

When Fran Adams died, her brother and sister, Michael and Kate, were bereaved by the loss of their younger sibling. When word reached them, they joined William in his private home office, where they cried and shared memories.

It was then they received the news that Fran had bequeathed each of her siblings five million dollars upon her death—a decision that both she and William had come to three years earlier.

Grateful, albeit shocked, Kate asked, "Why do you want to do this?"

"Fran and I had a joint directive of what we wanted to be done with our estates at the time of our deaths. For some odd reason, we always imagined that we would die at the same time; Fran called it, 'The Notebook pact,' like the book and film by that name. We never imagined living our lives as anything other than a couple. The only provision we made was that in the event of our deaths, our money would pass from one to the other. Estates of any size, in the thousands or the billions, pass between spouses as a non-taxable event."

"William, this is incredibly generous of you!" Michael said.

"It's a start on what Fran would have liked to happen for both of you. As you know, we decided several years ago that part of our giving back to the world would be covering the educational expenses of our nieces and nephews, and our support of them extends as far as they want to go in their schooling. Whatever it is, we—I mean I will always be there for them."

The meeting of the three of them ended in a long round of tearful thanks.

William's meeting with his two siblings, Andrew and Benjamin, went much the same.

Benjamin was not an academic, but a bohemian artist. Naturally, he was pleased with this unexpected five-million-dollar gift. The youngest of three boys, Benjamin slipped in and out of relationships. Always reserved, and without children, he was never as involved with people as he was with the challenge of a blank canvas.

Andrew, who had his parents' love of chemistry, became a professor of biochemistry. He was his happiest when faced with a new class of anxious and curious first-year students. The oldest of three siblings, Andrew was a late bloomer when it came to romance. But now happily married for eighteen years, they had a total of three children, two girls, ages sixteen and fourteen, and a son, aged twelve.

Afterward, Benjamin and Andrew agreed that they were overwhelmed with the size of William and Fran's legacy. They had no doubt they were blessed to have such a loving, supportive, and remarkably successful brother.

William headed into the issue of a prenuptial agreement with little forethought. What had quietly occurred to everyone else—particularly his bride-to-be—was an issue he ignored. As his friend and partner, James should have said something, but didn't.

It was only an innocent comment, made in jest by his regular and younger racquetball partner that started William to consider this delicate issue.

At home that night, as he sipped a fine aged Scotch in front of his study's fireplace, he looked out onto the bay and thought about what to do. The fog was so dense that it obscured the lights of nearby Sausalito and set off a cacophony of foghorns from passing cargo ships scurrying past Alcatraz Island.

I have to say something, he thought. Without signing an agreement before our marriage, Willow would inherit the bulk of my estate.

William took great pride in his oft-expressed belief that there was more to life than money, but half of his estate was currently valued at twelve billion dollars!

And what if there was a life beyond this life? An idea William silently contemplated many times since Fran's death. How would he ever explain to the woman who played a crucial role in assembling this fortune, his giving over half their estate, or possibly the entire estate, to a famous fashion model more than twenty-five years his junior?

"How should I tell Willow that I need her to sign a prenup?" William asked his law partner the following morning.

"Do what any negotiator would do," Finch advised. "Be open,

kind, thoughtful—and then present her with a prenup that offers her the lowest number you think she's willing to accept."

"But I have no idea what that number would be!"

"Oh, come on, William! You're a lot tougher on the company that provides our firm's cleaning services. Buck up, man. This is about safeguarding your family's fortune and your charitable gifts!"

James had reason to be enthusiastic about William pushing for a prenup. Since having introduced them, Willow had cut off all of the brief illicit encounters he happily anticipated for weeks in advance. As far as James was concerned, Willow needed to be taken down a peg or two.

"So, I'll start with a hundred million if the union should fail," William said, then quickly corrected himself, "No, two-hundred and fifty million, take it or leave it."

"She's a very fortunate girl to get that kind of money."

William winced. "I don't want to make a mess of this. I think I'll call Bob Ivan; he's done family law in Marin County for years. He must have some idea of formulas for settling on a reasonable amount."

"Bob would be a fine one to ask," James agreed, knowing that Ivan had a sharp eye when it came to the bottom line. "He's been on one side or another of enough Marin County divorce settlements that he probably knows a lot more about this than either of us."

"The hardest part is that I don't even know how to approach her about the whole business."

"Take her out to a great dinner, pour a lot of champagne into her, and get her to sign on the dotted line."

"James, be serious! I want to be fair to Willow. I also want to honor Fran's memory and the plans we made together both for our own families and for our foundation."

"Pick up the phone and call Bob Ivan; if nothing else, he'll get you on track."

Walking back to his office, Finch chuckled at his partner's indecisiveness. He'd love to be in the room when William and Willow had this conversation!

While William sat down to call Ivan, James, in the privacy of his office, slipped out his cell phone and tapped out Willow's number. It was time for the two of them to have a little talk. He doubted she'd blow him off so quickly this time, considering what he was about to divulge.

Willow was not pleased by James' insistence that they talk privately in a room he reserved at San Francisco's W Hotel. But when he warned her that she might be on the cusp of being "tossed out of her little Belvedere love nest," she panicked and wondered if William had somehow learned of her mad Russian violinist. She thought of ending the call. But Willow's default mode was to use caution in the face of uncertainty.

They met for drinks at the W Hotel's bar. There, Willow pressed him, "Tell me everything you know, James."

Instead, Finch reached into his inner pocket. Pulling out a room key card, he whispered in her ear, "You want some secrets, and I want some favors. Let's go upstairs and see if we can negotiate a settlement."

Willow hissed back, "This better be worth my time, not to mention effort."

"That's what I was thinking," James replied, flashing a smirk Willow had come to despise.

Upstairs, in a room he had booked for the night, James wrapped his arms around Willow's waist and buried his face into the sweet scent of her neck.

Pulling herself away, she turned to him and said, "I get it, James. You want to play."

"We haven't played in such a long time," he whined.

"This is what we'll do. You tell a little, then we'll play a little. Then you tell a little more, and we'll play a little more."

"Sounds like fun," James said as he casually undressed and slid into bed, lifting the blanket for her to come join him. Reluctantly, Willow undressed and joined him.

James wrapped his arm around her waist and pulled her close.

"Tomorrow, William is meeting with one of the top family law guys in Marin County. It's regarding a prenuptial agreement, and I know what he's going to present to you. If you want to know more, let's talk about it after we've had some fun."

Willow was annoyed. But being ever practical, she decided to take Finch up on his offer while silently pledging that this would be their final rendezvous.

As she anticipated, Finch's fantasies were quickly played out.

Stroking his chest lovingly, while imagining closing her hands around his throat, Willow asked, "Tell me what you learned, James?"

"William is going to ask you to sign a prenup that tops you out at two-hundred and fifty million dollars."

Most anyone would have smiled with delight overhearing that news, but James knew that Willow was not just anyone.

"That's not going to work," she said in a determined voice. "I'm not marrying Adams for a fraction more than one percent of his total worth."

"Not just anyone could do that kind of math so quickly, but you're not just anyone," James said as he attempted to kiss her neck, only to have Willow draw back quickly.

"Anything else?"

"Yes. I miss you."

Willow responded with a shrug. "Continue proving yourself of value, and perhaps we'll have more play dates like this." Willow dressed quickly while James propped himself up on two pillows and scrolled through his text messages. Relieved that the name Viktor Kozlov had not come up in their conversation and happy to know the financial offer William was going to present, she had no regrets about the time she had spent with James.

"No kiss goodbye?" James asked as she moved toward the door.

Willow gave a short laugh and considered how it would please her to take a small gun from her purse and shoot Finch between the eyes. For Willow, that brief fantasy was the highlight of the time they had been together.

CHAPTER FIFTEEN

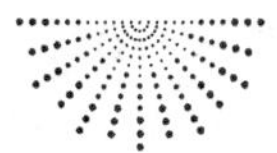

Once home, Willow mixed herself a drink—a glass of sherry with a splash of water—and contemplated what she would say when William broached the topic of a prenuptial agreement.

With a man of William's immense wealth, she never thought that the wedding day would arrive without discussing a prenup. But as the day grew near and William stayed silent on the topic, she toyed with the thought of half or more of his worth becoming hers; and that on the day of his death, she'd find herself one of the world's wealthiest people.

The thought of possessing such a fortune made her tingle. No doubt, two hundred and fifty million dollars was an impressive sum. Far more than she would likely earn in a lifetime regardless of her perfume's continuing success. But for someone who dreamed of a fortune beyond imagining, no figure in the mere millions had the feel of real wealth.

Willow put her finger into her drink and stirred it slowly as she considered her next move. Whenever uncertain, she returned to the advice that her father once gave her: "The best defense is a good offense."

If I wait for him to bring up the topic, I'm back on my heels, she reasoned. But if I raise the subject, then I'm the one looking out for his interests. Indeed, this was the best way to benefit from time spent in the arms of the repugnant James Finch.

William had known Bob Ivan for a very long time. He'd taken a tax law course from him when he was a student at Berkeley, and as a litigator, Bob was a legend in Marin County. At the same time, he was a rare bird who didn't quite fit into the modern age.

He worked out of a small office, with only one secretary and a law clerk. Nearing eighty, he worked harder and smarter than lawyers half his age. Unlike the new generation of specialists, Bob practiced in several areas of the law, from tax to family to property.

In fact, for many years, he served the town of Tiburon as its municipal attorney.

"William, how in the world did it not occur to you that a prenup would be needed?" Ivan asked as he swept an unruly mane of snow-white hair away from his piercing blue eyes.

When Bob stared in your direction, you inevitably felt compelled to speak honestly. William had no explanation. "I know it sounds idiotic, Bob. But I've been so enthralled with Willow that I didn't give it a thought!"

"What did you say her name was?"

"It's Willow Wisp."

"Come again?"

"She's an international celebrity model with her own line of perfume."

This time, a raised eyebrow accompanied Bob's curious stare.

William was tempted to mention that Willow graced the back

cover of this month's Vanity Fair, but knowing that would mean nothing to Ivan, he remained silent.

Finally, Bob asked, "I imagine she has money of her own?"

"Yes. She's done quite well for herself. Her attorney is my partner, James Finch. You remember James, don't you, Bob?"

Bob smiled and nodded.

"James tells me she's worth about twelve million."

"I imagine that's a lot of money for the kind of work she does," Bob said, as the curious expression remained on his face. "So, what do you want to offer her?"

"I'm thinking two hundred and fifty million dollars."

The point on the scribbling pencil in Bob's hand snapped as he looked up, stunned by what he had just heard. "Hell, I'll marry you for that kind of money!"

"I don't want to burst your bubble, Bob, but Willow's a lot cuter."

"That's okay; I can handle the truth."

"Seriously, Bob, what do you think I should do?"

Bob pulled at his ear and thought for a time. "With your wealth, the main issue we have to resolve is the cap that we're going to place on whatever share of your fortune comes to her in the event of a separation, a divorce, or your death."

"What would you suggest?"

"I would do an annual figure that increases for each year of your marriage. For example, it could start at fifteen million and end up at thirty-five million a year, over the next ten years. That would bring the total to the amount you suggested."

William nodded, "That seems like a sound approach."

"Of course, you need to consider what percentage of your estate will transfer to her upon your death. Your will needs to be updated, and naturally, all those provisions would be voided by a separation and/or divorce."

"Makes sense. Bob, I realize you know all the I's to dot and T's to cross. Can you have a draft to me by Monday? I want to discuss this with her sooner than later."

"No problem, William. I'm happy that you've found someone so special."

"No woman will ever take Fran's place."

"She was a remarkable woman. Still, you're a relatively young man. It's important that you have someone with whom you can share your life. Have you set a date for the wedding?"

"Yes! Mark your calendar for the twenty-third of next month."

"That soon? Well, I'll send a draft over to you in the next seventy-two hours."

Two days later, William hosted Willow for dinner at his Belvedere home. Willow, who had returned from a whirlwind tour of department stores in Denver, Seattle, and Portland, was pleased to learn that her perfume sales were steadily beating expectations as the tabloid coverage of "The Millionaire Model and The Billionaire Boyfriend" began heating up.

While magazines like People and Us were expanding coverage of the most prominent "fall/spring romance of the decade," the supermarket tabloids had already decided that William and Willow were front-page news.

All the attention embarrassed William, who had enjoyed a relatively private life up until now. But it pleased Willow, who knew that all publicity was good publicity.

After a meal of pasta with veal, sausage, and porcini ragu, Willow and William took their wine glasses into what had become their favorite spot, William's study, where they had held their first conversation on the night of the symphony's Black & White Ball.

As Willow ran her finger suggestively around the rim of her

wine glass, she said, "I want to bring up a sensitive subject, but something I think we need to discuss."

"Of course, sweetheart! What's on your mind?"

"Well, as I said, it's a sensitive subject…" She paused for emphasis.

"I'm always open to discussing anything," William insisted.

"Our wedding is getting closer by the day, and we haven't considered the subject of a prenuptial agreement. I think it's important we do that."

The very fact Willow was raising an issue he had tried desperately to put out of his mind impressed William beyond words.

"Are you concerned about protecting your estate?" William asked with a half smile.

"Now you're just teasing me! You know perfectly well that my millions are pocket change compared to your billions. No silly, you need to be protected, along with the wonderful foundation that you and Fran began. Not to mention any family and other loved ones you may want to designate."

William felt surer than ever that he could not have given his heart to a woman of higher principles. As highly as he thought of his delicate flower before this moment, his admiration instantly doubled.

"I'm not surprised that someone as dear and sweet as you would be thinking about protecting my foundation, and my other personal commitments and interests. As it happens, just a few days ago I contacted one of my old colleagues. He practices family law, among other things, right here in Marin County. I asked him to draft a prenup for us both to review."

"Oh, William, I'm so relieved to hear you say that! For the past several weeks I've thought that you would say something about this. But when you never did, I didn't know what to say."

Expert at crying on cue, Willow thought there would be no better moment than now, and she let her tears fall freely. "I'm, of course, happy that we're both blessed with great success, and I would never want the issue of money or material things to come between us. What's mine is mine, and what's yours is yours. That is as simple as an agreement can be!"

Willow knew that her choice of strategy was a calculated risk. Still, she was confident her performance would push William to be even more generous in sharing his wealth.

Overwhelmed with admiration for Willow's clear sense of dignity and independence, William swept her up in his arms and began to kiss her tear-stained face.

Then, holding her tightly, he carried her up to his bedroom and passionately kissed every inch of her perfectly proportioned body.

"No more talk of this nonsense," he insisted. "All I want to do right now is make love to you, and then sleep holding you in my arms."

"I am yours," Willow gulped helplessly. "I can't resist you. I belong to you, and I always will."

William left their bed early the next morning. He knew Bob Ivan started his day at dawn and he wanted to discuss with him a significant change to his prenup.

"I'm going to increase the amount from twenty-five to one hundred million dollars per year," William explained.

"Wow! And I thought twenty-five million was generous!" Incredulous, Bob said, "Do you mean the same terms, but just an increase in the annual stipend?"

"No, I also want you to move up the payments so that the first installment is transferred into her account the day of our wedding, and then another hundred million for each anniversary for the following nineteen years."

"That's twenty payments of one hundred million dollars a

year, starting on your wedding day, for a total of two billion dollars."

"Yes."

These may have been incredible amounts to Bob, but they both knew it was William's money they were discussing.

"Further, if Willow were to leave the marriage in the days, weeks, or months after our nuptials, that initial one hundred million dollars will be hers to keep!"

"Wow!" Bob said, clearly impressed.

"You have no idea what an incredibly special person I'm marrying, Bob. She brought up the topic of a prenup to me and suggested that she would leave with nothing more than what she had the day we married. I can afford to be a great deal more generous than that."

"Alright then," Bob said. "I'll make those changes in the numbers, and you'll have a revised draft agreement on your desk later today."

William thanked Bob and clicked off.

Two hours after William left for his office, Willow woke to the buzzing of her iPhone.

"Finch" flashed on the phone's display.

"Yes?" She said in a tone that dripped with displeasure.

"Your fiancé was very proud that his brave little Willow raised the subject of a prenup all by herself. He called you a woman of exceptional quality."

"You already knew that, James," Willow answered sweetly.

After a few moments of silence, Willow said, "I guess I have you to thank for that timely advice."

"You know how you can thank me."

"Got to go! William is calling," she said and abruptly ended the call.

Tossing the phone to the other side of the bed, Willow closed her eyes and hoped James had finally outlived his value.

Finch was not at all surprised that Willow was ready to dispose of him. The sooner she realized their relationship was more beneficial now than any time prior, the better. Happily, James imagined years of rendezvous with one of the world's best-known fashion models. Whether that pleased or displeased Willow was none of his concern.

It was hard to say what his role in bringing them together would be worth to Willow in the years to come—other than the hundreds of millions of dollars his prenup advice had already secured her. Indeed, Finch reasoned, it was worth more than a few rushed encounters at nearby hotels.

James fantasized taking Willow away to a South Pacific island for several days of sun and several nights of uninhibited passion.

He enjoyed the tension and the risk of pursuing Willow. It was even more thrilling now than when he had first provided her with insider-trading information.

In time, James was convinced, Willow would realize how badly she too needed him.

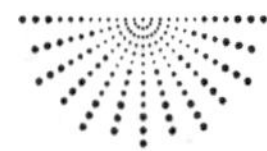

CHAPTER SIXTEEN

Keeping track of the continuing coverage of William and Willow became an obsession for Holly and Sylvia. When they met for a late morning walk on a sunny Saturday in the parking lot adjacent to Blackie's Pasture in Tiburon, all they could talk about was the famous couple.

"Did you see the story about them in last week's Us Magazine?" Sylvia asked.

Holly nodded enthusiastically. "I did! I thought the photo display of Willow throughout her career was pretty impressive. I would imagine that all this publicity keeps pushing up sales of her perfume."

"I wouldn't doubt that!"

"The wedding is getting so close; I guess it would be fantasizing to think that either of us will get an invitation," Holly suggested.

"Maybe—but I'm saving the date, anyway. It would make for an incredible column, don't you think?"

"Absolutely!"

At that moment, Sylvia's phone chirped. The display only read "private number." Showing it to Holly, she said, "Do you think I should get this?"

"Heck, yes! Could be one of your social butterflies with some juicy gossip."

She took the call, and in a moment squeezed Holly's arm. Sylvia's voice raised half an octave as she said, "Oh, Willow! Hello! How are you?"

"Hi, Sylvia, I know this is late notice, but I was wondering if you were around to go to a brunch or lunch with me today?" Willow asked.

"I'd love to, but...well, Holly and I are out taking a walk. We just left Blackie's Pasture and are heading to the far end of West Shore Drive."

"Ask her if she would like to join us—if she doesn't have other plans."

Holly, who could hear a pin drop from thirty feet, was vigorously nodding her head in agreement as Sylvia turned to look in her direction.

"Holly says she can make it too. Where do you want to meet?"

"How about Sam's Anchor Café?"

"When?"

"Well, since you're walking, how long would it take you to get there on foot?"

Sylvia thought for a moment. "I'd say forty-five minutes."

"Great. I'll see you at Sam's at noon," Willow said, and quickly clicked off.

"Well that was strange, here we are talking about Willow and William, and she calls."

"Has she called you often?"

"First time."

"She must have radar."

"I wonder what she wants?"

"I don't know," Holly said, "But this should be fun. I hope she tells us about the wedding."

"You don't think she'll invite us, do you?"

"I have no idea, but I'd sure love it if she did."

On any sunny weekend, Sam's, located on the small center strip of Tiburon's downtown, is always packed. Their expansive deck, complete with a boat dock, has fantastic views of Belvedere and some of the Peninsula's most stunning waterfront homes.

It can be a long wait for a table, particularly on a Saturday, but the café's owner, who had received a loan from William two years earlier to do an extensive renovation of the aging bar and restaurant, was quick to take Willow's call and reserve a water-side corner table for her party of three.

The restaurant's hostess was duly warned, "William Adams' lady friend Willow is coming in at noon with two guests; be sure they're treated well."

Neither Sylvia nor Holly recognized Willow, who approached the entrance to Sam's from the opposite side of Main Street in a new red Mercedes convertible with a specialty license plate that read, "WILLOW."

They waited at the door until she parked. Moments later, she strolled up to them in her standard public camouflage: oversized sunglasses and a wide-brimmed sunhat. Kissing both Sylvia and Holly on the cheek, she murmured, "I'm hoping to hide a bit, I've done a half-dozen events this week. I'm just not up for any more autographs."

"That's a beautiful car. Is it new?" Sylvia asked.

"William gave it to me last week! I love it! He's such a sweetheart, and what a cutie, getting me that specialty plate. He said it was an added engagement gift, but I thought the ring was more than enough," Willow said as she wagged her hand adorned with the new 12-carat diamond in front of both their astonished faces.

"Wow!" Holly exclaimed, feeling a bit weak in the knees.

"Do you feel safe wearing that out?" Sylvia asked, and immediately wished she hadn't.

"Come now, Sylvia," Willow chided her. "This is Tiburon, not Tombstone. There are diamonds everywhere you look. Given the size of this one, I'm guessing nine out of ten people think it's a fake."

Even though it was barely noon, the outside dining deck, bathed in full sunshine, was already full. Locals like Sylvia and Holly were accustomed to a long wait for an outside table. But when Willow asked for the table she had reserved, the hostess quickly grabbed three menus and with a welcoming smile said, "Absolutely, Ms. Wisp. Please follow me."

Seated at the best table, with a celebrity who was quickly becoming a household name, was rarified air that both Holly and Sylvia were delighted to partake in, even if only for an hour or two.

After a discussion that covered the lovely weather, the stunning views, and some details of the upcoming wedding, Willow got down to business. "I was wondering, Sylvia dear, what you think I could do to be more involved in the social and cultural life of Tiburon and Belvedere?"

Before Sylvia could speak, Holly jumped in and said, "What would you want to do that for?"

That stopped Sylvia in her tracks and caused Willow to laugh.

"Holly, I admire a woman who says what's on her mind."

Holly nodded. "Well, that's certainly me."

"I could be of more help if you told me what it is you're hoping to accomplish," Sylvia said.

"I think it would mean a great deal to William if I became more active in one or more of the causes that are important to the community. I've already told him that I'll get involved in the San Francisco literacy project he generously supports. But since we don't have much in the way of disadvantaged children here on the Peninsula, I thought there must be some event or cause that's important to the leading residents of Tiburon and Belvedere. I know from William that Pamela Botherton and Julia Hassie worked on some committees that Fran served on; perhaps that would be a good place for me to start if those projects are still ongoing."

"Yes, you're right, they did work together on at least one of our local committees, the McKegney Field beautification effort, along Tiburon Linear Park."

"Sounds interesting. Where exactly is that?"

"Most people know the property; they just don't know its actual name. Holly and I just walked by it earlier. You know Blackie's Pasture just off Blithedale Boulevard?"

"Of course, I love that statue near the entrance to the park of the old swayback black mare that gave the pasture its name."

"Well, if you follow that walking path from the parking lot going along the waterfront heading toward downtown Belvedere, Tiburon Linear Park adjoins the big open area where children play soccer on the weekends—that space is called McKegney Field. Let's just say it needs a considerable amount of TLC. The benches along the waterfront—the old playground, the landscaping—it's all been looking shabby in recent years."

With an excited smile, Willow said, "Sounds perfect. How can I get involved?"

"Are you sure you want to?" Holly asked.

"Yes, Holly, I'm sure. What's important to William is important to me."

"You could start," Sylvia said, "by hosting a lunch for Pamela and Julia. Reach out to them; I'm sure they'll be pleased to hear from you. Be sure to ask them who else they would like to have at the luncheon."

A sly smile lifted the cupid bow corners of Willow's lips. "I'll do just that! And I want the two of you to promise me you'll be there."

Sylvia nodded in approval, whereas Holly quickly asked, "Um…why would you want me there?"

"Besides the fact that I think you're refreshingly honest?" Willow asked as she raised an eyebrow. "Because I want to make sure that we get ongoing coverage of the good work we're doing in *The Peninsula Standard.*"

Remembering her long holiday list and the value of each box of Willow Wisp perfume, Holly grinned and said, "I can make sure you get all the coverage you need."

Not to be left out, Sylvia added, "I'll do my best to see you get the recognition you deserve for all your good efforts."

Sylvia decided that there would be no better time to broach the topic uppermost on her mind: "You must be getting excited about the wedding; it's getting so close!"

"Oh, I am, Sylvia—beyond words! And I have something I need to tell both of you"—she leaned in conspiratorially—"but I am so embarrassed, I didn't know how to bring it up."

Holly and Sylvia leaned in as well. "Whatever it is, certainly you can tell Holly and me," Sylvia assured her.

"I realized that with all my travels and appearance commitments, I didn't take the time to check on you and Holly regarding your invitations to the wedding—with a plus one for each of you, of course."

"Oh! My! That's very sweet of you!" Sylvia said. "I can't speak for Holly, but Jack and I will be thrilled to attend!"

"I'm in," Holly said quickly, wondering whom she would choose as her plus one. Then she had a quick thought. "You know, Willow, if you want to assure yourself of ongoing coverage in the local paper, you should invite my publisher, Rob, and his wife, Karin. That is if you have the room."

"Have the room? We're doing the reception at the house; I

suspect William and I will have two hundred guests before we've covered everyone on both our lists. Better to make everyone feel included than to have any hurt feelings."

Sylvia gave her a broad wink. "You're wise beyond your years, my dear."

Willow lowered her sunglasses. "I try, Sylvia. I try."

CHAPTER SEVENTEEN

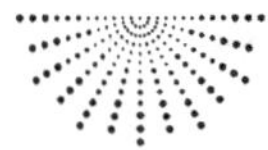

"Why in the world do I want to go to the Adams-Wisp wedding?" Rob asked as the small vein on the right side of his forehead began to pulse—a sure sign he was not pleased.

"I know high society events are not your thing," Holly explained. "But for starters, Karin is going to string you up alive if she finds out that both of you received an invitation to Marin County's wedding of the year—no, of the decade—and you tossed it in the round file."

"And who's going to tell her?" Rob said defiantly.

Holly batted her lashes and said sweetly, "I think that would be me!"

"I guessed that," Rob said, knowing he was swimming against the tide.

"Oh, come on, boss! It's going to be fun."

"Fun is a Saturday with Karin and the kids at Stinson Beach— not putting on a suit and tie and going to some obscenely extravagant wedding filled with pretentious people."

"You know, comrade, at heart you're just an old fashioned hippie. Look, as your mother told you when she'd drag you to those annual crab feeds at Star of the Sea Church, 'You're going, so just get over it.'"

Rob had Karin and Holly in his life long enough to know when he was outnumbered. The sensible thing to do was to embrace the upside of the situation. "Karin is always telling me that I never take her anywhere special. This should cover me for at least a year."

"God, you are one cheap son-of-a-gun!"

"Cheap? You know what this wedding is going to cost me?"

"Not sure, but it will be a tiny fraction of one percent of what William Adams is shelling out!"

"Do you think Karin's going to Belvedere's royal wedding without new shoes, a new dress, hair done, nails done, and God-only-knows-what-else done?"

"That's life in the fast lane, pal. Rob, think of this, we might all get our pictures in People Magazine!"

"Lucky us."

Christmas came early for Holly. The following day, a box arrived for her at the office with ten bottles of Willow Wisp perfume inside. More than half of her gift shopping for the year was already done! Holly thought happily.

Of course, Rob, Eddie, and a couple of other men on her list would expect something different than perfume. "Damn…men," she muttered to herself.

Sylvia called to report that she had received the same gift.

"It's lovely of her, but I imagine she wants something for it," Sylvia suggested.

"I think it's what she told us—good publicity from her local paper," Holly reminded her. "Fine with me. In fact, if Rob has to go out of town, I might give her a headline announcing Willow's been named our Woman of the Year."

Sylvia paused. "I didn't know we had such an award."

"We do now! Which brings me to my question—what can we do for Willow?"

"Well, I've called Pamela and Julia and told them about Willow's desire to lead the McKegney Field revitalization project. They both said they were delighted to have Willow involved."

"That's surprising. At William's party, it looked to me as if they were giving her the cold shoulder."

"Yes, but that was before they'd received their invitations to her wedding."

"Gosh! When Willow wants to make friends, she doesn't waste time!"

"I should say not. I imagine that's how she climbed so quickly from small-town kid to the top of the fashion world. When Willow sets her mind to doing something, nothing gets in her way. She's like a force of nature."

"If she can take care of a good part of my shopping list every Christmas, she's okay in my book."

"When I first interviewed all the local society gals about Willow, I thought she'd have some rough going if she wanted to fit in. I suppose I was wrong," Sylvia admitted. "It looks like the future Mrs. Adams is off to an impressive start."

CHAPTER EIGHTEEN

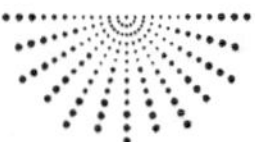

By the week of the grand event, the story of Willow and William's romance had moved out of the Belvedere Buzz column and onto the front page of *The Peninsula Standard*, which particularly delighted Sylvia because it appeared under her byline.

Rob was pleased knowing that Sylvia—and now, Holly—had an inside track in covering the one story in Marin that was attracting national and even some international attention.

The day of the wedding was picture perfect: cloudless sapphire-blue skies, temperatures in the mid-seventies accompanied by a gentle breeze.

Before the ceremony began, William and Willow's guests sipped and savored Krug champagne that came at a per-bottle price that even the unimaginably wealthy newlyweds considered excessive. It was one more extravagance dismissed with a casual shrug.

Holly, who had been pleased to crash the "get to know Willow party," was delighted to witness firsthand this display of opulence provided by an army of wedding planners, orchestrated by San Francisco's premier party czar, Stanlee Gatti.

Both the welcoming reception and the exchange of vows were staged on the manicured lawn to the side and back of the estate, a place from which attendees had a clear view of the bay framed by the Golden Gate Bridge. Later, a sit-down dinner was set for the home's expansive third-story outdoor deck.

William told nearly everyone that he was marrying the woman who reinvigorated his life. His tone was calm, confident, and excited. He had the sophisticated demeanor of a mature Hollywood film star as he waited for his bride in a tailored Armani suit under an arbor draped with white roses that had arrived early that morning.

At precisely four o'clock, a string quartet that frequently performed at San Francisco's Davies Hall began an expertly rendered interpretation of Felix Mendelssohn's Wedding March.

The assembled guests rose to greet the bride, who was escorted down a gold carpet soon covered with white rose petals tossed by two flower girls.

Willow was a vision in a couture gown designed especially for her by Henri LeBon. It had one hundred and twenty feet of platinum silk fabric, stitched together with platinum silk thread. At first, LeBon insisted that the gown was a wedding gift to his muse. But eventually, she convinced him to accept a payment of two hundred and fifty thousand dollars—exactly half of the gown's retail cost.

Earlier, Willow considered wearing a dress designed by Renee Strauss and Martin Katz. The silk bodice was laced with over one hundred and sixty carats of diamonds. It wasn't the fact that LeBon would have been livid watching her walk down the aisle in someone else's creation, but the realization that William might find its twelve-million-dollar price tag excessive, even for this all-important day. Willow was tempted to point out that the gown's diamonds could be removed the following day and sold to LeBon's lover, Allard, the Parisian jewelry designer, for a tidy sum, but thought better of the idea. Why give William the notion that she would ever consider recycling her diamonds?

James, who had served as his partner's best man at his first wedding, was once again at his side. William's brothers, Benjamin and Andrew, and Fran's brother, Michael, were his groomsmen.

Even though she had virtually no female friends, Willow realized it would be odd not to have any bridesmaids, so she chose Fran's sister, Kate; her longtime agent, Adele, and her personal assistant, Andrea. The latter two knew each other well, having worked closely in coordinating Willow's countless number of public and private events.

During their fitting, Andrea shared her surprise at having been selected. "Granted, in the past, I've had to juggle a lot of men in her life, but I don't think I've ever taken a call from any woman claiming to be Willow's friend."

Adele expressed similar surprise. "Over the last few years, I've spoken to you far more than Willow. She's professional, and always in a hurry to end our conversations. I didn't think I'd be invited to the wedding, no less asked to be a bridesmaid."

Willow could tell that her father, Oscar, felt uncomfortable escorting her down the aisle. Frankly, she would have preferred many other men in her life for this honor, but that could have invited awkward questions from William. Like so many other aspects of her complicated life, this was a conversation that could wait until after the wedding.

As for Willow's relationship with her parents, nothing had changed: they were always proud of her success, but hugely disappointed by all their shared suffering as a result of what they called "Willow's challenging adolescence."

Gloria often spoke of concerns regarding her daughter with colleagues at the school where she taught and at Saint Patrick's second-hand shop where she volunteered. Nearly all had suggested counseling, but Oscar adamantly opposed the idea. "Between work and out of office meetings, I have little enough time for myself!" he claimed repeatedly. In his view, none of the unpleasantness between the three of them was the fault of anyone but their only child.

On this day, however, hearing Oscar bemoan the deep chasm between child and parents was not acceptable.

"It's Willow's day to shine," Gloria patiently reminded her husband, "All we can do is be here for her. I wish we had the chance to meet William over these past months, but from everything I've read, he sounds like a lovely person."

Oscar nodded, but he couldn't dismiss the question that had plagued him since Willow was a teen:

Why had she spiraled out of control?

With William making their threesome a foursome, the Bukowskis posed and smiled for photos. Gloria was pleased that Willow was set for life, but quietly saddened to think that it would likely be years before she would again be in the presence of her famous daughter.

J ust as the afternoon sun began to disappear behind the Marin Headlands on the opposite side of Richardson Bay, William kissed his new bride, and once again, the string quartet played The Wedding March.

As per Stanlee's instructions, the newly betrothed couple walked off to a room in the back of the home for a few minutes of much-needed privacy. The wedding party moved upstairs for a champagne reception, which was to be followed by a four-course dinner.

Finally alone for a few fleeting moments, William embraced Willow. "I can't believe you are mine forever."

"For eternity, my dear sweet William," Willow cooed.

James was livid with Willow for persistently failing to respond to a single one of his many calls. None of this could have happened without me, he mumbled angrily to himself. Still, James was determined to keep a smile on his face throughout the long evening ahead.

To mitigate his growing resentment, he busied himself by talking with other guests explaining how shocked he was that Willow and William had formed themselves into such a happy couple.

"I thought, after a year, William needed to have a little fun," James explained to one circle of guests. "He was so isolated after Fran died so unexpectedly. Willow seemed like the perfect distraction. I've never played Cupid, but this time I'm glad I did."

When the happy couple emerged from their cocoon, their guests surrounded them to toast to their future happiness.

LeBon, not unexpectedly, was the most flamboyant. After tapping one of the many gold rings he wore on his fingers against a Waterford crystal champagne flute, LeBon declared, "I've read and watched and heard the news about this fabulous couple's nuptials, so I decided to come from Paris to see for myself. Well, for once, all these news people have told a true story! They are fabulous! Mr. William Adams, you can have my Willow for today, and for a romantic honeymoon"—the crowd chuckled—"but afterward, I expect her back at work! Before long it will be the holiday season once again, and we have perfume to sell. We poor working class people have to get up every morning and go to work, you know," LeBon added, looking directly at William as he winked playfully. "Here's wishing a long and happy life for the woman so many women, and a few men would love to be—my darling Willow Wisp!"

Despite straining to understand his heavily accented English, everyone raised their glasses and drank to the newlyweds' good health.

❧

Holding down one of the far corners of the patio were Sylvia, Jack, Karin, Rob, and Holly, who kept looking around in amazement.

"I wonder what's the combined worth of all the people on this patio?" Holly said.

"You mean morally, or financially?" Rob asked.

"Oh, honey," Karin sighed. She tugged at his sleeve in the hope that he'd behave himself. Up until now, she was surprised and thankful that he had.

"Well, morally, I have no idea," Jack offered. "But I'd say financially, if Adams represents one hundred percent, maybe everyone else combined adds another five percent, probably less."

"Really?" Sylvia said as she continued to be amazed by the size of William's fortune.

"Of course, I have no idea what that French fruitcake, LeBon is worth—" Now it was Sylvia who tugged on her husband's sleeve in the hope that he too would behave.

"The Bothertons, the Hassies, the Greens, and the rest of her posse are worth a few scattered millions," he continued. "Likely, most of that in the value of their homes. But all that is just pennies compared to Adams' fortune."

"You and your numbers," Sylvia muttered, hoping for a change of topic. She looked around, fearful that her sweet but socially inept husband might be overheard.

"I can't speak for the rest of you, but I'll settle for a million of my own," Holly said. "I don't mind if that's just pocket change to William Adams."

"I would be perfectly happy as well," Karin added. "No complaints."

"What you're seeing is the one percent at play," Rob added.

Holly rolled her eyes. "Here goes Comrade Timmons!"

"Really, Holly?" Rob fired back. "Doesn't it bother you that the price of Willow's dress could have provided expanded facilities for the Bay Area's homeless population?"

"Yeah, I suppose. But it doesn't bother me half as much as the fact that I could go to classes at Curves for the next ten years, and still not fit into her wedding dress."

"Settle down, you two," Karin shushed Rob and Holly, whom she often referred to as her "two oldest children."

Hoping to change the topic, Sylvia pointed to the sky. "Here comes another one of those news copters! We're at Marin County's wedding of the decade! Let's forget about the expense of it all and just have a good time."

"You're right, Sylvia," Rob said. "After all, it's not our money."

"Here's to the millionaire model and her billionaire boyfriend," Holly said, tipping her champagne glass toward her friends.

"Say, that's not a bad line," Rob said excitedly. "We should use that as our headline."

Holly laughed as she shook her head. "You're a little late pal. That's what the tabloids have been calling their relationship for weeks. You've been too busy covering the repair of potholes in Mill Valley to notice."

"Somebody's got to pay attention to the things that matter in the lives of us commoners."

"Behave yourselves," Karin said, trying to keep their banter from distracting her from the spectacle she was enjoying firsthand.

Holly announced that she was going to "mingle," and wandered off into the crowd. Discovering Allard sitting alone at a table, she sat down and introduced herself. She suspected that he was LeBon's boyfriend or husband, having noticed the two of them sitting together during the wedding ceremony, but, always curious, she wanted to know more.

"What do you do?" she asked.

"I make jewelry in my studio in Paris, which I sell all over Europe. Sometimes here in L'Etats Unis —I mean, America."

"I love jewelry! But I guess what you make is a little too expensive for me."

"Tres cher, oui? But you never know, come and see me sometime at my shop on Boulevard St. Germaine. Maybe I could do something special for you," Allard said with a broad smile.

"I would love to do that. I was in Paris once—the year I graduated from college. It's a beautiful city."

"Oui, it is beautiful. Tres joli, mais tres cher."

The two had little in common but felt an instant kinship for one another. "Oui, tres joli," Holly said with a smile, and then moved on.

Dinner was served just before eight. The festively lit veranda took on the look of a Venetian palazzo as night settled in.

The lights of San Francisco twinkled in the distance while the guests were served a four-course meal catered by Saison, Willow's favorite eatery, and arguably San Francisco's most exclusive restaurant with a tasting menu and wine pairings beginning at four hundred dollars per person.

The evening's meal began with individual servings of white sturgeon caviar presented over cured, smoked sturgeon belly, which included a gelee made of the fish's grilled bones.

Looking at the small black dots of caviar, Holly raved, Sylvia was hugely impressed, and Rob took a pass, hoping some bread would soon arrive.

The next course brought a small square of Japanese butterfish. One edge of it had been quickly pressed against coals and heated lightly before being served with a dot of black vinegar. Presented with a piece of pickled horse mackerel on thin toast with crème fraîche, all of which prompted Rob to mumble to Karin, "Now I know how Willow stays so thin."

For Rob, things didn't get much better with the presentation of the main course: roasted pigeon, which as their server explained was "wrapped in cherry leaves and aged for thirty-eight days, until it was tender but resistant." The waiter took a deep breath and continued. "This wild game is then garnished with olives, as well as cured Asian pears, a beet purée, cured plums, bitter chocolate, and cherry blossoms."

"Wow," Sylvia exclaimed. Jack raised a doubtful eyebrow over what he had just heard.

"Sounds like a dressed-up version of roadkill," Rob muttered to Holly, only to be rewarded with an elbow to the ribs.

Karin, seated to the other side of Rob, said, "You'll never have another meal like this."

Rob rolled his eyes and said, "Okay by me." Like Jack, he contented himself mostly with pieces of various artisan breads placed on each of the tables, along with warmed brown butter.

Later that evening, to their delight, both men agreed the wedding cake was the best dessert they had ever tasted.

"You missed out by not trying that blackened Japanese butter-fish," Holly insisted.

"I couldn't eat that, Holly. It looked like something I might have found on the floor at Smitty's," Rob said with a wince.

Willow was delighted with how the afternoon and evening were progressing. Secretly, though, she wished that Kozlov had been there to see her whisked away by her beloved billionaire. Unfortunately, he had a weekend commitment in Sydney, Australia.

Of all the lovers she had spurned for William, Kozlov was the one guilty pleasure she was determined to keep. She remained anxious about the coming toast of William's best man, and her least favorite guest, Finch. But as was tradition, after the meal and before the cake, James rose and tapped on his champagne glass for attention and began to speak:

"By now, most of you know my story about introducing William and Willow, and how delighted I have been seeing the two of them grow together in love. Fran Adams was an extraordinary woman, and Willow knows well she could never hope to take her place. But, in Willow, William has found a woman of unique charm and beauty." Finch smiled benignly at the beaming couple.

"In the many years that I have served as Willow's attorney, she learned how much I value her exceptional qualities, not to mention her extraordinary beauty. It has made me very happy to see how, over these past months, my dear friend and partner has come to appreciate Willow's wisdom, beauty, and her joy for life." He paused, then lifted his glass. "I would ask that you stand and raise your glasses with me in a toast to Willow and William's future happiness. Here's hoping they will be blessed to share their love with each other for many, many years to come."

It was a brief performance that earned James high praise from all in attendance. Even Willow kissed him on the cheek, then whispered into his ear, "I'm glad you value my 'many excellent qualities.' And I hope you know that we are at an end."

"My dear Willow, I will never think of our shared pleasures as being at an end."

"There's a difference, James, between attraction and coercion."

"In the happy spirit of the occasion, I'll just act as if you never said that."

"Don't! James, I mean this in the nicest possible way: Get lost!"

To Willow's delight, Finch seemed wounded by her words. Perhaps it was too much champagne that brought out his vulnerable side. Whatever the reason, she hoped that James finally heard what she so badly wanted him to understand: their naughty little trysts were a thing of the past.

But seeing the disappointment in Finch's eyes wasn't the best part of her day. Willow's greatest joy came in knowing that she was a hundred million dollars richer than when she had started her day. A remarkable increase in her total worth! That, more than everything else, made this a day to remember.

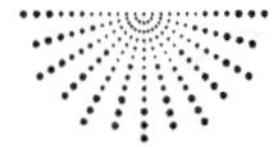

CHAPTER NINETEEN

In the week following the wedding, Belvedere Buzz again appeared on the front page of *The Peninsula Standard* just as Rob assured Sylvia it would.

This time, when she made her obligatory round of calls to Pamela, Julia, Cynthia, and Vivian, she heard nothing but praise. As usual, Pamela's comments set the tone for what she would later hear from the others.

"Sylvia, I don't have to tell you the doubts I had about Willow when she and William Adams first became a couple. But I've been very impressed with everything I have heard and seen since. I know that I found their age difference off-putting, but of more concern was her celebrity status. I find people with even a remote connection to the world of celebrity to be utterly unreliable. Still, in a short period, so much has changed. Her commitment to the park revitalization project is very encouraging. I see it as evidence that Willow Adams wants to be an active and contributing participant in the betterment of our small but wonderful community."

As Sylvia's fingers raced across her keyboard, she wondered if Pamela would ever pause to take a breath.

Apparently not. Without hesitating, she continued: "So many

of our celebrity residents will make an appearance at one of our events, but it's rare to see someone like Willow, rolling up their sleeves and getting to work."

By the time all four of the Peninsula's social stars weighed in on the subject of the newly minted Mr. and Mrs. William Adams —now the preferred label for Belvedere's top couple—Sylvia had enough glowing comments to fill three columns. Her offer to chair the McKegney Field project played a critical role in changing hearts and minds regarding Willow, but inviting the four ladies and their husbands to the wedding sealed the deal.

Thanks to the efforts of her two most devoted fans, Holly and Sylvia, Willow's charm offensive continued in her absence during a two-week honeymoon she and William enjoyed at the Castadiva Resort on Italy's Lake Como.

Their most time-demanding task was inserting flyers into all six thousand home delivery copies of *The Peninsula Standard* inviting readers to the groundbreaking ceremony for the Tiburon Linear Park renovation.

Neither of them had any doubt that there would come a time when Willow would look for some return on the kindness she showed them with her gifts and invitations to the wedding. But, as Holly told Sylvia, "If Willow keeps taking care of me, I have no problem helping out with whatever cause she wants to support!"

When Willow returned, she worked the phone, coordinating fundraisers held at the Bothertons' and the Hassies', and smaller events, like afternoon teas hosted by the Greens and the Buckleys.

Willow was quickly learning all the local traditions and

customs. One that she found particularly fascinating was the Belvedere Ball, which was held annually alternating in location between the area's two yacht clubs. On that night all the ladies would put on their most exquisite jewelry and recapture some of the grandeur of Old Peninsula society.

Each one of the ladies in their small circle had a different theory as to how this bejeweled competition began.

"I suppose," as Pamela explained, "it was nothing more than an opportunity to show off your finest pieces." Willow, of course, was enchanted by the idea.

Pamela took Willow to her bedroom and slid open a panel located inside a generously proportioned walk-in-closet, where she had secured her jewelry. Inside a hand-painted box was a lovely pendant. It was old but impressively designed, even by today's standards.

"It's a classic piece," Willow said sweetly.

"It belonged to my mother, and it's very special to me."

"Diamonds, emeralds, and rubies, set in antique platinum—that is special," Willow exclaimed as she came in closer for a better look.

"I see you know your jewelry."

"I think precious stones set in exquisitely designed pieces are great works of art."

"I feel the same way," Pamela explained, as she closed the case and slipped it back into its hiding place.

"Pamela, I'd lock those up if I were you."

"I've thought about it, but it's so well hidden, and our crime rate is so low in this area, I just don't worry about it."

Two weeks later, Willow paid a similar call to Julia, who like Pamela, thawed almost to an adoring puddle in her presence.

Willow brought with her an antique diamond pendant she had just acquired through a trusted San Francisco broker.

"I'm just so excited about this piece," Willow said happily.

"You've got a right to be, Willow! It's exquisite."

"I just love fine jewelry; I know Pamela has some lovely heirloom pieces."

"Oh, those old things?" Julia said with a dismissive shrug. "Come, let me show you something better than anything she has!"

Feigning excitement, Willow followed Julia to her bedroom. There, she was made privy to Julia's hiding place, which was no more elaborate than Pamela's safe place, tucked away behind a false panel in her walk-in closet.

Julia had several pieces she was proud of, but she lovingly lifted and placed down on her vanity a bracelet that she called, "my favorite piece of all. It has been handed down through three generations, beginning with my grandmother."

Willow was impressed. It was a beautiful work, adorned with multiple carat diamonds and sapphires.

"Oh, it is lovely," Willow said excitedly. "You must enjoy wearing it."

"Most years it comes out only for the Belvedere Ball."

"You should wear it more often," Willow said.

"One day, I'm going to have this piece improved; I need to strengthen the clasp and do a few other things. I think until I do, I'll just trot it out once a year for the ball."

Thanks to the work of her trusted jewelry broker, Willow was building an excellent collection of antique pieces as well.

Late one night, when William was away on a two-day business trip to New York, Willow sat by the fire and considered how naughty it would be to relieve both Pamela and Julia of their precious jewels. She could barely tolerate being in the presence of either of them, but knowing that she had deprived them of something they held dear would give her great joy.

Just like stealing a high school rival's most valued possession, she would remove their favorite jewels when they were not paying attention. In Willow's view, it was a temptation too great to resist.

CHAPTER TWENTY

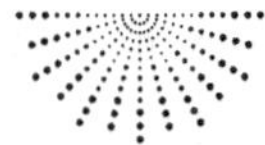

Those who wagered that the marriage of the millionaire model and the billionaire boyfriend would not make it six months lost their bets. Eight months after William and Willow exchanged vows, their bliss continued.

Tired of sending James' persistent calls to voicemail, Willow obtained a new cell number, which for a brief time appeared to have done the trick.

William asked if she intended to quit as the face of Willow Wisp perfume. But after her first trip to Paris for an event at Bon Marche, she concluded it would be foolish to walk away from all of the fame and success she had worked hard to create.

"You would never let your millions stand between us, would you, mon cherie?" LeBon asked while the two sipped champagne in his design studio.

"Why should I fade into oblivion just because I've turned thirty? I've decided that I will wait and let the public tell me when it's time to leave the stage. All of this is too much fun...Paris, London, Tokyo, New York, Los Angeles, Rio, all have the nightlife and excitement I love. Belvedere is a beautiful place, and I have a gorgeous home, but peaceful surroundings and manicured lawns can be found in a well-kept cemetery! I've got too much living to do to give this all up for a lifetime of eternal peace."

"Agreed, my dear. But come, we're meeting Jacques for dinner, and he's always furious with me if I'm late."

"But Henri, being late might earn you a good spanking, which I thought you appreciate?"

"I do, but Jacques—he does not spank, he pouts. What fun is there in that?"

The wedding and all the publicity surrounding it had made the perfume more popular than ever. Willow was the woman most twenty-something single women wanted to be. And now thirty-something married women thought of her as their ideal as well.

Somehow, word leaked out that Willow's prenup entitled her to a payment of one hundred million dollars a year starting on the day of her wedding. Securing such a lucrative agreement made her that much more of an icon to her adoring fans.

Jacques, who was waiting at the dinner table when Henri and Willow arrived, exchanged kisses with both of them. Without delay, Willow declared, "Jacques, I have something that I have been excited to talk to you about."

"What is it, my dear?"

"You know how much I adore diamonds and other precious stones?"

"Certainement, mon cherie."

"Well, I've begun acquiring old estate pieces, and I thought that—"

"Absolument! I'll do it," Jacques said, realizing that she wanted to harvest gems from old pieces and reimagine them in new designs.

"I'm so glad to hear that! I brought them with me and put them in a case that's in the safe at the Georges Cinq. Can I bring the jewels over tomorrow afternoon and we can discuss some possible designs?"

"Mais oui! It will be exciting to see what we can create together."

❧

Later that evening, Willow fell into her bed at the Georges Cinq.

The room could not have been more romantic. With softwood accents, adjustable lighting, and a bed that was fit for a queen and her consort, everything was perfect.

Now, Willow thought, all I need is my mad Russian.

Just before midnight, her wish was fulfilled. Viktor Kozlov walked up two floors from his room and softly tapped one of his highly insured hands on the door of Willow's suite.

After a brief exchange of greetings, they lunged at each other and spent much of the night making love.

At a time when the busy streets of Paris fell into a rare silence, between three and four in the morning, they sat by the fireplace and spoke of their dreams and disappointments.

"I do not understand why you should not leave this man!" Viktor exclaimed.

"Viktor, in just four months, on the date of our first anniversary, I receive a second one-hundred-million-dollar payment. It's hard to leave anyone when that kind of money is involved!"

"Yes. But you do not love this man. You love me."

"Of course I love you, silly! But William has been very kind to me. And very generous!"

"With me, you can travel around the world. I will make a special performance for you as much as you like."

"I know, my love," Willow said softly as she tenderly kissed the hands that delighted audiences everywhere. "Give me a little more time. Perhaps after my second anniversary, I'll consider leaving William. By then, I will have a total of three hundred million dollars. That should be enough to keep me comfortable no matter how foolishly I behave."

"Sometimes, I think you more crazy for your dollars than you are for me."

Willow stopped herself before confirming for Viktor what to her was a ridiculously self-evident truth. Lovers come and go, but with care and attention, great fortunes last a lifetime.

Avoiding further discussion, Willow took his famous features in her hands, kissed him tenderly first on his cheeks, and then hungrily on his mouth.

Elated to be with her and disappointed that it would not be for longer than a few hours, Viktor lifted her up in his arms and carried her back to bed.

At five-thirty in the morning, Willow told Viktor to dress and rushed him out of the room.

"I don't need the maids or the staff running into you on your way out my door and selling a phone camera photo to the tabloids."

"You treat me like Russian peasant," Kozlov said indignantly, as he searched in and around her bed for his underwear.

"Don't be ridiculous, Viktor! I don't let peasants anywhere near me! You of all people should know that!"

Willow left a wake-up call for two o'clock that afternoon and instructions to the housekeeping staff that she not be disturbed. The only item on her calendar for that day was a late afternoon meeting with Jacques Allard.

Down in the hotel's lobby, Parisian private investigator Roger Guilbert waited patiently for the celebrity model with the famous face to come down from her room. As in all surveillance work, his most significant challenge was staying alert while waiting long hours for his target to appear. He watched the lobby, the exits, and the elevators, shifting his eyes and letting them rest in one place for only a few moments.

At three-fifteen, more than seven hours after he arrived, Guilbert's patience was rewarded as he observed Willow carrying a green clutch and strolling confidently across the marble and gold-accented lobby, out to the street and into a waiting car.

Guilbert went to the third-floor storage room, where a ladder and coveralls identifying him as a member of the hotel's maintenance staff were left for his use.

Using a passkey he had paid a hotel security officer one thousand euros to borrow for twenty-four hours, he entered Willow's room, placed a Do Not Disturb sign on the door handle, and then put the storage room ladder near the foot of Willow's unmade bed. Carefully, Guilbert removed the device designed to look like a smoke detector. He then went into the lavishly appointed bathroom, contorted himself to reach inside a discretely placed storage cabinet that held a variety of scented candles and scented soaps to remove the room's actual smoke detector, which he then snapped back into place.

Leaving his maintenance uniform and ladder back where they belonged, and after exchanging polite nods with two members of the hotel's cleaning staff, Guilbert exited the hotel hoping that his hidden camera and audio recording device had captured a show worthy of his fee plus expenses.

Willow was delighted to find Jacques alone in his shop. The last thing she needed was to deal with the endless questions of the ever-curious LeBon.

Closing early, Jacques escorted Willow up to the small elegant apartment that he kept above his shop. Both shared a passion for precious stones and the bold designs of Bulgari, a topic they had often discussed backstage while watching LeBon prepare for one of his elaborate Paris fashion events.

As he handed her a small glass of sherry and they toasted to "all things beautiful," Jacques showed her a few of his favorite creations from large books he had on jewelry design, many of which were devoted to the work of Bulgari.

"Well, as you may have heard, I've come into a little money," Willow began.

"Ah, oui, I recall hearing something about this," Jacques said, as they exchanged smiles.

"So, I have spent some of my money collecting several estate pieces. Here, let me show you." Willow opened her green clutch and removed three glittering necklaces and an assortment of other pieces—mostly rings and pendants, all of which were wrapped separately.

Of the dozen pieces, undoubtedly the two most notable were Pamela's necklace of diamonds, emeralds, and rubies, and Julia's beloved heirloom, a sparkling bracelet adorned with multi-carat diamonds and sapphires.

"My goodness!" Jacques exclaimed as he carefully examined each piece with his jeweler's loupe. Willow knew he was impressed with this array of handsomely cut gems, mostly set in gold and platinum.

"All of it is lovely, mon cherie. The sapphires, emeralds, and rubies are all dazzling. Have you looked at the cut of this four-carat diamond? It's beautifully done. How did you acquire these pieces?"

"I have a trusted broker who locates them for me, everywhere from Singapore to Zurich to Los Angeles. He's terrific and very discreet. After all, if someone learns that Willow Adams is the interested party, the price suddenly doubles."

"Having a trusted broker is very important. You want all of your pieces to have been obtained honestly."

"Absolutely!"

"So, I'm sure that between your love of precious stones and your broker, you did not come to me for another appraisal."

"No, silly boy!" Willow said with an innocent smile as she tapped his arm playfully. "I want you to use these stones to design several exciting new pieces."

"Really?"

"Why not? Nearly all these are vintage designs, and I want something modern, dazzling, and..."

"In the spirit of Bulgari, mais oui?"

"But of course, monsieur. You know me too well."

"I imagine you know that it would be more economical to just acquire the gems that you want for the piece that you are designing than to purchase antique pieces such as these."

"Yes. At first, I thought about doing just that. But a few of these pieces I've had for many years. When I first acquired this antique necklace and bracelet, for example, I thought I'd like to keep them just as they are. But then I fell wildly in love with Bulgari, and I decided I'd be a lot happier if I had all these pieces reinvented in tribute to his genius."

The truth was that the few pieces that did not belong to Julia, Pamela, or other friends and family of Willow were merely a ploy to provide cover for this cache of stolen jewels.

"How soon could you transform these into new works?" Willow asked.

"We'll start with some design sketches and go from there. Once you approve my concepts, we'll settle on a price. I can have the sketches to you in two weeks."

"Wonderful! Let's shoot for September. I want to have new pieces by the time William and I celebrate our first anniversary."

"I will make it my top priority." He reached for her hand. "Willow, thank you for entrusting me with all these beautiful gems."

"Jacques, think nothing of it. Where would we be without friends we can trust?"

❀

At the same time Willow and Jacques were busy discussing how many of her precious stones should be placed in various new settings, Guilbert was back in his office examining the result of his surreptitious video recording.

He was so pleased with what he saw that he quickly picked up the phone to call his client.

"This video of Willow and Kozlov is stunning," Guilbert explained in the perfect English he acquired as the result of being raised in London by a French father and an American mother.

"It's that good?" his employer asked.

"Good? No, it's incredible!" Guilbert was not boasting. He was stunned by the quality of the image captured by a tiny camera inside a faux smoke detector.

"Make me two copies on SD memory cards and send them to my office. I'll wire you the balance of your money the moment I receive your package. Remember to send me your out of pocket expenses, too. I only want there to be one more payment exchanged between us."

"Done. I'll put it in an air-express pack for shipment tonight."

Guilbert had no reason to doubt his client. He had worked for him in the past, usually in the area of corporate espionage. As Guilbert uploaded the digital file onto two empty memory cards, it was difficult to resist the urge to make an additional copy. What a handsome price this video would bring on the open market, he thought.

But Guilbert took his responsibilities seriously. As tempting as it was, he knew that the original product of both his risk and ingenuity would remain locked away in his safe to be removed only for his own viewing pleasure.

CHAPTER TWENTY-ONE

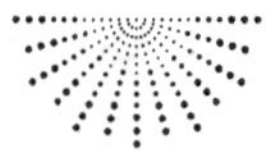

Willow laid peacefully in the fully reclined sleeper seat on her morning nonstop aboard Air France to San Francisco. She was pleased with her trip. The public appearances went well, and the Georges Cinq was the perfect reward for two days of long hours. As she told William on her call shortly before takeoff, "I don't know what I find more exhausting —the fans or LeBon."

Predictably, William told her what he had before, "You could always put an end to your traveling days. You have the money never to work another day in your life if you choose."

"I know, dearest. But I'm just an old-fashioned working girl. I'll give it up one day, I promise."

"It's your decision darling. But please hurry home. I miss you."

"Darling, you're all I've thought of every moment since I landed in Paris."

Of all the highlights of her brief trip, the afternoon spent with Jacques was the most pleasurable. She happily enjoyed visions of the gorgeous new jewelry she would be showing off at her first appearance at the Belvedere Ball. Poor Pamela and Julia would be sick over the loss of their favorite pieces, never suspecting that their missing gems would be there hiding in plain sight.

Willow smiled with delight. It was all such wicked fun!

James finally had what he wanted. Best of all, it had cost only five thousand dollars to obtain. By the time he came into the office on the morning after speaking with Guilbert, the two SD memory cards he had ordered were sitting on his desk. The package contained a vinyl binder labeled, "Confidential - Business Prospectus."

Taking a small blade from the center drawer of his desk, James sliced open the back of the binder and carefully removed the two small memory cards. Both, of course, were unlabeled.

He placed one inside a card reader device and inserted it into a port on his laptop.

A high definition picture soon appeared on the screen. Finch was mesmerized by what he saw: eight minutes of high definition video, complete with sound, that quickly identified Willow and Kozlov in the throes of passion.

Just as Guilbert had touted, the video's quality was impeccable. Uploaded onto the Internet, on perhaps an offshore pirate server, it would cause an international sensation within hours.

Of course, that was not Finch's preferred use for the video evidence of Willow's unfaithfulness. Ideally, it would serve as the perfect pressure point to get what he wanted from Willow: not just an occasional rendezvous, but whatever else he might find of value.

For example, William had a nasty habit of keeping investor information to himself. No one was in a better position than Willow to snoop about William's home office.

James sat back for a few moments as he considered his next move. How was he to arrange a meeting with a woman who had stopped taking his calls? Thankfully, Willow had realized it would be challenging to drop William's business partner as her attorney. Too many awkward questions might arise.

When all other channels of communication appeared to be cut off, their professional connection was undoubtedly his best choice. James picked up one of his office lines and buzzed his secretary.

"Please get Willow Adams on the phone."

"Mr. Finch, I believe she's in-flight returning from Paris at the moment."

"Check on that, then ring me back. I have some papers to send over to her."

Less than a minute later, his secretary rang back.

"Our driver confirmed that he is planning on picking up Mrs. Adams at SFO at two-thirty today. Her flight is due in on time."

"Good, I'll have a package ready for our driver to take to the airport. Please see that he gets it so Mrs. Adams will have it when she arrives."

"No problem, Mr. Finch."

James took one of the two memory cards and locked it in his office wall safe. The duplicate he placed inside a small envelope. Across the front, he wrote, "Call my private cell number after you review this."

He sealed the envelope and taped it to a white presentation binder that contained one of the many investment opportunity pitch portfolios that he received daily.

This should get her attention. James handed off the sealed package to his secretary, who placed it in the hands of Mike, the firm's longtime driver, with instructions to be sure Mrs. Adams received it with the message, "Mr. Finch said the contents require your immediate attention."

CHAPTER TWENTY-TWO

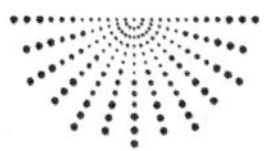

Willow glided confidently through San Francisco's International Terminal. The immigration and customs officer who scanned her passport gave her a knowing smile as he welcomed her back home to the United States.

Less than twenty minutes after stepping off her flight, Willow texted her driver that she was on her way out of the terminal. As she approached the curb, Mike glided up in a black Mercedes sedan. Tipping his hat in welcome, he lifted her two bags and placed them carefully in the trunk.

"Did you have a good flight, Mrs. Adams?" Mike asked as he slid back in behind the wheel.

"I did! Those new first-class sleeping pods are so comfortable; much better than what they had before."

Mike smiled in the rear view mirror while thinking: You should try being my size and flying coach on a long flight. At least your little behind fits into the cheap seats!

What he actually said was, "Before I forget Mrs. Adams, Mr. Finch wanted me to be sure that you got this package. There is some important content that requires your immediate attention."

"Thank you, Mike," Willow responded unenthusiastically.

For the first ten minutes of the ride north toward the city center, Willow left the envelope unopened. She was quite convinced that it was one more desperate attempt by James to get her attention. She tried closing her eyes, determined not to look at whatever it was he had sent her.

Twenty minutes later, as Mike drove out of the city and onto the Golden Gate Bridge, she pulled out the envelope and removed the investment portfolio. *Why would that idiot bother me with this investment opportunity trash?*

Then Willow saw the small invitation envelope taped to the other side of the prospectus.

As expected, the message on the outside of the envelope was yet another plea to call James' private cell. But what made her heart skip a beat were the next two lines:

"This regards your night at the Georges Cinq. From what I could see, you had a great time!"

Oh my God, Willow thought as a chill went through her. Finch knows about my night with Viktor! How did he pull that off?

With great hesitancy, Willow opened the envelope. Noting that it contained only one thing—a small SD memory card—she suspected the worst.

Thankfully, only Mrs. Jackson was home when Willow arrived. William was out at a tech conference south of San Francisco in Mountain View.

She slipped the memory card into a key, and within moments her worst fears were confirmed. She held inside the scream and the temptation to smash the twenty-five-thousand-dollar vase that was inches away from her. Instead, without further thought, she called her tormentor.

James was sitting alone in his office, wondering how his

scheme was progressing when Willow's number came up on his display.

He barely stifled a laugh before answering, "James Finch. How can I help you?" he began teasingly.

"Son of a bitch," Willow said in a low scream.

"I'm sorry, who is this?"

"You know who this is, you SOB!"

"Wow! That is no way to talk to the man who introduced you to your favorite billionaire. At least I think he's your favorite; you might have one or two others by now for all I know."

Willow closed her eyes and imagined how delightful it would be to jam a kitchen knife into James' frozen heart.

Naturally, she held her tongue. After a few moments of silence, Willow asked, "Where, and when?"

"I find the W hotel so conveniently close. I'll have a key waiting for you at the front desk. Let's go with the name Boyle. Mr. and Mrs. James Boyle. But this time let's make it an evening rendezvous. Say, seven tomorrow night? Wear something sexy. I've missed you terribly."

To show how convinced he was that the ultimate power in their relationship was his, James clicked off before Willow had the time to reply.

With Mrs. Jackson downstairs, Willow wisely chose to muffle her scream by burying her face in a couch pillow embroidered with the words, "There's No Place Like Home." Collecting herself, she requested that Mrs. Jackson draw her a warm bath. "I'm exhausted after that long flight," she purred.

On one level, Willow was furious with James. On another, she reluctantly admired his ingenuity. Locating an operative in Paris and arranging to have her tryst with Viktor recorded in a hotel with the security of the Georges Cinq must have cost him a pretty penny.

Soaking in a warm tub allowed the long miles of a nearly

twelve-hour flight to dissolve and permitted her to focus on the most important subject at hand: handling James.

In this game of cat and mouse, it was her turn to make the next move. True to Willow's penchant for intrigue, it wasn't long before she had a plan.

❧

Willow arrived at the W nearly an hour before Finch. At the front desk, she introduced herself as Mrs. James Boyle. She was handed a key and headed straight to their fifteenth-floor room.

She had spent the day consulting with a security person on the use of a hidden camera. She explained her interest as the result of suspicions over a possibly dishonest member of their household staff.

In truth, Willow wanted a camera to record her in bed with James. She considered it almost laughable: duplicating the stunt James had his operative perform in Paris.

She would be ruined with William if he were to see a video of her at play with either James or Viktor. But the video of her with James would end his relationship with William and ruin both his marriage to Jade and his standing among San Francisco's elite law firms. It was a nuclear option, but what choice did she have? You launch your video; I'll launch mine!

As instructed hours before by the security consultant, Willow quickly learned the many ways that a small video device could be hidden. It took her a minute to replace the digital clock on the hotel room's nightstand with the one she had just purchased. Within moments, she was ready to catch their show.

At just a few minutes past seven, there was a soft rap on the door.

She was surprised James didn't strut in and play lord of the manor. Why didn't he use his own key?

Hesitantly she asked, "Who is it?"

"It's your favorite pussycat."

What game is that idiot playing now? Willow thought as she opened the door.

James was wearing one of his standard-issue gray suits but held the mask of a cat over his face.

"Is this some new game you've dreamed up?"

"No. This is just my being cautious. I told the front desk that our room smelled of cigarette smoke. They graciously arranged for us to have another on the sixteenth floor. Follow me, my little kitten." Willow did what she was told.

As she stepped into their sixteenth-floor suite, Finch moved in to enjoy his victory, whispering in her ear, "Don't you think one video between us is enough for one week? I'm crazy about you, but I'm not a fool."

She would have to wait for another opportunity. Right now, James was holding the kill shot. Willow needed to work harder and smarter to earn a kill shot of her own.

CHAPTER TWENTY-THREE

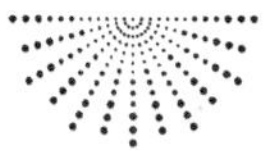

While Willow was imagining delicious ways of destroying James, the rest of her life was proceeding according to plan.

Jacques delighted her with the design sketches he sent two weeks after their Paris meeting. The pieces he recommended—one a bold bracelet that wrapped itself around her delicate lower arm, the other a stunning piece to adorn her neck—were both in the spirit of Bulgari creations for Elizabeth Taylor.

Allard's price for the work was more than reasonable. Willow sent an email back, offering to double his fee if he could cut the time of their completion in half. She envisioned the moment that Pamela and Julia would see these stunning new pieces adorned with precious stones that had once belonged to them.

With her first anniversary soon arriving, along with a second one-hundred-million-dollar payment, twelve thousand dollars more to assure these pieces came on time was a pittance.

Allard was more than pleased to oblige. He cleared two other projects from his schedule and focused solely on completing Willow's new pieces.

On the Monday afternoon before the Belvedere Ball, Willow, Sylvia, and Julia gathered at Pamela's for a planning meeting on a McKegney Field benefit auction and dinner.

After the business portion of their meeting concluded, Willow shared with the other three women how excited she was about attending her first Belvedere Ball.

Willow boasted proudly, "In keeping with the tradition of wearing our finest jewels to the ball, when I was last in Paris I asked my favorite designer, Jacques Allard, to design two new pieces just for the event. I'm looking forward to all of you seeing them."

The women expressed excitement about seeing these new creations and repeated stories about wearing, as Pamela explained, "the same old, same old."

"But, Pamela," Willow said in protest, "I think those pieces you showed me were all lovely. Oh, Sylvia, I don't know if you've ever gotten a good look at Pamela's pieces, but they are exceptional."

As Willow had hoped, Sylvia expressed great interest in seeing the pieces.

While the women nibbled at their cookies and sipped their tea, Pamela rose from her chair and proudly headed off to her bedroom to show off her heirloom pieces.

When they heard a blood-curdling scream, all three women leaped out of their chairs and raced in the direction of Pamela's bedroom. On the floor of the walk-in closet, they found Pamela sitting on the carpet, looking wild-eyed and mumbling in disbelief, "They're gone, they're all gone. How could that be?"

"What?" Julia shouted, instantly concerned about the safety of her own jewels.

Sylvia went down on her knees and placed her arm around Pamela.

"This is impossible!" Pamela declared angrily.

"Could it be your maid?" Julia asked.

"No!" Pamela snapped. Not that she'd admit it, but three months earlier, in one of his belt-tightening moods, her husband, Peter, declared that weekly maid service was no longer needed. "The children are grown and gone." Pamela knew he could have also said, "And you do nothing all day!" But he didn't dare cross that line.

Julia suddenly announced that she was late for an appointment with her eye doctor. In truth, of course, she was headed home to check on her jewels.

The scream Julia let loose moments after arriving home was remarkably similar to that of Pamela's. "Son of a bitch!" Julia shouted, standing alone in her closet with tears streaming down her face.

Julia was tempted to call Pamela immediately, but waited an hour, giving herself the time to return home from her imaginary doctor's appointment.

After spending a good part of the night comforting his wife, the next morning Judge Peter Botherton came into his chambers and asked his longtime friend, Marin County Sheriff Jack Canning if he would be so kind as to put his best man on the theft of his wife's jewels.

Eddie was less than thrilled to be dealing with a hysterical Marin County socialite who had suffered the indignity of a robbery. Undoubtedly he'd hear from her about the "social decay threatening our community's way of life."

Having learned that Julia was also a victim of this daring jewel thief, Pamela wasted no time in calling Sylvia.

"Sylvia, when is your next deadline?"

"Tomorrow. Why?"

"Because we have a major crime wave going on in our supposedly safe community!"

Sylvia was amazed to hear that Julia's gems had vanished as well. Possible headlines raced through her mind, with "Jewel Thief Terrorizes Peninsula Residents" being the one she chose. Minutes later she called Rob to get his go-ahead.

"Absolutely," Rob said without a minute's thought. "Currently our front page lead is the Tiburon Town Council approving the renovation of public restrooms near the ferry landing. I think we'll lead with the jewelry heists instead. Great work, Sylvia!"

When Eddie arrived at Pamela's home, both she and Sylvia greeted him.

"Sylvia writes for The Standard," Pamela declared, reasoning that would put Eddie on his best behavior and increase his desire to bring the case to a satisfactory conclusion.

Eddie turned to Sylvia. "You work for Rob?"

"Oh! You know Rob?"

"I do. In fact, Sylvia, we met the day of Fran Adams' funeral service."

"Oh, yes of course. So, it's okay with you if I write a story about your investigation?"

"Sure. I'm not a private investigator. I work for the people of Marin County. A free press is an important part of what makes our system work." In truth, Rob was the only journalist Eddie actually trusted. His years of being a detective did little to alter that view.

Eddie knew that local politicians and real estate agents hated to see stories about high-end homes being burglarized. Elected officials because they disliked hearing they did not budget enough for public safety, and realtors because robberies of wealthy dwellings put a ding in home values.

None of this, of course, concerned Eddie. "They can give all of Marin County back to the Coast Miwok Indians for all I care," he told Rob after an especially stressful week.

Pamela took Eddie back to where her jewels had been kept. He did a thorough inspection of the closet. Eddie then walked around the house checking every ground floor window, plus the front and back doors.

"I see no evidence of forced entry. No tampering with any of your windows or doors. You say you have no maid or cleaning service?"

"That's correct."

"When was the last time you saw your jewels?"

"When I brought Willow Adams back here to show them to her."

"Isn't that the model who married William Adams?" Eddie asked, already knowing the answer.

"Yes, that's her," Sylvia said.

"Well, the wife of a billionaire is an unlikely suspect," Eddie said with a short laugh. "Do you have any photos of these pieces? And did you ever get the jewels appraised for insurance purposes?"

Pamela gave an affirmative nod in response to both questions. "I'll look for photos and the appraisal, and call you when I find them," she promised.

Eddie looked around for another few minutes, then slipped one of his business cards into Pamela's hand. "Call me when you have those photos and information. If someone is attempting to resell your jewels, the sooner we can get the word out to Bay Area dealers the better."

"Detective Austin, will you be heading over to Julia Hassie's home next?" Sylvia asked.

"Yes. You're welcome to follow if Ms. Hassie doesn't mind your being there."

"I'll call her now. I'm sure it will be okay. I'll meet you over there."

"By the way, call me Eddie. Any friend of Rob's is a friend of mine."

❧

As Sylvia suspected, Julia was every bit as devastated as Pamela by the loss of her jewels.

"Your arrangement, with the hidden panel inside the walk-in closet, is very similar to that of your friend, Mrs. Botherton. I'm just curious if one of these hidden nooks inspired the other."

"Yes. I got the idea for mine from Pamela's. Why would that matter?"

"It might mean nothing. I was curious as to whether you both had the same carpenter making these pocket hiding places."

"In fact, we did."

"Could you look up the date that work was done, as well as the contractor's name, and send it to my email?" Eddie asked, handing her his business card.

"Of course, I'd be happy to do that. But you don't think that someone with the construction firm might have done this, do you?"

"I have to check all the possibilities. One thing you also have in common with Mrs. Botherton, there are no signs of forced entry. I looked at the doors and windows, both at her home and now at yours. To the best of your knowledge, nothing else was taken, damaged, or moved. In other words, whoever did this seems to have gone straight to the spot where these gems were kept and removed them. That's very peculiar. As a general rule, burglars will grab anything of value they can easily take. Do you have any cash in the home?"

"Not much, but some, perhaps three hundred dollars."

"And where is that kept?"

"Right there in the top desk drawer. It's just so we can have some cash on hand."

"Have you checked to see if it's still there?"

"No, but I will right now," Julia said as she walked across the room and pulled open the drawer and looked inside. "Yes, Detective Austin, it's right where I last saw it."

"Okay," Eddie said as he made a quick note in his spiral pocket pad.

"It's frightening to think that I had a jewel thief in my home!"

"To help in the recovery of your jewelry, send me any names and contact information that you have for any cleaning service, maintenance, and repair workers who have been in the house in the past three months. And remember the contact information for the people who did the carpentry work on your closet panel area."

"I'll pull that list together for you by this time tomorrow."

"Also, consider carefully when you last saw or wore your jewels. Mrs. Botherton told me she rarely wore hers."

"I'm the same way. I often go months without checking my pieces. But I did show them to Mrs. Adams not long ago. That's the last time I can say with certainty that they were there."

"Okay. Well, look at your calendar and see if you can pinpoint that date when you showed the jewels to Mrs. Adams. It will help us to narrow our search. Don't forget to send me any photos you have of the pieces, with or without you wearing them."

Julia bid Sylvia and Eddie a tearful farewell. Sylvia gave her a reassuring embrace and promised to call later.

Once outside, she asked Eddie the question that was uppermost in her mind. "How odd that Willow Adams was, in both cases, the last person to see the missing jewelry."

"It is, and that would make her my number one suspect if she had any logical reason to want their jewels."

"Oh, I agree! I'm sure it's just a bizarre coincidence."

"That would be my guess."

This curious coincidence was discussed in detail later that day when Pamela and Julia met for tea and sympathy. Joining them was Sylvia, who brought along a printout of her story for *The Peninsula Standard*.

Both Pamela and Julia agreed that they did not like seeing their names in a story about something as sordid as a jewel robbery, but they understood the importance of putting their stories in print. As Eddie pointed out to both of them, "Publicity about the robberies will put jewelry dealers on notice that several valuable heirloom pieces might soon be appearing in the marketplace as being legitimately obtained from estate sales."

"I regret that this gives our community a black eye," Julia told Sylvia dismissively.

But Pamela convinced her otherwise. "We dedicate ourselves to making this one of the Bay Area's best places to live. I'm sure the local police and real estate agents would rather not see this story in print, but the truth is that crime happens, and we'll never be as safe as we could be if robberies like these were swept under the carpet."

"I hate it, but you're right," Julia said in a tone of resigned disgust. "Sylvia, go ahead and do what you must! It's our civic duty to inform our community that brazen criminals lurk in our midst."

Sylvia gave them both a sympathetic smile and held back any hint of how tiresome she found their pretentious behavior. This was a good story, and she was thankful it was exclusively hers.

Sylvia's instinct proved correct. It was rare for a story in one of the Standard community newspapers to catch the attention of other media outlets. That had not occurred since its lead coverage of the shocking revelations in the case of Sausalito's gossiping gourmet. To Rob's delight, Sylvia's story was picked up—not just in San Francisco, San Jose, and Oakland, but as far south as Santa Barbara, as far east as Reno, and as far north as Seattle.

The robberies were still topic number one when the Peninsula's best-known families gathered for the Belvedere Ball.

Not to be outdone, Pamela and Julia wore stunning pieces that were rented from a nearby jeweler and insured with separate coverage riders to assure their safe return. Pamela complained bitterly to Julia, "I feel like a fraud wearing rented jewels!" But, she put on a brave face that night for the rest of her social set.

Willow, on William's arm for most of the evening, was having a fabulous time. Three days earlier, her two new jewelry pieces had arrived from Paris.

Filled with many of the gems extracted from Julia and Pamela's missing pieces, these new creations also contained two emeralds that once belonged to Willow's grandmother. The same ones that had disappeared from her mother's collection fourteen years earlier, leading to never-resolved accusations and bitter exchanges between Willow and her parents.

To dance at this glittering event with two of her bereaved victims nearby gave Willow indescribable delight. And to know that two stones from one of her earliest jewel thefts were included made her evening complete.

On the Monday morning following the ball, Judge Botherton, weary of listening to his wife's mournful cries over her lost jewels, placed a second call to his longtime acquaintance, Sheriff Jack Canning, who in turn invited Eddie to come to his office for a working lunch.

Keenly aware that the sheriff was sensitive to the public pressures all elected officials experience, Eddie had no doubt this invitation was prompted by Canning's need to push for progress in the case of two robberies the media was calling, "The High Society Heists."

After deli sandwiches served on the sheriff's long conference table were finished, Canning got down to business. "Are you making any progress with the Botherton and Hassie robberies? I'm starting to take some real heat on both cases."

"To be honest, I'm at a dead end."

"No suspects?"

"I wouldn't say that. I've got one perfect suspect."

"So, why are you not moving toward making an arrest?"

"Simple. She's the wife of one of the world's wealthiest people."

"Come again?"

"You've heard of Willow Adams, the supermodel who married William Adams last year? She's been my prime suspect since I first went to each of the two crime scenes and interviewed Judge Botherton's wife, Pamela, and her pal, victim number two, Julia Hassie."

"You've got to be kidding me!"

"Both Botherton and Hassie tell similar stories. A few weeks before the thefts they showed Mrs. Adams the jewels they wear to the annual Belvedere Ball. Both walked with her into their bedrooms to pull the jewels out of pocket panels they had installed in their walk-in closets. Subsequently, Adams was in their homes for charity event planning meetings, and both victims say that they were with Adams the last time they saw their jewels."

"Wow," Canning muttered, shaking his head.

"Wow is right! Not a dime was lifted from either home; the only items missing were the jewels. You and I both know that if they had the same house cleaner and they showed him or her where their jewels were kept, and the next time they looked their jewels were gone, that cleaning person would be in custody right now."

"Exactly!" Canning said with a nod. "But the only person you know who did see these jewels and knew exactly where they were kept has no obvious motive."

"That's the problem. Jack, I went through both homes on the day that I interviewed the victims. I then went back to each with crime techs, to double check. Nothing to indicate a forced entry had occurred. I doubt Hassie and Botherton decided to cook up some crazy insurance scam because they vastly overspent their household allowances—although, let's face it, in the years we've been dealing with Marin's high society families, we've seen some pretty nutty stuff. So, unless someone beamed down from the Starship Enterprise, we have no logical suspect other than Willow Adams."

"And no evidence that these two shared some handyman, or any other service person, even a masseuse who came into the home in the time between their showing these jewels to Willow Adams and their disappearance?"

"Zip. I worked both women to be sure they provided me with all the relevant names and dates for any service people who may have entered the home. Nothing matches up, and I sure wish it had. The carpenter used to create these in-wall hiding places for both women's jewels was the same, but he retired and moved to Huntington Beach years ago. Still, I checked him out, the guy is clean as a whistle, no priors, not even a moving violation," Eddie added with a laugh.

"Damn!"

"Tell me about it. Normally, we'd put Willow Adams under a

microscope. But, come on—first of all, it makes no sense! Secondly, her husband could have you, me, and the entire department crucified just for the fun of it."

"I suppose she could be a kleptomaniac."

"Absolutely! And to satisfy my curiosity, I discreetly did some checking, but I was hesitant to get too close. If the department starts snooping around a little too vigorously, it wouldn't be long before we found ourselves facing a furious William Adams."

"I certainly can't disagree with that," Canning said, seeing his hopes of winning another term as county sheriff going up in smoke if someone with the money of a William Adams decided to back his next opponent. In an election in which no more than forty thousand dollars was ever spent, Adams could crush Canning's hopes for re-election with pocket change.

"I mean, it's not unheard of; there have been at least two successful film stars arrested for shoplifting," Eddie explained, knowing his boss was no longer listening.

"You've done great work, as always," Jack said, as he patted Eddie on the back and walked him toward the door.

He had taken the matter of the robberies as far as he could. It would remain an "open investigation," but Eddie knew that as far as the sheriff was concerned, this would stay an inactive case. The media would soon move on to the next crime story, and the chance that any opposition candidate would use this unsolved case to argue against the sheriff's re-election was a far smaller risk than infuriating someone who could cause the sheriff lasting political harm.

Over lunch later that week, Canning privately shared with Judge Botherton Eddie's findings.

The judge, whose name would soon appear on the same ballot as Canning's, decided it was more prudent to take the ample insurance money covering the vanished jewels and put the entire business behind them.

"I've had my doubts about that Willow woman since I first met her," the judge announced with a shake of this head. "It's a shame that she was able to wrap herself around William Adams, but he's not the first man of great wealth to fall for a beautiful young woman."

As for his distraught wife, the judge would focus her attention on the exciting idea of acquiring new pieces and making her promise that only the two of them would know where in the house these new jewels were hidden.

CHAPTER TWENTY-FOUR

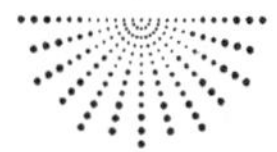

illow's days of happiness continued, starting with William and her going off to a private resort in Tahiti to celebrate their first anniversary.

The blue-green waters, the endless blue skies, the spacious home that sat on a nearly deserted strip of beach, and staff anxious to meet their every expectation; all added to her bliss.

Willow took with her the two new prized pieces done by Jacques Allard. She wondered if she should send more gems his way from a few other pieces currently owned by the group she thought of as FOB—Friends of Botherton. She was still relishing the thought of having Pamela and Julia sitting nearby while their diamonds, rubies, emeralds, and sapphires were literally inches away.

But the next grand Belvedere Ball was nearly a year away, and Willow had more pressing matters on her mind—principally, getting out from under the thumb of James Finch.

While she had only suffered through one loathsome encounter with him at the W Hotel since the video of her night in Paris with Viktor had emerged, Willow did not doubt that James would be planning other acts of coercion.

As she rocked gently in a hammock, delighting in the touch of a gentle tropical breeze, it occurred to her that perhaps she could turn the tables on James by getting closer to his wife, Jade. She and Willow had a cordial relationship but had never been close. If they were to become friends, James might consider his pursuit of her no longer worth the risk.

And what about that spectacular video that Finch held over her and Viktor? Certainly, it was possible to locate Finch's operative. James would claim his motive was to reveal Willow's deceit, but his withholding the video from William gave credence to the theory that James' real purpose was to place pressure on Willow.

This was a different nuclear option. Finch could destroy her relationship with William with proof of her affair, but having just received a second hundred-million-dollar payment after passing their first wedding anniversary, perhaps that was enough? Better still, she and Kozlov would have a chance to live happily, and very comfortably, ever after. But was such an outcome possible with the volatile maestro? As for James, his banishment from William's firm would ruin his standing in the close-knit San Francisco legal community. A reputation built by James throughout his professional life would vanish in an instant. Arguably, Finch had the most to lose.

Still, the next eight anniversary payments would make her an additional eight hundred million dollars wealthier and that, to Willow's view, was the difference between vast wealth and extraordinary wealth.

While not sure which path she should pursue, she no doubt had options. The very thought brought her relief. Other women might worry about jealous husbands, but William carried himself like a man who didn't have a care in the world.

The first full day Willow was home from Tahiti, she called Jade and suggested she join her, Holly, and Sylvia on Saturday to hike the trail through the Tennessee Valley.

On the phone, Willow poured on the charm. "I don't know why I hadn't thought to call you before."

To Willow's relief, Jade sounded happy and grateful that she had reached out.

"I'd love to walk with the three of you. I spent time with Holly and Sylvia at the wedding; they're both delightful. But Saturday morning I'm meeting some girlfriends for a wine tasting up in Napa. Can you make it Sunday instead?"

"I've got a promotional commitment for a Willow Wisp product event in Denver on Sunday. How about the following Saturday?"

"That should work," Jade responded happily. "I'll leave it open. Perhaps we can meet for breakfast before we hike."

"Wonderful, I'll call you Monday, and we can plan where and when to meet."

Willow clicked off and looked outside her bedroom window on a bright blue day. Richardson Bay was quiet with only a few boats crossing between Sausalito and Tiburon. The beauty of the scene matched the delight Willow felt in taking a significant step forward in freeing herself from the relentless pursuit of the scheming Mister Finch.

On Friday afternoon, William returned home from an investment conference in Aspen. Willow found him seated at his desk going through papers sent over by his office.

As she bent over to kiss him on the forehead, he shared with her that he had a ten o'clock tee time Saturday morning with Judge Botherton at Peacock Gap. "Would you like to join us and make it a threesome? It's been a while since you got out for a round of golf, and I'm sure Pete would enjoy seeing you."

"No, no. Go and enjoy your game. I promised Holly and Sylvia that we'd all walk the Tennessee Valley and I need some girl time." The judge's behavior seemed odd to Willow on the night of the Belvedere Ball, and while she enjoyed the occasional round of golf, she was convinced that Pamela's husband was a good deal more astute than his chattering wife and her friends. A hike with the ever-gracious Sylvia and Holly would be far less stressful.

Holly was running late—not unusual for her on a Saturday morning. They planned to meet at the trailhead by nine-thirty, but it was past that time when she met Sylvia at the commuter car park located under an overpass of Highway 101. From there, they planned to ride together into Tam Junction, and out along Tennessee Valley Road.

In recent years, the trail had become increasingly popular to the point there was often limited parking left for hikers, hence the choice to take just one car the last two miles to the trailhead. As Sylvia got into Holly's car, she said, "I'm going to call Willow and tell her we're running a little late."

Willow's cell rang without response.

Sylvia frowned. "She's not answering. Let's get there as soon as possible."

From Tam Junction to the trailhead, the road is forested and filled with curves. Holly drove quickly, but not recklessly. When they arrived at the off-road parking area, they looked around for Willow or her car and found neither.

"I'll try her number again," a frustrated Sylvia said in a clipped tone.

"Don't be mad at me," Holly insisted. "She certainly didn't drive off because we're fifteen minutes late! Anyway, if she had, we would have passed her car on the way in. There is no other way back to the main road."

After another unanswered call to her cell, Sylvia said, "She obviously isn't near her phone. What do you think we should do?"

Holly laughed. "I think there's a good chance the princess overslept. Let's give her five more minutes then head out toward the beach. We didn't get up this early on a Saturday to chat while standing in a parking lot."

"You're right. She probably forgot to set her alarm and just overslept. I'll send a text and let her know that we left the parking area a little before ten, and we're heading out toward the beach."

As Sylvia did that, Holly scanned the cars in the lot. "That car of hers is so recognizable; I just want to take one more look."

Sylvia did a few stretches and said, "Darn! I was really hoping to see Willow today. I wanted to ask her if she and William were going to appear at the community picnic next weekend—the one they hold every year in the park adjacent to Belvedere City Hall. I've been trying to get her as much positive local press as I can, and that would help."

"Trust me, Sylvia, she couldn't get more ink from us if she married Rob. And she's not that crazy."

Willow's no-show did nothing to change the fact that it was a beautiful day for a hike. Holly, an avid walker, was in fine form as usual, which put pressure on Sylvia to keep up. Neither of them bothered to look at their phones on the trail out to the beach or back because cell service in this mostly undeveloped part of Southwest Marin County is nearly non-existent.

Holly walked the final third of a mile briskly back to the trailhead as Sylvia struggled to keep up. When they reached the parking area, they checked their phones' displays and were dismayed to see no missed calls or messages.

Disappointed, they got back into Holly's car for the short drive back to the Manzanita commuter lot.

Typical of a busy Saturday, cars were now parked along both sides of Tennessee Valley Road for nearly a quarter of a mile before the designated parking area.

Suddenly, Sylvia shouted, "Stop!"

"What's wrong?"

"I just saw Willow's car!"

"Did it say 'WILLOW' on the plate?"

"I couldn't see the plate, but I'm pretty certain it was her car."

"Okay, let me park, and we'll walk back and check."

Holly put on her flashers to get the jerk in the Maserati behind her to slow down as she pulled into the first available spot on the side of the road. It was just a few hundred feet beyond where Sylvia had seen Willow's car.

A cold chill ran down Holly's spine as they approached the cherry red Mercedes SL 550 Roadster with white leather seats. She had hoped to see a different license plate, but there it was:

WILLOW

Simultaneously, they looked inside the car and spotted Willow's iPhone in its gold glitter case, lying on the passenger seat.

"I guess she forgot to take the phone with her," Sylvia said with a shrug.

"That's strange; have you ever seen Willow without her phone?"

"Well," Sylvia said as she paused, searching for an answer. "She's been here before. She knows the cell service is hopeless along the trail. So maybe she just left it in the car."

"True, but you would think she would have taken it with her

so she could have called us from the trailhead if she didn't see us. Generally, you have cell service up until there."

"Do you remember when we got here?" Sylvia asked.

"I think it was almost nine-forty-five when I picked you up, and we parked a good deal closer to the trailhead."

"She had to have parked well after us to be this far back. She wouldn't have parked here unless she came twenty or thirty minutes after us."

"Somehow we missed her, I suppose," Holly said with a shrug.

"Is that possible?"

"There is that one spot along the trail, about two-thirds of the way to the beach, where the trail bows out to the right. She might have forked to the left. The two paths are not far apart, but they're separated by some high vegetation, so sure, it's possible we could have missed her along that stretch of the trail."

"Well, now what?" Sylvia asked, bewildered and somewhat weary under an increasingly hot sun.

"I suppose we could leave my car here and we could walk back to the trailhead and wait there for thirty minutes or so to see if she comes back up from the beach."

"I don't think we have any other choice."

Holly and Sylvia tried making small talk while they waited at the trailhead, but the subject inevitably came back to the question of where Willow might have gone. The time passed slowly, and with no shade trees, they grew increasingly uncomfortable. After forty minutes, they reluctantly returned to Holly's car.

Along the way, Sylvia said for the umpteenth time, "There must be some logical explanation for this."

Holly was tempted to tell Sylvia to stop chattering, but she recognized it was her way of expressing concern.

To their disappointment, Willow's car sat just where they had found it an hour earlier.

"There's a little diner up behind the strip mall at Tam Junction that serves great huevos rancheros," Holly said. "Let's go there, get something to eat, and try to figure out what to do next."

They slid into one of the booths by the diner's front window. The old diner looked more or less as it had since it opened for business forty years earlier. After ordering their food, Holly took charge. "After we eat, let's drive back up Tennessee Valley Road. If her car is still there, I'm going to drop you back at your car, then try to get ahold of Rob. I'm sure he'll suggest we speak to Eddie Austin."

Sylvia frowned. "Do you think that's necessary? Perhaps we're overreacting."

"I'm not sure. But I know that whatever Eddie does will be a lot more than the two of us can accomplish."

"Holly, you don't think Willow's in any trouble…do you?"

"I have no idea! Right now, I'd just like to know where she is!"

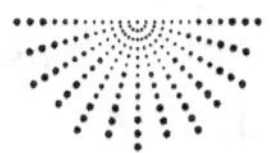

CHAPTER TWENTY-FIVE

Neither Holly nor Sylvia were surprised to see Willow's car where they had seen it last. They discussed leaving a note on the windshield but reasoned that made little sense, considering that by now they had left several voice messages on her phone.

Ten minutes later, after dropping Sylvia off, Holly was determined to push for a plan of action. On the short drive from the Manzanita car park to Rob's house on Filbert Drive in Sausalito, Holly thought about what she would tell her boss. As of now, she had only questions without answers.

Holly felt a sense of relief when she saw Karin outside in the home's small side yard playing with Micah and Alice. The children ran to Holly, each grabbing one of her hands as she stepped out of the car. "Holly, do you want to make cookies with us?" Alice asked. "Mommy said we could make peanut butter cookies if we ate all our lunch and we did!"

Holly kneeled down and gave each one of them a hug and said, "That sounds like fun, but right now I need to speak to your daddy."

"He's over at Eddie's house," Karin said. "Eddie and Sharon got one of those do-it-yourself IKEA dressers for Aaron's room, and they were both going nuts trying to assemble it."

"Sounds like fun, huh?" Holly said, looking up from where Micah and Alice had dragged her down onto the lawn.

"Okay, kids. Let your Aunt Holly up. I'm sure she'll promise to come back later to try your peanut butter cookies." Reluctantly, the children helped Holly up off the grass.

Sensing there was something troubling her longtime friend, Karin asked, "Is everything alright?"

"Probably, but it's a long story. I'll come back and tell you over a warm peanut butter cookie and a cold martini," Holly answered with a wink and a quick kiss to Karin's cheek.

A frustrated Eddie greeted Holly at the front door with a quick kiss on the cheek and a suggestion that she follow him back to Aaron's room. "Rob is trying to assemble the mother of all do-it-yourself projects," he explained as they walked down a long hall. "If the genius who writes these instructions for IKEA is found murdered, I'm not working the case. There would be way too many suspects!"

On the floor of Aaron's bedroom, Rob sat surrounded by a collection of screws, pegs, tools, handles, and boards of various sizes.

Rob looked relaxed and confident about finishing this life-sized jigsaw puzzle. He was, however, surprised to see his assistant on a Saturday. "So, what's up Holly? Came to join the fun?"

"I wish. Could you, me, and Aaron's daddy talk for a minute without the K-I-D?"

"Hey, I'm no kid," Aaron shot back, perched on his bed and enjoying his father's frustration over the assembly of what his mom and dad described earlier as his "new, big boy dresser."

"See, Holly?" Eddie said with a smile, "Kindergarten's not just for coloring books and building blocks anymore. Aaron's a future spelling bee champ!"

"Yeah, I've heard," Holly said. "I'm very impressed. Soon they'll be teaching them how to write computer code."

Eddie ruffled his son's hair. "Aaron, your Mom is out back in the garden; could you go help her so the adults can talk for a bit?"

"Okay," Aaron said, obviously displeased, as he headed toward the back door of the house.

"So, what's up?" Eddie asked.

Holly recapped the day's events. "At first, I was sure Willow had just overslept. But when we saw her car and knew she had come at least a half hour after us given how far back she parked, we just hung around at the trailhead and waited for her to show up. When I went back to check on the car after Sylvia and I had lunch, it was over two hours since we had first spotted it. In that time, an eighty-year-old could have walked through the valley, out to the beach and back. It just doesn't make sense!"

Eddie nodded. "Okay, I get it. Well, let me do a couple of things. First, I'll get one of the sheriff department's patrol cars to keep an eye on her vehicle. If it's still there around dusk, I'll have it towed and brought to our lockup in San Rafael."

"Will it just be placed in impound?" Holly asked.

"No, it will be towed to a secured evidence lockup area. The hope is that it's kept clean before we have the crime lab staff look it over. But let's not get ahead of ourselves. It might seem impossible now, but this could all have an innocent explanation."

"What about William Adams?" Holly asked. "Shouldn't someone contact him?"

"We'll give it another hour. Say, around three-thirty. See if you can get him on the home line and ask him to give me a call on my cell. I know you've got Willow's home number."

"Okay," Holly said, as her gut tightened with worry.

"Did Willow mention to you or Sylvia any plans to meet

someone else? Perhaps someone who offered her a ride when the three of you did not connect earlier today?"

"I asked Sylvia that when we had lunch. Neither of us heard her say anything about meeting anyone today. Eddie, I'm getting more worried by the minute."

"Just take it one step at a time, Holly. Ninety-nine times out of a hundred these situations turn out fine. Nothing nefarious, just one big misunderstanding."

Holly thanked him and wished Rob luck as he continued to do battle with his "easy-assembly" project.

CHAPTER TWENTY-SIX

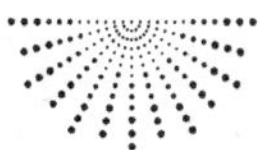

A little past three-thirty, Holly called William Adams on his house phone. She had no other contact number, and she hoped that Adams would remember her.

Mrs. Jackson answered the phone. After just a few moments of waiting on hold, Adams, to her relief, came on the line.

"Yes, hello Holly, this is William Adams."

"Yes, hi. I was wondering if you've seen or heard from Willow?"

"No. In fact, I just got home fifteen minutes ago from a round of golf. Willow told me last night that she planned to walk the Tennessee Valley with you and Sylvia this morning. Is everything all right?"

"I don't mean to worry you, but Sylvia and I have both been a little worried. Willow never met us for our walk. After trying her phone with no luck, we just thought she overslept, so we walked without her. But about an hour later, when we left the parking area, we saw her car parked along the side of the road. Her phone was on the passenger seat. We went back to the trailhead and hung around for close to another hour, but she never appeared."

William felt his chest tighten as his mind flashed back to that terrible day in Tahoe when he first reported Fran missing to the ski patrol. He willed himself to put any negative thoughts out of his mind and stay focused on the moment.

After a brief awkward silence, Holly said, "Rob Timmons, who is the publisher of The Standard, you met him at the wedding, has a very close friend, Eddie Austin. Eddie is the lead investigative detective for the Marin County Sheriff's Department. Eddie asked me to get a hold of you and give you his contact number. He has a patrol officer checking on Willow's car. If it's not picked up by dusk, sometime after seven, he's going to have it towed to the sheriff department's secure lot up in San Rafael near the Civic Center. Let me give you his cell number so you can talk to him directly. Eddie's a terrific guy. I know he'll do everything he can to help."

William's hand had a slight tremor as he wrote down Eddie's contact information. "Thank you for your concern, Holly. Willow has lots of admiration for both you and Sylvia. I can't imagine why she would not reach out to you if something else had come up."

"I agree. Well, hopefully, this will simply be a big misunderstanding. Call Eddie. I'm sure he'll help you get this sorted out. When Willow shows up, ask her to call me. I'd like to know everything is okay."

Eddie arrived at the Adams' mansion less than an hour after he and William spoke.

As he drove up to the estate, Eddie remembered his relief when he was told by Jack Canning to back away from investigating whether Willow Adams knew anything about Pamela and Julia's jewelry. The suggestion that Willow had anything to do with the missing gems was perfectly logical and utterly ridiculous at the same time. But Eddie could not shake the uncomfortable feeling that perhaps Willow had gotten in over her head with some less than desirable characters. Could there be a connection between her suspicious behavior and her disappearance? That thought ran in a loop in Eddie's mind as he pushed the front doorbell of the Adams' mansion.

William himself answered the door and led Eddie into his study. "Since Holly's call, I've been worried. Is there any further news?"

"I got a call from one of our deputies on my way over here. Your wife's car is still on Tennessee Valley Road. We'll do another couple of checks, and then, if it's okay with you, we'll tow it to our secure lot in San Rafael."

"Holly mentioned you suggested that," William said softly. "At what point would she be considered a missing person?"

"As a rule, we go with a minimum of forty-eight hours, and often longer, before declaring someone missing. In spite of what people see in police dramas, it's at the discretion of the particular department in which the disappearance occurs."

"I'm at a loss; I have no idea what's going on," William said as his voice wavered. "Holly must have mentioned that my wife is something of a celebrity. Any day of the year, she might be somewhere different. Still, someone close—myself, or her assistant, Andrea, or her talent agent—knows where she is at any given time. I checked with Andrea. Her next scheduled event is tomorrow afternoon in Denver. What's disturbing is the thought that her car is still sitting out there on Tennessee Valley Road! I mean, she goes to meet Holly and Sylvia for a walk, parks her car not far from the trailhead and then has someone pick her up, and she takes off in another direction? That doesn't make much sense!"

"I agree, Mr. Adams."

"William, please."

Eddie nodded. "It doesn't make sense. But, more often than

not, these things turn out fine. Have you been here at the house all day?"

"No, actually when I left, Willow was still in bed. I was meeting an old friend, Peter Botherton, the Marin County judge, for breakfast and a round of golf up at Peacock Gap. I got back here a little before three. When Holly called, that was the first I heard about any of this."

Eddie kept the surprise to himself that William had spent a good part of his day with Pamela Botherton's husband. This entire situation, Eddie thought, was getting stranger by the minute.

"And from the time that you left this morning until now, have you looked at your cell phone's display to see if you missed a call, text, or voicemail from your wife?"

"I hadn't until after I spoke with Holly. There's been nothing from her, which also makes no sense. So now what?"

"If the car is towed to our lot, and we don't hear from you or your wife, come Monday the crime lab techs are going to start going over every square inch of her car."

"What does that entail?"

"Standard procedure is that you have to treat the vehicle the same as you would a crime scene."

William winced at the suggestion.

"Every loose item is removed and checked for fibers and prints," Eddie continued. "They'll start with the engine and finish at the trunk, examining everything in between. They'll vacuum out the car's interior and check what they collect for hair, skin, and more. It's all about looking for things that are not supposed to be there. More than likely, they'll use luminol as well, to see if they can bring out any bloodstains that might have been wiped away because blood leaves a chemical signature."

"I met you before," William suddenly announced.

"Yes, you told me about your grandfather's work in developing luminol."

"That was at Fran's service. Why were you there?"

"Rob Timmons at The Standard is my closest friend; we grew up together in Sausalito. Sylvia Stokes suggested we attend her service along with Holly. That was a sad day."

"Yes, I was walking around in a trance that day. But I do remember our conversation."

Eddie wisely chose not to praise the buffet at Fran's service. Ready to change the subject, he said, "Hopefully, by this time tomorrow, we will have had a good laugh over what turned out to be a colossal misunderstanding."

"Before the ski patrol's search for Fran, they told me, more or less, the same thing—not to worry, she was probably taken off course and was trying to make her way back through a deep snowpack. In truth, she was already dead. So you can see why Willow's disappearance is bringing back some painful memories."

"I completely understand. In fact, if you like, I'll ride out to Tennessee Valley Road with you, and we can see the car. Just keep one thing in mind, if you've got a spare set of keys, at this point it would be unwise of you to get inside her car."

"I understand. But, could we at least open the trunk?"

"Well..."

"I had a buddy in college whose father picked up a hitchhiker near his home in central Florida. This is over thirty years ago. The guy robbed his dad and locked him in the trunk where the police found his body the next day. I'd hate to think she was lying in there suffocating in that trunk! It would just be a great relief to know she's not in there."

"I've yet to come across an airtight car trunk. My guess is, it being Florida, your pal's dad died from heat exhaustion. Not to mention, if she were in the trunk she would have heard Holly and Sylvia when they walked around her car. She would have banged or called out to them. Still, I respect your concerns. When we get there, I'll open the trunk, but I'll do it with gloves on. After we look inside, we shut the trunk. And no touching the rest of the vehicle, okay?"

"Fair enough. I don't want to get in the way of you doing your job, and I appreciate the extra support you're giving me."

On the ride over, William asked, "Do you think she was the victim of a carjacking or a robbery?"

Eddie shook his head. "In this part of Marin County, it's nearly impossible to carjack someone in broad daylight without anyone noticing. Additionally, had it been a carjacking, the odds are your wife would have been left at the side of the road as the thief drove off."

When they pulled up next to Willow's car, Eddie slipped on a pair of surgical blue nitrile gloves, asked William to stand back to avoid placing additional prints on the car—or more importantly, rubbing against a perfect print that might provide a critical clue.

The trunk was spotless. "Wow," Eddie said, trying to lighten the moment, "I don't think I ever managed to keep a trunk this clean."

When there was nothing else to be done, William was still reluctant to walk away. Eddie knew why. It felt like he was leaving his wife behind.

On the ride back, Eddie asked a handful of questions about how William and Willow met, why she kept working, and how often she went on the road for work.

When they arrived back at the Adams' house, Eddie said, "I can't tell you not to worry because I know this doesn't make a lot of sense. Here's my card. Please call me immediately if she shows up. I'll make certain you're the first to know anything we learn after her car is examined on Monday. Hopefully, you will have heard from her before then."

William struggled to focus on Eddie's directions. He was polite but badly shaken. With each passing hour, both men knew there was an increased cause for concern.

CHAPTER TWENTY-SEVEN

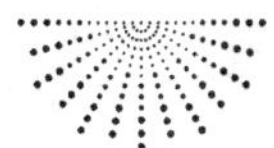

Monday morning, two crime lab technicians began the methodical process of going over every square inch of Willow's vehicle.

The following morning, Eddie reached out to William, who by then had cleared his calendar for the week.

"There are no signs of a struggle having taken place inside the vehicle. No scratch marks on the seats, let alone anywhere else, and no hair or skin other than what particles all of us shed every day of our lives. To that end, I do need your help with something."

"Whatever I can do," William said, feeling the knot in the pit of his stomach that he had lived with for more than two days now.

"I'm going to have a deputy come by your home in the next hour to pick up a hairbrush that belongs to your wife and a comb or hairbrush that you use. If you would place them into two separate plastic bags, that will help us make a positive match of hair and skin cells found in the vehicle and help us distinguish if there was an unknown third person in the car."

Eddie paused, then added, "We did find two spots on the driver's side seat that had been bloodied and wiped clean. Unfortunately, we can't tell if that happened on Saturday or a day or two before that. It was small, trace amounts of blood, and it could be something innocent like a scratch or small cut."

"Could it mean something more than that?"

"Perhaps, but any trace of blood has to be noted as a formality."

"Anything else?"

"Not much. Neither of the two doors indicates that there was an attempt at forced entry. We can't be certain, however, whether it was your wife or someone else who left the car where it was found. What we do know is that there is no evidence of tampering with the ignition system. It appears that your wife drove the car to the spot where we found it. Finally, your wife's cell phone left in the car showed no outbound calls made on Saturday, but several missed calls from both Holly and Sylvia."

"What now?" William asked feeling increasingly desperate.

"I've been assigned to the case. For now, it's filed as a missing person. I'm going to start by interviewing Holly and Sylvia, to get their full accounts of the sequence of events before their scheduled hike on Saturday."

"Detective, will you keep me posted?"

"Every step of the way I'll let you know where we stand."

It was noon that same day when Eddie came by the offices of The Standard.

"Where have you been? I'm starving!" Holly declared as Eddie handed her a roast beef on rye from Venice Gourmet.

"She gets grumpy when she hasn't been fed," Eddie muttered to Rob, as he handed his friend his requested meatball hero.

Rob shrugged. "She's grumpy all the time. Claims I pay her too little and expect too much."

"Some people are never satisfied."

"If you two are done, let's get down to discussing Willow's disappearance," Holly said, as she stole Rob's pickle.

"Hey," Rob barked, noticing her petty theft.

"What do you need a pickle for when you're eating a meatball hero? I'm the one with the roast beef on rye."

"Okay, you two, let's not fight over a pickle."

"Yeah, Rob. We've got a mystery to solve."

"You know, Holly, you missed your calling. You were on Warren Bradley's case like a bloodhound," Eddie offered.

"Don't forget she was there when you nabbed the guy. Not fully dressed, but she was there," Rob added.

"Okay, if you boys are done having your fun, let a girl get involved just once with the wrong guy and you never let her forget!"

"She's right Rob; it's not like he was a serial killer."

"Let's get down to answering the most important question of the day—where in the world is Willow? In fact, speaking of missing, where are those salt and pepper chips I asked you to pick up?"

Eddie fished around in one of the two bags he brought in with him, found the chips, and tossed the bag to her.

"So, where oh where is Willow Wisp?" Rob asked.

"Damned if I know!" Eddie snapped back.

"No clues in the car?" Holly asked.

"It was pretty clean. Luminol revealed that there had been a couple of small blood smears on the driver's seat that got wiped down, but that doesn't tell us much. We were hoping for the prints of someone who wasn't supposed to be in that car, and on that front, we came up with zilch."

"Eddie, I know you well enough that you must have a couple of working theories by now," Rob said. "So, what's your gut telling you and what, if anything, have you told Adams?"

"I'm keeping pretty tight-lipped with Adams. If he had anything to do with her vanishing, I take my hat off to him. He's giving the best performance of a concerned spouse that I've seen on or off the big screen."

"Poor guy," Holly said. "With what he went through with his first wife, he must feel like this is part two of the same nightmare."

"So, what's on your mind, Eddie?" Rob asked.

"Willow vanished over seventy-two hours ago. She might have appeared a bit flighty, but up until she missed that personal appearance in Denver on Sunday afternoon, she's been a professional her entire career. She has not missed a single appearance date. At this stage, I believe she was abducted, murdered, or both."

"Got a hunch as to which of those two might be the right answer?" Holly asked.

"Sadly, yes. Murdered."

"That's a gruesome conclusion," Rob said, putting down his sandwich. The tone of the conversation was making it increasingly difficult for him to swallow.

"Why murdered?" Holly asked, quickly losing her appetite.

"If it was an abduction, it's reasonable that as the wife of a billionaire, Adams would have been approached regarding a ransom demand by now."

"True," Rob nodded.

"Further, she doesn't fit the profile of the disgruntled wife who decides to leave her husband and run off to some far-flung corner of the world with a secret lover. For starters, having her face on perfume bottles from Moscow to Melbourne doesn't allow her to blend into a crowd easily. And if she had decided to run off, her car would likely have been found at one of the Bay Area's three major airports. But it wasn't. Her car was left along the side of the road as if she was out for a Saturday morning hike through the Tennessee Valley."

"But where is the body if she was murdered?" Holly asked.

"Possibly in those woods that run alongside Tennessee Valley Road. Or a thousand and one other places if she was abducted while walking up the road to the trailhead."

"Oh, God," Holly said pushing her food aside and starting to tear up. "I didn't want to think about it, but all weekend long I kept wondering, what if Willow were lying dead somewhere in the woods?"

"Okay, kiddo," Eddie said, handing her some tissues. "It's just a theory. Maybe I'm off the mark. I certainly hope I am. But the first thing you learn in my line of work is never to ignore the obvious."

"The same goes for the business of reporting," Rob said.

"There are acres of wooded fields around Tennessee Valley Road, and she might have been dragged off in a dozen different directions. But I'm not going to look elsewhere until the area within a half-mile of her car has been checked completely."

By Wednesday morning Eddie had rounded up five sheriff's deputies to join him in searching the woods near where Willow's car was found. They met up near the horse stables a few hundred feet from the trailhead's parking area.

"This is your party, Eddie," Deputy Nat Tompkins, one of the department's longest-serving officers, said. "How do you want us to proceed?"

"If the body of Willow Adams is somewhere in this area, I imagine we would find it within the quarter of a mile from the trailhead back to where Adams' car was located. Along that stretch, there are four pullouts where drivers often pull off. We've all been around Marin County long enough to know that people pull into these areas to do everything from smoking dope to having sex. If Mrs. Adams was killed, it's reasonable to suspect that her killer grabbed her near one of these spots. The crime tech team who went over the car found no trace of anyone being in her car other than Mrs. Adams or her husband."

"So I suppose you're looking for us to split up and check the woods around each of those parking pullouts."

"That's right. You, Mike, and Buck take the pullout nearest to the trailhead. Bettie, Craig, and I will take the first one beyond that. Fan out about five hundred feet in each direction. Search the area for about twenty minutes looking for leaves bunched together, broken branches, anyplace that seems recently disturbed. Afterward, walk down the road to the next location, and we'll do the same thing at the remaining two pullouts. Please tread lightly. If my hunch is right, we might be walking into the middle of a crime scene."

"If we come up empty, what then, Detective Austin?" Bettie Sheryl asked.

"Then, this afternoon, I'll be back with a team of search dogs to check again," Eddie answered. "One other thing, we've got three patrol cars out here right now. So far, we've been able to keep this celebrity case off the radar and out of the press. I'd like to keep this quiet for as long as we can. Let's take our cars and park them behind the stables, then walk to our search areas."

"That adds another half mile to the distance we're walking," Deputy Mike Palmer complained.

"Give me a break, Mike! All of us could use the extra exercise."

"What do you want us to say if one of the nosy old buzzards taking a hike asks what we're doing?" Tompkins asked.

"Tell them we're checking for fresh tracks of a mountain lion because we've had several reports. That will send them off in the opposite direction."

That gave Eddie's posse a much-needed laugh. "Nothing gets people moving faster than those two words—mountain lion," Craig Neufeld declared. "But why are you trying so hard to keep this hush-hush, Eddie?"

"Do any of you remember a year ago, when the southern part of the county was crawling with paparazzi covering the wedding of the millionaire model and her billionaire boyfriend? We've been able to sit on this for the last few days, but the moment it gets out that Willow Adams is missing—or worse, murdered—you can forget about preserving any crime scene. If we do find a body or at least evidence of a crime, we can secure the area before it's trampled over. We won't be able to do much about the media circus, but we can put up a tent and barriers around the area. Of course, if there is a body out there, there's a chance the site has already been disturbed by everything from ravens to bobcats. But maybe we'll get lucky and come up with shoe prints, or possibly more than that. So let's keep alert and play smart. Hopefully, we'll catch a break, and we can get this done without a team of search dogs, which would surely get the locals talking."

On occasion, a curious passerby did stop to ask whether something was going on. The roaming mountain lion story sent the curious scurrying back to their cars.

Just a year earlier, on a trail going up Mount Tam, a mountain biker was attacked and killed by a female lion fearing for the safety of her cubs. Mountain lion attacks, particularly fatal ones, are as rare as deadly shark attacks in coastal waters. But this recent encounter dampened the interest of the most intrepid hikers and kept people on the trails most frequently traveled.

The first and second pullouts appeared to be undisturbed. There had been no noticeable movement of leaves, which were still scattered about from the previous fall, and recent showers had softened the ground with some much-needed moisture.

After the two search parties had regrouped as planned, Eddie, Bettie, and Craig took the next pullout down the road, while Nat, Mike, and Buck headed to the fourth and final pullout.

Eddie was particularly interested in this third site because it was the one with the deepest wooded section behind it, and best hidden from cars heading to or from the trailhead and stables.

After Eddie and the two deputies walked the half dozen feet down into what for most of the year was a dry creek bed, they went still further into a shade-covered stand of trees. Even though the sun was high enough by now to provide adequate light, the canopy of leaves created enough shadows to encourage Bettie and Craig to put on their flashlights so any possible disturbance of the surrounding landscape could be seen more clearly.

Separately, they both saw areas where leaves and fallen branches appeared to have been moved. All three checked carefully and found nothing. After going as deep into the woods as they thought reasonable, and stepping carefully to avoid any sleeping rattlesnakes, they turned around and headed back following the same path. Bettie kept pointing the beam of her flashlight up and around to her right. Craig, who was standing on the other side of Eddie, swept the perimeter to his left.

"Wait a minute," Bettie said in a soft voice. "Take a look over there."

With the help of her searchlight, she noticed a pile of leaves that stood out from its surroundings—a possible sign it had recently been stepped upon or moved about.

"Let's take it slow and easy," Eddie cautioned. "If we've got something, we want to leave the area as pristine as possible," Eddie said as he directed Craig to pick up a couple of fallen branches.

As they slowly moved closer to the spot, each of them thought they detected the smell of perfume. Bettie said, "That's her perfume—that's Willow Wisp! I'm certain; my sister sent me a bottle for my birthday. I love that stuff."

They used their sticks to slowly and carefully clear away a pile of leaves. Their efforts revealed a clear vinyl garment bag. Inside was the nude body of Willow Adams encased for the world to see. She was lying on her back, her cornflower blue eyes wide open and her skin a macabre mix of chalk-white and gray.

Craig, embarrassed for the deceased celebrity, turned away. Bettie, after a time of staring slack-jawed at the corpse, ran back into the woods and deposited her breakfast of eggs, ham, and toast.

Eddie stood silent, transfixed by the sight of Willow. It was an image he was sure he'd never forget. "Dear God," Eddie murmured. "So much for fame, wealth, and beauty."

CHAPTER TWENTY-EIGHT

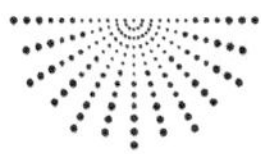

It took less than an hour for the circus to arrive. Powerful portable generators and lights were placed on one side of the road leading to the Tennessee Valley trailhead.

Under a large white tent was the site where the body had been discovered. Over a much broader area, yellow tape cautioned the curious, "Crime Scene Do Not Enter."

On the opposite side of the road, the first of what would soon be a long line of broadcast satellite vehicles parked to begin reporting on the shocking murder of the millionaire model.

Max Brownstein, the county medical examiner and a longtime friend of Eddie's, arrived during this early flurry of activity.

"From what I can see, this area has been mostly undisturbed," Max said, obviously pleased. "Between slipping the body into this bag and dousing it with perfume it either did not attract, or more likely repelled, coyotes, raccoons, bobcats, or any of our other four-footed friends interested in digging up the site and disturbing the corpse. At least for the ninety-six hours, give or take, she's been out here."

"We caught a break on that count," Eddie said, hands shoved in his pockets, feeling a chill in the air, discomfort with the macabre scene, or both.

"Well, the victim is obviously in good condition. Her killer took care of that. Obviously, I'm going to have the body removed to the morgue for a complete examination. That will leave this area for the crime techs to work over. From what I can see, without even attempting to turn the body over, it's likely the victim was struck from behind one or more times."

"How so, Max?"

"When you get in a little closer, you can see the back of her hair appears to be caked with blood that has turned dark and gelatinous over the last four days. Nothing bleeds like a blow to the head because the scalp is highly vascular. Back at the morgue, we're going to have to spend time washing that area down and cutting her hair loose from this bag. I'm guessing we've got quite a mess back there."

"I've got to reach out to the victim's husband. With the news trucks starting to gather, it won't be long before the news is out everywhere."

"I wouldn't want your job, Eddie," Brownstein said.

"Trust me, Max, the feeling is mutual."

Eddie called the Adams residence. Mrs. Jackson answered the phone and told him that William was working in his home office.

"Please tell him that I have some information for him. I'll be there in twenty minutes or less. In the meantime, Mrs. Jackson, if Mr. Adams receives any calls from the media, please do your best not to put those calls through."

Mrs. Jackson, having been told by her employer how impressed he was with Detective Austin, was determined to honor his request. She couldn't help but wonder if those words of caution were an ominous sign.

Eddie knew that as soon as the media storm began, Adams would be the number one suspect for many people. Personally, he considered that theory a ten-to-one shot at best. Still, it wouldn't hurt to see for himself how the billionaire reacted to the sad news.

Once inside the Adams home, Mrs. Jackson led Eddie to William's office, where he was invited to take a seat.

"Any news?" William asked, attempting to sound upbeat.

"Yes, sir. Unfortunately, it's the worst possible kind."

"Oh, God," William said, as he lowered his head and quietly began to weep. "How many men do you suppose have had to hear this kind of news twice in their lives?"

Eddie was tempted to point out that William's first wife died in an accident and the second at the hands of a deranged killer, but that would fall well short of helpful. Instead, Eddie explained the location where the body had been found, while avoiding details such as Willow being stripped nude, placed in a garment bag, and the bag doused with her signature perfume.

"The medical examiner just had Willow's body taken up to the morgue. They'll want you up there to make a formal identification. Any time between now and the end of the day will be fine."

"Would I be imposing to ask if you might take me up there? I can have my driver bring me back."

Eddie thought for a moment and then answered. "Sure, I'd be happy to do that."

"Thank you, detective. I'm a little numb right now. I suppose I should call Willow's parents, but I don't have their number. They live in Larkspur."

"Give me their last name."

Moments later, Eddie handed William the number. William called the Bukowskis' home number and left a simple message for either of her parents to call his private cell.

"Willow never told me much about her parents. I knew it was

a difficult subject for her. I was always tempted to ask why, but I avoided the topic. It was unusual to me. Fran and I were both very close to our parents. Now that Willow is gone, I feel I should have asked her more about their relationship. I might have better understood the distance between them. I suppose many of us put off discussing difficult topics until it's too late."

Wwhat William had to say on the ride up to the Marin County morgue was a continuous stream of consciousness. Eddie reasoned it was William's way of maintaining his sense of balance.

"The one difficult thing about being married to Willow was all the media attention," William explained. "You can't be one of the world's wealthiest people and be married to a celebrity model, and not be followed by every jerk with a camera looking to sell a photo to one of the tabloids. To a great extent, their readers don't care about some nameless billionaire. But let one marry a famous model half his age, and they'll be on that story in an instant."

Eddie nodded silently.

"You know, when you first came to see me Saturday afternoon with the news that Willow was missing, I thought of asking—perhaps insisting—that some massive search of the entire area be done starting Sunday morning," William went on. "But I knew that would lead to a media circus, and I thought, what if this was much ado about nothing? I'd never want to do anything that would embarrass Willow. I just kept telling myself that somehow this would all turn out fine and Willow would be coming home to me."

William's knees buckled when an attendant pulled down a sheet to reveal Willow's face. Instantly he knew it was his "perfect flower." Still, he was genuinely shocked at how different she looked in death. Standing there with just Eddie and an attendant, William began to weep as he leaned into Eddie to help maintain his balance.

"This makes no sense! Why would anyone want to hurt someone as sweet and loving as Willow?"

To Eddie, it was a powerful reminder of something his mother explained about the power of family. "No one on their death bed asks if their stocks went up or down that day. They talk about the people they loved and the people who loved them."

Standing shoulder to shoulder with one of the world's wealthiest men and seeing the depth of his grief, Eddie was more convinced than ever of just how right his mother's words had been. Aware of William's distress, Eddie stayed with William until he left the morgue with his driver.

Driving back to the crime scene, Eddie knew he owed Rob and Holly a call. More importantly, they might help him fill in some of the blanks he was facing in untangling the story of Willow's life.

When Rob answered the phone, Eddie asked if Holly could pick up the extension. That caused both of them to anticipate good news—or bad news.

"We found Willow's body near one of those pullouts off Tennessee Valley Road."

"Oh, God!" Holly exclaimed.

"Unbelievable," Rob added.

"Holly, can you get ahold of Sylvia, and ask her to come up to your office, say around ten tomorrow morning? Rob, if you can, please join us. I have something I want to discuss with the three of you."

"Come on, Eddie! Don't leave us hanging," Holly pleaded.

"Sorry, I'm going to have to for right now. I've got to follow every lead, and you and Sylvia might be able to help me do that. Rob, I need you there in case we send out for refreshments."

"Very funny," Rob barked.

"Give me a break, pal. That joke I just made at your expense was the first laugh I've had all day. Between finding Willow and spending the last ninety-minutes with William Adams, this hasn't been a fun day."

"I hear ya, bro. Okay, see you tomorrow. Let Karin and me know if you need any coverage for Aaron tonight."

"Thanks, pal. We should be fine. I'll see you both in the morning."

When William got home, he called his brothers, then he called Fran's brother and sister. He began to cry during each call but felt a desperate need to connect with family.

Finally, he called his partner James.

"But I didn't even know she was missing. I don't believe this!" he said insistently.

"I learned Willow was missing Saturday afternoon when I returned home from a round of golf with Pete Botherton. I hadn't said anything to you or anyone over the last few days because I didn't want to cause concern when there was nothing we actually knew."

"William, I'm so sorry to hear this."

"She was perfection," William said.

James rolled his eyes and thought of the many things that Willow was. Perfection was nowhere on that list.

James' mind was racing when he got off his call with William. His first thought was about all the calls that he had made to Willow over the past several months. He wondered if that would contribute to him becoming one of the suspects in her murder.

No, I should be fine, James reasoned, in spite of the knot in the pit of his stomach. I was her attorney. Her advisor. Conferring frequently with a top client is not unusual.

But, of course, there was the operative he hired in Paris, Roger Guilbert, and the sex video that his surveillance produced. Could that somehow leak out? Would anyone believe that he had done it to warn his longtime partner and friend about his wife's infidelity? That required a leap of faith that, at least for the moment, James was unable to make.

Before nightfall that day, news trucks lined both sides of Tennessee Valley Road with their long satellite transmission arms fully extended, beaming live from the site where Willow Wisp's body had been found.

In response to the media's persistent demands, Sheriff Canning called a press conference for the following day, Thursday, at two o'clock. Eddie would happily avoid the event, but as lead investigator, he had no doubt Canning would place him front and center.

William too was bombarded with interview requests. In response he released a brief statement, expressing in part, "A deep sense of loss and profound pain over the tragic death of my beloved wife." He followed those words with a simple request: "Please respect my family's need for privacy during this difficult time." In spite of this plea, he had little expectation that the media's pursuit of him would abate.

ddie arrived back at the crime scene tent to check on the work of a team of specialists who were covered in protective clothing in the hope that they would not further contaminate the murder site.

"How's it going?" he asked Debbie Salem, the county's lead forensics tech. "No fun, I suspect."

"We would have preferred if the body had been found in, let's say, a less challenging environment," she replied with her usual half smile. "Human hairs and traces of DNA are all a lot easier to find on a carpet, a bedspread, or a kitchen floor than here in the great outdoors. But as always, we work with what we have."

"It's never easy, is it?"

"That's why I get paid the big bucks, right?"

"Ha! Really? I never knew that."

Debbie playfully smacked Eddie's arm. "If you think that's true then I've got some marshland over in the East Bay I'd like to sell you."

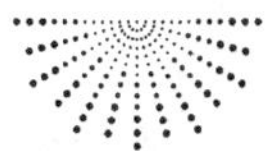

When Eddie walked into Rob and Holly's offices at ten the following morning, he was carrying an extra-large cup of black coffee from the Starbucks directly across the street.

"You look like you saw a ghost," Rob announced, noting that his friend appeared to have gotten very little sleep.

"I guess you could say that. I can't shake the image of Willow Adams' eyes staring up at me. In fact, when we found her, one of my deputies ran off and lost her breakfast behind a tree. If I wasn't the officer in charge, I might have done the same. Talk about unsettling," Eddie said as he gave an uncharacteristic shutter.

Rob nodded. "There are days that I wouldn't do your job for all the money in the world."

"Funny, that's how I feel about running a string of community newspapers," Eddie laughed. "I guess we were both cut out for the professions we chose. So, where are Holly and Sylvia?"

"They should be back any minute. Holly took Sylvia out for some fresh air. They're both stunned by all this."

"Join the crowd. Willow's husband looked crushed when I took him up to the morgue. It's not been all that long since his first wife died in that skiing accident, and now his second wife is murdered. I don't think all that money he's worth means very much to him right now. He looked like he had been kicked in the gut."

At that moment, Holly and Sylvia walked back into the office, both with red-rimmed eyes. Apparently, they had shared a good cry.

"I know all three of you have a full day ahead, so I'll get right to it," Eddie said, choosing to ignore the fact that Holly and Sylvia were obviously badly shaken by the news. "I'm looking to both of you to fill in some blanks regarding Willow's life. There's a lot about her that has me puzzled, but one aspect in particular. Sylvia, you were with me when I interviewed Pamela Botherton and Julia Hassie. I know you could tell what I was thinking after those interviews."

"Well, yes," Sylvia admitted. "You felt that, somehow, Willow was involved in the theft of those jewels. But at the same time, you and I both knew that made no sense."

"Exactly. Here's where I need the help of both of you. Organize a timeline from the moment you met Willow, up until the time she vanished on Saturday. As best as you can, try to remember every encounter: What did you discuss? Anything she told you about her friends, the people she liked, disliked, and perhaps those who disliked her."

"So, essentially, starting from the time I met her at the Adams' home when they had their meet Willow party going forward," Sylvia said.

"The party that I crashed and now wish I hadn't," Holly said with a short laugh. "Okay, we'll do it. But I'm guessing it's going to be this weekend before we can work on that. I think you know that Rob, Sylvia, and I have a crazy schedule today. We've got a deadline for the Peninsula edition, and on top of everything else we normally do, pulling the Willow story together is going to be pretty intense."

"No problem. But it would be great if you had something for me by Sunday night."

"Level with us, Eddie. I know you've got some angle on this?" Rob asked, unable to resist his reporter's curiosity.

Eddie nodded. "Okay. In a nutshell, I think it's highly unlikely that Willow is the random victim of some bloodthirsty nut job. My hunch is that someone lured her to that spot. Someone she knew, who came prepared to kill her. I know all of us have a lot on our plates for the next couple of days, so I'll explain further tomorrow night at Smitty's. I'll leave you with this; I suspect there is an awful lot that we don't know about Willow Adams. That said, the more we can learn about her the closer we might be to understanding why she was murdered and coming up with one or more likely suspects. A good place to start is getting the two of you to journal all those things you remember about her."

Eddie paused for a moment, while Sylvia and Holly started thinking about every encounter they'd had with Willow.

"Before I run off, any suggestions on how I should handle this late afternoon news conference? Jack Canning wants me in his office an hour before we meet the press, and I know he's going to push me out front."

"Keep all your cards close to your chest," Holly suggested immediately.

"There's no other way to play your hand in my line of work," Eddie responded.

"Then you know the best line of all is, 'Here's what we know at this time.'" Rob added.

"Which, in this case, is not a whole hell of a lot," Eddie conceded.

"It would be helpful if you could let people know that you think Willow was not the random victim of a crazed killer," Holly said, trying to pick her words carefully.

Instantly, Rob knew what Holly was thinking. "I've been peddling news in the Bay Area for many years now. People around here love spending nine or ten months of the year outdoors. If you can tell them that Willow was not a random victim of a crazed killer ambushing people on coastal hiking trails, you'll take a lot of heat off the department right away."

"Thanks for that. I see your point. The Hillside Strangler and the Trailside Killer didn't do much for people's enjoyment of nature."

"And when voters are fearful, politicians are unhappy," Rob said as he patted Eddie's shoulder and wished him luck in front of a press corps eager for answers from an investigator who had little to say.

After Eddie had hurried off, Rob turned to Sylvia. "I know you wanted to talk about your column regarding Willow."

"It's just hard for me to be objective about all this. I was very fond of Willow. I don't think she was perfect, I don't know if any of us are, but I'd like to believe that her heart was in the right place."

"Sylvia, I want you to call your piece, 'Remembering Willow Adams.' It should be a personal remembrance of the friend you lost. What do you think, Holly?"

"I agree! You should sit down and write the story of the Willow you knew—how hard she worked to become a valued member of the community, her generosity of spirit, all the things that made her special."

Sylvia nodded and valiantly attempted a smile. Since she looked as if she were back on task, Rob suggested that she open her laptop and write the piece before leaving their office.

"I suppose that is a good idea. My deadline is in a few hours anyway." Suddenly, Sylvia frowned. "But what about all this Eddie was saying? Perhaps Holly and I don't have any idea who the real Willow was. The disappearance of those jewels Willow was the last to see is one very odd example."

"Well Sylvia, that's called a follow-up story. Right now, I need seven hundred and fifty words on the Willow you knew. Make it kind, loving, and personal. Remember, you're a society columnist, not a crime reporter."

❧

Later that day, after Sylvia had left for home, and the Peninsula edition was completed and transmitted to the printer, Rob pulled a bottle of Johnny Walker Blue Label from his lower desk drawer and called Holly into his office. "I don't know about you," he said, "but I think we've earned a shot of the good stuff today."

"I'm with you, pal! Make mine a double."

As he poured her drink, he asked, "What did you think of Eddie's theory about Willow? Did she have a secret life?"

Holly shrugged. "I can't speak for Sylvia, but I thought Willow was interesting, in part because she was probably a little crazy. I presumed most of it was related to her being rich and famous."

"What does that mean?"

"Well, if you're a person of modest income, as you know I am, boss—"

"You know Holly, Karin and I aren't in the top one percent either."

"True. But in Marin, in towns like Sausalito, Ross, Mill Valley, Tiburon, and Belvedere, there are so many wealthy people, there are a lot of times when you feel like you're sitting outside a big party tent."

"How so?"

"Just a few feet away—inside that tent, you can hear the laughter, the cheers, the clinking of champagne glasses—and it's all wonderful and exciting, but deep down you know that you're not a part of it all. You're outside, merely overhearing the party.

"I knew Willow did what she did for Sylvia and me because we could help her meet goals she had. I never understood why that socialite community nonsense was important to her, but I didn't care. I loved being in the company of someone who was recognized from Berlin to Beijing, from London to Los Angeles. Not to mention being married to one of the world's wealthiest people. Willow was one of those rare opportunities I have had to peek inside the tent that's reserved for the rich and famous only. Like going to the wedding of Willow and William. I agreed with you, the food was not really my thing either, but the ridiculous extravagance was amazing to see from a front row seat. Oh, and getting all those insanely expensive perfume bottles I could hand out as holiday and birthday gifts were pretty sweet as well."

Rob chuckled. "I'm glad to hear you say that. For a time I thought you were star struck."

"I'm not the star-struck type. But, even little things like when Sylvia and I walked onto the deck at Sam's Cafe and although the place was packed, which for you and me would have meant a long wait, they seated Willow immediately and at one of their best tables. It was all pretty special, and I'm sorry to see that end. But, more importantly, I feel terrible for Willow that she died so young. There was something big missing from her life. I have no idea what that was. I do know this: Willow was proof that fame and wealth don't make a person whole."

"Holly, you're a born philosopher."

"Maybe. Or maybe it's just the scotch talking."

By the time the afternoon press conference got underway, the anticipated media storm was raging in full fury.

For Eddie and Jack, this was anticipated. "Any time you have the words 'celebrity-slaying' and 'unanswered questions' in the same sentence, you're going to find yourself in a feeding frenzy," Canning muttered before they stepped out onto the stage.

With Eddie at his side, Canning was hoping to say as little as possible. The media hammered away for forty-five minutes, finding various ways to ask the same three questions:

"Are there any leads?"

"Do you have a person or persons of interest?"

"How was she killed, and was a murder weapon recovered from the scene?"

To the media's frustration, Eddie and Jack handled the situation with the caution of experienced law enforcement officers. As discussed before the press conference, they revealed their working theory that Willow was the killer's intended target and not the random victim of a deranged killer.

When pressed for details on how they knew this, they took turns repeating variations on the same theme: "We're not prepared to go into that at this time..." or, "Releasing further information as to why we believe the victim knew her assailant could jeopardize our investigation."

The two concluded with the usual pledge: "As soon as we have more we can share, we will." Everyone knew that was an empty promise, one that was unhappily passed along to readers, listeners, and viewers.

Pamela and Julia had their own theories regarding Willow's murder.

"Perhaps she was working with some underworld characters in the robbery of our jewels, and she got in a little too deep. Maybe she stole from them as well," Pamela suggested, having long since decided that Willow was the only possible suspect in the disappearance of her jewels.

"Really?" Julia responded, as the two shared tea and sympathy, still wounded from the loss of their now-forgotten jewels. "But why would a woman worth hundreds of millions be interested in our gems?"

"I have no idea, Julia. But I could read between the lines of Detective Austin's questions. She was his only suspect. She had knowledge and opportunity; the only mystery is, what in the world was her motive?"

"Look at the bright side, Pamela. We no longer have Willow to worry about, and we received handsome final settlements from our insurance carriers. I thought those new pieces that Willow wore to the Belvedere Ball were exquisite. Maybe we should approach her jewelry designer in Paris—what was his name? And see if he can create something equally stunning for us?"

Pamela's lips slowly curled into a smile. "Allard was his name! And Julia, that's a marvelous idea!"

CHAPTER THIRTY

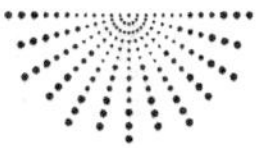

Eddie listened to the radio on his way to a meeting with Max Brownstein. He was happy to hear that one theory he shared at the press conference was being discussed: Willow's killing was not a random act.

He felt sure this would bring a call from William Adams looking for details. Eddie welcomed that. With every passing hour, he was increasingly confident the key to unlocking Willow's murder lay in the unusual aspects of her life.

Eddie found the county's medical examiner sitting in his office in a meditative state.

"So, what have you got for me, Max?"

"Not a pretty picture. Sit next to me. I want you to see this computer animation; it illustrates the actual murder with remarkable precision."

Brownstein had a fascination with the violent act of murder—something Eddie found both compelling and unsettling. Newly enhanced 3-D computer imaging added to Max's curiosity.

"The victim was struck from behind with the rounded side of a ball-peen hammer," Max explained. "From the angle of the impact, we now know that the killer was right-handed and likely several inches taller than the victim."

"That's a great start."

"After we removed all the matted hair, shaved the skull, and cleaned the wound, the method of murder became quite apparent. Removing the back of the skull we saw the massive damage to the brain, and the cause of death was then clear. Here, let me show you. Watch what happens to the skull and then the brain after a blow like the one the victim suffered."

Brownstein clicked his keyboard's space bar, and the animation began. "For clarity, this is in slow motion. As the back of the skull is struck, that rapidly spreading gray shadow you're seeing is the massive amount of blood released by the impact. A dozen different blows to the head can lead to a dozen different outcomes, but it's likely your killer was hoping to accomplish one fatal blow. There was certainly no holding back. The victim's killer struck with considerable force, and the use of that particular hammer helped to assure the outcome."

Max paused the program. "Now, let me replay this. There is one particular aspect I want you to see carefully." He pushed another key, and the animation restarted. "This shows us that as the dark shadow spreads, the brain is being compressed and forced downward."

"What does that mean?"

"It means the blood released inside the skull was so considerable that it caused an extreme amount of downward pressure. That pushed the victim's brain into the base of the skull, where the spinal cord enters."

Brownstein used a laser pointer to circle the area on the screen indicating the portion of the brain he was discussing. "This opening is called the foramen magnum. It's where the brain stem controls respiration. With this degree of compression, the victim almost certainly died within minutes of being struck, due to asphyxia. Given the amount of damage from this strike, death was an inevitable outcome."

"The husband is going to want to know if she suffered."

"This happened very quickly—almost like a bullet to the back of the head, although the injury pattern is substantially different than that of a gunshot. Loss of consciousness would have been nearly immediate. There was no point at which she could have regained awareness. The power of the strike was simply too great."

"Do you think the killer was an expert at using a hammer as a weapon?"

"Eddie, that's a tough one. When you consider the extent of the damage, your first instinct would be to think that. But a ball-peen hammer was a well-chosen weapon. It's relatively light, but it has a forged head that makes it a good deal stronger than the more typical, and heavier, claw hammer. I suspect that the killer was someone who had a tremendous animus toward the victim. Killing someone with a hammer blow is rare, and there is a psychotic viciousness to this act that we don't see very often."

"Any theory about the killer's use of that plastic garment bag?"

"I thought that was a compelling bit of theater, plus it served the killer's lethal intentions."

"Assuring the victim's death regardless of the success of the hammer strike, I suspect."

"Exactly," Max responded. "When someone gets a bang to the back of the skull, they could be unconscious for minutes, hours, days, or longer. Unless your killer was highly trained—and I think this was more luck than expertise—the only certainty they had was to strike a blow with sufficient force. The body length garment bag was added insurance to, pardon the pun, seal the deal. As it turns out, the killer bowled a strike. After that, the need for the garment bag to suffocate the victim was redundant."

"You on board with my theory that our killer knew their victim? This was not the act of a random crazed fan?"

"The psychotic aspect of the murder leaves me a bit unsure. Obviously, it was a targeted hit. Certainly, your killer came well prepared. Beyond that, I suppose the motive itself remains a mystery. But I think the killer was looking to expose their victim," Max said using air quotes. "One would think that was their twisted logic in stripping the victim and dousing the garment bag with her famous perfume. Now whether the killer was driven by personal animus or simply delusional hatred, that's not my area of expertise."

"A good amount of preparation went into this killing," Eddie said as the computer images of the fatal blow replayed in his mind.

"My guess is the killer repeatedly practiced using that hammer. In fact, that hammer might have been acquired for this one purpose. All I can say with a high degree of certainty is the killer had a set plan of action and executed it to perfection."

"The chances of us recovering the murder weapon at this point are probably nil."

"No easy breaks coming your way on this one."

"Not yet, but you have to keep plowing ahead. We'll catch one or more lucky breaks. At least that's what I keep telling myself."

When Friday rolled around, Rob, Holly, and Eddie were glad to see their workweek end. They celebrated in their usual way: meeting at Smitty's for happy hour.

"I could use two days off," Eddie began. "One more microphone gets stuck in my face, and I might come out swinging."

"Easy, big fella," Rob said while patting Eddie's shoulder.

Eddie was relieved just to be back in the presence of two trusted friends.

"Tough case, huh?" Holly asked.

"It's always tough when it's high-profile. Between Willow's celebrity status and William's fortune, it doesn't get any higher—at least, not in Marin County. We're already getting calls from local politicians who want to know if we're making any progress. We keep reminding them that it's forty-eight hours since we found the body, and the killer wasn't considerate enough to leave their business card."

"So, where are we?" Holly asked, crossing her legs and staring intently at Eddie.

"Calm down, Nancy Drew! We are making progress, but so far there are more questions than answers."

"Eddie, you can guess what my sidekick, Ms. Drew, and I want to know: what cards are you keeping close to your chest?"

Holly slid closer to tighten their small circle.

"Well, the killer didn't leave a business card, but there was a note in that clear zip-up garment bag she was found in," Eddie shared after reminding them of their long-standing bond of secrecy.

"When was it found?" Holly asked quickly.

"When her body was removed from the bag she was lying in, nude and face-up."

Holly shivered at the thought. Suddenly the vision she had of Willow's lifeless body grew more vivid and more disturbing.

"Where was the note?" Rob asked.

"It was inside a zip-lock bag, nailed to the base of her spine. We suspect the killer used the same hammer that struck the fatal blow to drive home their message."

"I'm starting to feel a little sick." Holly put down her cocktail on the small table between them and pushed it away.

Rob pointed at the bar's back wall. "If you're going to be sick, the ladies' room is over there."

"I'll be okay, smarty-pants."

"What did the note say?" Rob asked.

"'Forever young!'"

Holly's mouth fell open. "That's it?"

"No. On the next line, it said, 'A Devoted Fan.'"

"God, that's creepy!" Holly added.

"Can they get anything from a handwriting sample?" Rob asked.

"No such luck. Whoever this crackpot is took the time to cut out all twenty-two of the note's letters from magazines and paste them down on a note card. It was quite a work of art."

"Wow," Holly murmured.

"And this is why you could say at the press conference you were sure the killing was not a random act. Willow Adams was the intended target," Rob reasoned. "And I thought you were going on the hunch you shared with us Thursday morning."

"There's more. The outside of the garment bag her body was placed in was doused with Willow Wisp perfume—enough that the scent was still noticeable when we found the body. It certainly kept the woodland creatures away. The site looked untouched at the time we located the body."

Holly, hungry for more details, asked, "Where does that leave you?"

"With either a whack job or a killer who would like us to think he or she is a deranged fan. I'm going with the latter. I can't imagine Willow pulling off to the side of the road for anyone other than someone she knew. From what little I know of her, I doubt she'd stop for a stranger in distress if their hair were on fire."

"I think you're right," Holly said with a nod. "I also believe she stopped for someone she knew—or, at least, thought she knew."

"Not to mention walking a hundred and fifty feet back into the woods with her killer," Eddie said.

"Unless, of course, she was forced at gunpoint," Holly suggested.

"But remember, Ms. Drew, this was somewhere around 9:30 on a Saturday, and while the pullout nearest to where she stopped is next to a usually quiet two-lane road, at that time of day, during the dry season, there is a steady stream of hikers driving toward the trailhead."

"So why would the killer want the police to think he or she was a crazed fan?" Rob asked.

Eddie shrugged. "To throw us off I imagine. If you're chasing after some nut job fan, unless you got lucky and found something in a letter they sent to their victim or a clue that led you to their front door, you might chase down leads that turn into dead-ends for a very long time. On the other hand, if the killer was someone Willow knew, the field of your search gets much smaller and a lot easier to manage."

"Any chance of a carjacking?" Rob asked.

"Adams asked me that as well. But, between her home and where her car was found are pretty open roads, and it is broad daylight, there is not much opportunity for a carjacking without someone seeing something and calling it in. Nope, she had a reason to stop and pull off the road before reaching the trailhead. I'm betting she was ambushed, not carjacked."

"Makes sense," Rob said, confounded by all the blank pieces in the puzzle Eddie was struggling to complete. "But if it was someone she knew, how did they know she was going to be driving down Tennessee Valley Road at that time on a Saturday morning?"

"That's what we're trying to figure out. Neither Holly nor Sylvia had been told by Willow to expect anyone else. Surely, several pieces of the puzzle are missing. We're looking through phone records of Willow's cell, her husband's cell, and the Adams' home phone for the two weeks before the murder. We want to see who called in and who called out; that might be a significant help."

"And what's with this whole thing about Sylvia and me writing down all we can recall about Willow?"

"As with any case, I'm always looking for a thread you can pull to unravel relevant details that occurred before the crime. I'll bet the bank that Willow had a whole bunch of little secrets. Teasing out if she did know something about those missing jewels is as good a place to start as any."

"But, Eddie," Holly said, "why in the world would she take those jewels? On top of having a billionaire for a husband, she had a prenup that gave her a hundred million each of the first ten years of their marriage!"

"I know, Holly. It's bizarre. But it's not any stranger than a highly successful Hollywood star being arrested for shoplifting. Maybe she loved the thrill of the caper. Maybe it's the cry for attention therapists talk about. And if she was into theft for thrills, God knows what else she might have been getting herself into. Maybe she cheated the guy who was fencing jewels for her. Maybe she knew too much about something she wasn't supposed to know anything about."

"And you think the husband is in the clear?" Rob asked.

"I've given that a lot of thought. It's unimaginable to me that he killed her—not to mention the vicious way in which she was killed. And don't share any of this with Sylvia, or anyone else. We're going to have to feed the news mill something by Monday afternoon when we hold our next press briefing. I'm saving our conclusion regarding the murder weapon for the ladies and gentlemen of the press for dessert. The funeral is later that same afternoon, and the reporters are all going to be looking for updates by then to go along with their evening coverage from outside the church. If nothing else, the grizzly nature of how Willow died should keep them happy for a few more days."

"Wow!" Holly exclaimed. "This whole thing is like a car wreck! You don't want to look, but at the same time you can't look away."

"That nicely sums up my job during too many weeks of the year," Eddie said as he called for the check. Rob stopped his hand as Eddie reached for his wallet.

"This time is on me, pal. There are weeks our job can be a grind, but this is one week I'm glad I dig up stories and not bodies."

CHAPTER THIRTY-ONE

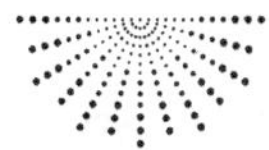

On Saturday morning, Holly and Sylvia met at Caffe Acri, a coffee shop across from the picturesque Tiburon waterfront. It was tempting to sit there and stare out at sailboats framed by a bright blue sky. But they both had work to do: documenting the various meetings and conversations they had with Willow. Hopefully, that would reveal pieces of her life they had previously ignored.

As they stared down at their pads and pens sitting next to mugs of coffee, Holly muttered, "This whole thing stinks."

Sylvia nodded. "You're right it does."

"Last week at this time we were walking through Tennessee Valley, wondering how we could have missed seeing Willow."

"I know," Sylvia said, as her lower lip trembled slightly. "I kept telling myself there must be a simple explanation like she overslept, or forgot and went off with a friend to do something else."

Holly tried hard to keep all of Eddie's information to herself, but after getting Sylvia to swear an oath of silence, she told her that Willow was struck down with a single hammer blow to the back of the skull. After all, in forty-eight hours Eddie was going to share with that information with the world.

Sylvia began to cry quietly. She repeated one word several times: "Why?"

"Buck up, Sylvia, we've got to do our bit to help Eddie find her killer. But this idea of writing a history of our experiences with Willow doesn't make as much sense to me as putting our thoughts together on what we found odd and unexpected in the time we spent with Willow." Holly picked up her pen and asked, "What would be first on that list?"

Sylvia leaned in. "For starters, I always found myself wondering why she had no other friends. Over the time that we knew her, I can't recall a single mention of any personal friend. Which is one big reason I found it hard to imagine she had gone off with some friend instead of meeting us. Obviously, she had some professional acquaintances, but I can't name one person, other than the two of us, from outside the world of modeling and the promotion of her perfume, that she ever mentioned."

Holly nodded in agreement. "I know! I told myself that she didn't have time for a social life because she was too busy with travel, photo shoots, and personal appearances."

"And, didn't you find it strange that she reached out to us to identify some community effort that she could spearhead? I would think that would be the outcome of a conversation with William. Fran was very active with community causes, and William was aware of all her activities."

"I remember sitting at Sam's Café and asking her why she would want to get involved with something like the McKegney Park project! She didn't seem to like any of those society gals, particularly Botherton and Hassie."

"I just thought she wanted to make a place for herself with the local social set, something I assumed William had urged her to do."

Holly's eyes got wider. "And then their jewelry disappears."

"I was with Eddie when he interviewed Pamela and Julia.

Willow was the only obvious choice for having committed the theft, but then there was…" Sylvia shrugged.

"All her money, right? How could someone so rich care the least bit about their antique bracelets and necklaces?"

"If she liked old estate pieces, she had the money to buy them by the basketful," Sylvia said as she stirred her coffee and stared down at her cup. Suddenly, she looked up. "Did you notice the odd interaction between Willow and her parents on the day of the wedding? If that had been our daughter, Jack and I would have been beaming. She's an international celebrity, and she's marrying one of the world's wealthiest men—and a dear, sweet man at that. That's what any other parent would define as a blessed day! But from what I could tell, Willow barely exchanged ten words with either one of her parents. I don't remember a single hug between the three of them."

"I saw the same thing. They acted more like distant relatives who were seeing each other for the first time in years."

"Something must have happened years ago, I would imagine, that caused a terrible rift in their relationship," Sylvia declared. "Whatever that was, it apparently went unresolved."

"Do you think there's a chance that Willow chose a project headed by Pamela and Julia so she could get close to them?"

"I suppose, but that takes us back to why would she want their jewels. Any piece of jewelry William didn't want to buy her, she could easily have bought on her own."

"Maybe she was ticked at the two of them about something, and taking their jewels was her way of striking back."

"Well, I overheard the two of them saying some nasty things about Willow at the party William held for her. More importantly, I think Willow overheard Julia and Pamela as well. I thought Willow put that behind her when she invited both of them to her wedding, but maybe not."

"I suppose you could file that under the old rule of keeping your friends close and your enemies closer."

"The sum total of all this," Sylvia said slowly while stirring her coffee, "is Willow clearly had some serious issues."

"More to the point, did those issues play a role in her murder?"

"Perhaps…"

"I have a suggestion," Holly said as a smile flashed across her face. "I'm going to look online at Willow's senior class at Marin Academy. I want to find a few of the women who graduated the same year. Why don't you call them with the excuse that you're doing a follow-up story on Willow's life? Maybe we'll find out something that will help us to understand why she had no old high school friends at the wedding—or for that matter, from any other time in her past. Then, at the funeral on Monday afternoon, you could find Willow's parents at the reception and tell them something sweet about their daughter and mention the follow-up article you're doing on Willow's life. See if you can get an interview with one or both of them. I don't know how revealing they'll be, but we both know there must be a lot they're keeping to themselves."

"Absolutely!" Sylvia responded.

"Eddie feels certain Willow knew her killer," Holly added. "If he's right, who would hold that much vengeance for her? At this point, I'm pretty sure there were at least two sides to Willow's personality. Hell, there might have been a half dozen for all I know. If we can get some people from her past to tell us more about the Willow they knew, maybe this whole puzzle will start falling into place."

CHAPTER THIRTY-TWO

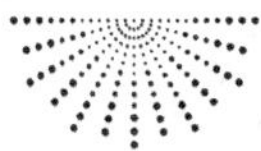

Debbie Salem called Eddie on Saturday afternoon to share a bit of good news. "I thought you'd like to know that we pulled two pieces of physical evidence from the scene," the forensic tech explained.

"I'm all ears," Eddie answered.

"First, at the end of a twig lying under those leaves that were pushed together to cover the victim's body, we found some light blue fibers. We've identified the fibers as coming from a denim material backpack sold by REI. It's not much, and there is no way to assure that some innocent hiker did not leave those fibers there at an earlier time, but given where these fibers were located it's a potentially significant find."

"I imagine the killer's supplies were in that backpack—the hammer, the plastic garment bag, the perfume, the nail, and the note. Plus, whatever else he, she, or they took from the scene."

"I suspect the killer put on a pair of nitrile gloves after the victim was struck from behind," Debbie added. "We didn't lift any prints off the garment bag, the note, or that nail in the victim's spine. As all of us suspect, the killer came well prepared for the job. Eddie, I'm sorry and frustrated that we didn't get more."

"Thanks for what you have done. The backpack is a nice little break. What's the second piece you found?"

"We made some casts of a bike tire's tracks that were approximately four feet from the location of the body. The upside is the tire's imprint was made in soil that was soft enough to give us a clear image, and certainly close enough to the scene of the killing to also make it relevant. The downside, it could be just another tire print belonging to some unrelated mountain bike passing through the woods in the days before the crime."

"It's better to have tire tracks than not. I'm glad you were able to get them. Was there any indication that the bike had gone beyond the spot where we found the body?"

"No, there was not. The biker might have leaned the bike against a tree and then carried the bike out from there. But the tracks did not continue beyond that point."

After thanking Salem, Eddie sat back for a moment at his kitchen table. From there, he could hear Sharon and Aaron playing hide-and-seek in the backyard.

I'd love to find that backpack and that ball-peen hammer, he thought. But probably within an hour of the killing, it was all tossed along with the bike tires in one of a thousand dumpsters.

If I had done this, dumping all that evidence is the first thing I would do, Eddie thought. But, who knows? This wasn't the work of a professional killer. This feels more like a crime of passion. Most amateurs slip up one way or another. Starting, perhaps, with a recent purchase at Marin's REI store, located in Corte Madera's Town Center, of a light blue denim backpack.

Two hours after they met in Tiburon, Holly called Sylvia to give her the phone numbers of three women who were in Willow's high school graduating class.

The moment Sylvia hung up with Holly, she called the first

name on the list. Randi Franks picked up after two rings, and Sylvia poured on the charm.

"Yes, I've been reading about Willow. It's regrettable," Randi offered.

During the first five minutes, their conversation centered on the shocking news, then Sylvia subtly moved to a deeper level. "Covering Willow and working with her, I was surprised by the lack of close friends she had. Everyone in her life had a business or community connection, but there didn't seem to be any personal friends, especially ones from her past, such as an old high school friend. Not even one at her wedding."

Randi sighed. "I'm more than happy to share with you my theory as to why that would be, but you must not use my name in your story."

"This is strictly confidential, for background use only," Sylvia promised.

"I hate to speak ill of the dead," Randi hesitated.

"No, don't worry," Sylvia assured her, "We're off the record."

"Well…in truth, Willow was both a sneak and a thief."

"Really?"

"In time, she burned every girl in Marin Academy's senior class. If she did not go after your boyfriend, she'd swipe something else of yours. It could be anything, a favorite pen, a music CD; I knew one girl who lost the gold cross her grandmother gave her! It simply vanished from her gym locker one day. She couldn't figure out what had happened, but a few other girls and I knew. We called it 'getting Willowed.'"

"Wow," Sylvia said as she attempted to minimize the degree of shock in her voice. "Why do you suppose Willow would do something like that?"

"I have no idea. But I can give you the names of some of the other girls in the class who went through the same thing. They might know more than me."

Sylvia took down the names but had no real intention of

calling them. However, their contact information could potentially be of value to Eddie.

"Why do you suppose Willow was lashing out against these girls? Was she a social outcast? Was she angry with a particular group of girls?"

"Willow was an equal-opportunity thief. I'm not exaggerating when I tell you that she crossed just about every girl in our senior class. It was weird. No one was ever quite sure what set her off. But from our sophomore year on, every girl learned to stay out of her way. No one trusted her, and no one wanted to be her friend."

If Sylvia thought there was any exaggeration on Randi's part, it was dampened by the list of names she shared. "Start with Suzie Steiner," Randi suggested. "She would love to talk to you. Willow took both her boyfriend and the antique watch that her grandfather left her. It was pretty sad."

"Just one more question. Why didn't any of you speak to your teachers about all this?"

"We all talked about doing that but decided against it. Better to just be more careful about our possessions than to get Willow angry with us. Sounds silly now, but back then, we were all terrified of her."

Sylvia's conversation with Randi was so revealing that she immediately called Holly to share what she'd heard and tell her of the list of names her interviewee had provided.

Holly's only two comments were, "Oh, my God!" and, "That's incredible!"

"I'm just curious if you're thinking what I'm thinking?" Sylvia asked.

"You mean about the Botherton and Hassie robberies?"

"Yes. It's unbelievable—but I suppose it was Willow; it certainly matches up with her past behavior."

"Perhaps Ms. Wisp was a sociopath," Holly murmured.

"How do you define sociopath? I don't think I really know."

"I've dated my fair share," Holly assured her. "I was a Psych major, so you'd think I'd know better," she said with a sigh. "Sociopaths have aggressive and impulsive behaviors. They have a complete disregard for the rights of others. With her classmates, she followed a sociopath's view that what's mine is mine, and what's yours is mine too. Let's be honest; you would have to have a mental health disorder to be worth a fortune and want to steal the property of other people. I'm sure it gave her some kind of rush. For sociopaths, the norms of right and wrong just don't apply."

"How could Willow fool someone as astute as William Adams?"

"Sociopaths know how to say the right thing—and to push all the right buttons. They know what society expects of them, but they have this uncontrollable desire to do the opposite."

"I guess it helped that she was gorgeous," Sylvia murmured. "But that still leaves the biggest question of all, did she die for her sins?"

"I have no idea," Holly replied, "but given her behavior, I'm starting to think the list of Eddie's suspects is getting longer by the minute."

❦

Holly could not let the weekend conclude without reaching out to Eddie to share what Sylvia had learned.

"I'm not surprised," Eddie responded casually. "Did she ever mention to you a guy named Kozlov? He's a well-known concert violinist."

"Willow never mentioned him to me. I don't think to Sylvia either. But considering all we've learned about Willow in the last twenty-four hours, I'm sure there's a good deal more we don't know. What about Kozlov put him on your radar?"

"Phone records, which reveal that he and Willow called each other dozens of times over the past year. I don't know anything about her taking violin lessons. I think it's a pretty safe guess they were having an affair. It took me less than a minute on the Internet to learn that Kozlov was linked with Willow romantically before she met William Adams."

Holly gave a low whistle. "Willow certainly kept busy!"

"And do you remember anything about a James Finch?"

"His name never came up that I recall. But wait a minute, I did meet the guy. He was William Adams' best man. His law partner as well, if memory serves. Kind of a full-of-himself, fast-talking guy. What put him on your radar?"

"He's the only guy who rang Willow's number as often as Kozlov."

By Monday morning, Eddie was beginning to feel more confident about unraveling Willow's unusual life. Her slaying was still topic number one for Bay Area media, and Eddie knew it would be a blessing to clear this case as soon as possible.

He and Canning huddled early in the day to discuss their one o'clock press conference. At three, Eddie planned on arriving at St. Stephen's for Willow's memorial service.

"Anything interesting turn up in the call records of our celebrity victim?" Canning began.

"A few items raise questions that need answering."

"Such as?"

"One is a Viktor Kozlov. He's a famous Russian violinist who renounced his citizenship and became a British citizen. He and Willow were an item before she and Adams married."

"From what I've read, she was an item with half of the big names in Hollywood, plus a sprinkling of NBA, MLB, and NFL standouts," Canning muttered.

"True. But her lasting relationship appears to be with Kozlov. And given the calls between them over the past year, you start to wonder if they were..."

"Fiddling around?" Canning said with a smile.

"Exactly."

"Well, I know you're not seriously looking at William Adams as a suspect, but at a hundred million dollars a year, he might think that kind of money should have bought him a little fidelity if nothing else."

"Yeah, you would think."

"What else do you have?"

"This attorney—a guy named James Finch. He's a senior partner in Adams' firm. Could be nothing, but a lot of calls between him and our victim as well. More accurately, incoming calls made from him to her. There must be ten calls for every call she returned. Maybe nothing. It just strikes me as unusual. I'm going to Willow's funeral service later today. I pulled up a picture of Finch from his law firm's website. I'm going to buttonhole him and arrange an interview for tomorrow if possible. Perhaps I'll catch him off-guard and get a real feel for him."

"Any others?"

"Yes, two, both in Paris. She had the same number of calls inbound and outbound in this instance. One of them is her designer and partner in the creation of that perfume, Henri LeBon. The other guy is Jacques Allard. He's a jewelry designer. I'm just curious about what she may have been up to with him."

"Still working the jewel thief angle?"

"One of my contacts at The Standard, the local columnist for Tiburon and Belvedere, learned that Willow certainly had a habit while in high school of taking what didn't belong to her. Apparently, that wasn't limited to jewelry; it extended to boyfriends as well."

"Wow, Eddie, I'm getting the feeling our victim was a handful."

"I've had that feeling for quite some time."

For dramatic effect, Eddie and Canning leaned on Max to join them and put on a little show for their afternoon press briefing.

"Nothing too gruesome," Eddie explained to Max. "Just a bit of that computer modeling you made of the hammer striking the back of Willow's head."

"You think you're going to satisfy the media's appetite with that?"

"Trust me, Max, they'll eat it up," Eddie said confidently. "It's unsettling but way too dramatic to ignore."

"Anything else?" Max asked.

"Yes. I'm going to mention that we have fibers that were left behind by the killer," Canning said.

"But we have very little of that, and no way to know if it's connected to the killer," Max emphasized.

"I know that, but at least it sounds like progress," Canning explained. "Better still, if our killer is watching, it will start him thinking. The first person who pops up and asks what kind of fibers, I'm going to reply that 'discussing the nature of our evidence could impede an ongoing investigation.' That might make our killer sweat a bit, which is undoubtedly a good thing.

"Okay, guys, it's your show," Canning reminded them. "The sooner we can get done with this, the happier I'll be."

"Don't worry," Eddie said as he put his arm around Max's shoulder and added, "It's just a bit of show business."

"You mean like when Macbeth said, 'It is a tale told by an idiot, full of sound and fury, signifying nothing.'"

"Something like that, Max," Canning said with a laugh.

CHAPTER THIRTY-THREE

The press conference went well but ran long. Eddie arrived at St. Stephen's Episcopal Church shortly before the memorial service began. The first thing he noticed was television satellite trucks lining Bayview Avenue as reporters, camera operators, and producers all jockeyed for position on the usually quiet street.

Anticipating a rush for the limited available seating inside the sanctuary, Holly, Rob, and Sylvia arrived thirty minutes early and held on to one extra space for Eddie. As he slipped in between them, he whispered to Holly, "All the usual suspects, I imagine?"

Eddie craned his neck to observe those seated in the pews. "Do you know where Finch is sitting?"

"He and his wife are seated to the right of William Adams," Holly responded.

"And the couple to his left?"

"Oscar and Gloria Bukowski, Willow's parents."

"Quite the family photo."

"Hardly!"

"Do you see LeBon and Allard?"

"They're seated in the second pew behind Adams. LeBon is the one in that dramatic white double-breasted suit, with the black carnation on his lapel. Allard is to his right."

"Sylvia, when the service ends, buttonhole the Bukowskis," Eddie said and then turned back to Holly. "Pull Allard aside. I'll introduce myself to James Finch. Rob, keep an eye on the buffet and make sure to save me a donut; I haven't eaten since breakfast."

"Very funny!" Rob muttered. "By the way, how did the press conference go?"

"A breeze. You were so right to suggest that Max show his animation of the hammer blow's impact. They sat there like kids at a magic show. Nothing like the reality of a violent homicide to satisfy the appetite of hungry reporters."

Rob nodded. "They love anything that will shock their readers or keep their viewers from changing channels."

Just then, the organist began to play Rock of Ages.

"And the show goes on with all those satellite trucks parked outside," Eddie added in a whisper.

"Lights, camera, murder," Rob replied.

Except for William and LeBon, there were few tears shed during the brief service.

Sylvia dabbed the corners of her eyes several times, but Holly reasoned that was more for the loss of innocence than the loss of Willow.

Sylvia assumed none of Willow's classmates were in attendance. Most of the attendees were there for William. The Bothertons, the Hassies, and most of Belvedere's social elite stayed away. No doubt a sign that Pamela and Julia had been quietly sharing their suspicions regarding Willow and their missing jewels.

At the end of the short service, the gathering stood to follow William and the minister to the church's reception hall for an elaborate afternoon tea. Sylvia intercepted the Bukowskis, as

Holly re-introduced herself to LeBon and Allard, and Eddie walked just steps behind Finch.

In the church's spacious glass-enclosed space, the attendees—mostly William's immediate neighbors, his family, partners and employees at his law firm, and various other business ventures spoke in hushed tones regarding the unsettling nature of Willow's murder.

Sylvia began by reintroducing herself to Gloria and Oscar.

They all agreed that it seemed like a short time since they had been together at Willow and William's wedding.

"Willow and I spent lots of time together, working on local community projects. She dedicated herself to the causes she chose," Sylvia said with a sympathetic smile.

"I never knew Willow to do any charitable work," Oscar exclaimed with evident surprise.

Sylvia smiled, ignored Oscar's comment, and pushed ahead. "Oh, she was very determined to do what she could for her adopted community. In fact, I'm writing a piece about your daughter's community volunteer work for this Friday's edition of *The Peninsula Standard.*"

"I don't think there's very much we could tell you about Willow, at least not about her life for the last ten plus years," Gloria murmured in a soft, tired voice. "She moved out of the house at eighteen, less than a month after she graduated from Marin Academy. I'm sorry to say that we had minimal contact with her after that."

Sylvia hoped to stay on task, but the nature of Willow's relationship with her parents struck her as remarkably odd. The only thing she could do was to follow Rob's advice: "If you reach a sensitive point in your interview, don't let it throw you. Just keep pushing forward. Maintain your balance and momentum, or you could lose the most important part of the story."

Hoping to provoke a response from Gloria, Sylvia declared, "Willow seemed happy and sad all at the same time."

Gloria shrugged. "I never knew her to be satisfied, I can tell you that. The moment she achieved one goal, she was on to the next."

"Sounds like an admirably ambitious young woman."

"Admirable?" Oscar said abruptly.

Anxious to escape an unintended and awkward confession, Oscar feigned hunger and wandered off toward the buffet table. Gloria took Sylvia by the hand and walked her to a far corner of the room. "My husband is very uncomfortable talking about Willow," she said just above a whisper as Sylvia, several inches taller, leaned in. "The two of them had a terrible relationship! I learned, over time, to forgive Willow, but my husband never could."

"Forgive Willow?" Sylvia asked attempting to feign surprise. "What could cause such a terrible divide between the two of them?"

Gloria pursed her lips. "I don't want to see any of this in the story you're doing. You must promise me that."

"Absolutely," Sylvia said quickly. "I had great affection for your daughter. We're completely off the record."

Gloria looked down at her hands, which she kept tightly clasped. "Before Willow finished middle school, things in our home began to disappear."

"What sort of things?"

"At first, small, rather unimportant items. I lost a hat, a pair of sunglasses, and some perfume. Oscar lost a Willie Mays auto-graphed baseball. He was very upset about that!"

"Did you think it was Willow?"

"No. Instead, we changed house cleaners—twice, in fact—until we realized it had to be Willow. But it was more than a year before the situation got even worse."

"What happened?"

"Oscar's parents' wedding rings vanished. His mother gave them to him shortly before she died. They had great sentimental value, and Oscar was devastated when they could not be found. Then, my grandmother's diamond bracelet went missing. I won't go into the details, but Willow was the only one, besides us, who knew where any of these pieces were kept."

"Why did you tell her where they were if you suspected her?"

"We told her before all this. Willow was our only child! If something terrible had happened to us—a car accident, or whatever, she'd be the only one left. We wanted her to know where to find the few valuables we had. Of course with the loss of these other pieces, we could no longer ignore the obvious."

"At this point, you must have asked her about all this?"

"Of course we did. Willow vehemently denied everything. In fact, she was very angry with us for confronting her. But after her school contacted us about classmates claiming that she had stolen from them, we confronted her again. It only resulted in more anger and more denials. Nothing we did made the situation better. We suggested counseling—not just for Willow, but the whole family. She put up a stone wall and wouldn't discuss it."

For the first time that day, Sylvia saw Willow's mother cry.

She wrapped an arm around Gloria's shoulder and said, "I'm so sorry to have upset you. Please know that wasn't my intention."

"No, my dear, you did nothing wrong. Willow's relationship with us has been the greatest source of pain in our marriage. And now, with her death, we know that we'll never have closure regarding any of this. It's simply devastating."

"None of this was ever resolved?" Sylvia asked embarrassed by her own persistence.

"Our lives as a family unraveled. When we got nowhere with suggestions of therapy, Oscar wanted to get the police involved! It was terrible. By her senior year of high school, Oscar kept everything of value under lock and key. We were constantly on alert. He even locked away his wallet and my purse at night. It was a great relief when Willow's income from modeling allowed her to move out and live on her own so soon after she completed Marin Academy. She had nothing to do with us after that. Holiday and birthday messages, our cards and gifts, all went ignored and unanswered. Oscar had the locks to our house changed. That for me was the saddest part of all."

Sylvia could not imagine the stress all this had caused. "I won't write a word about any of this," she assured Gloria. "My heart goes out to both of you."

"Thank you, Sylvia. Oscar and I know none of this will ever be resolved. Willow barely spoke to us at her wedding, and not a word from her in the year plus since. We constantly pray for answers, but in the meantime, life must go on."

❀

Holly was thankful that Allard and LeBon were undisturbed at the reception, except for a brief moment when William came over to thank them for traveling such a great distance.

After William had his say, Holly walked over and reached out her hand. "How nice it is to see you both again! I'm Holly Cross. We met at Willow's wedding."

"But, of course!" Jacques smiled, as he took her hand and kissed it.

Henri nodded nonchalantly, but Holly read his disdainful expression as: "Who is this peasant to disturb my time of grief?"

Holly ignored Henri and pressed on. "As I'm sure both of you were, I was devastated by Willow's death."

"And you are, again?" Henri sniffed.

Twit! Holly thought instantly. But she smiled sweetly and said, "I'm the editorial and production manager of the local community newspaper. Willow and I spent lots of time together working for charitable causes." Turning to Jacques, Holly added, "We want to do a story about Willow's stunning jewelry. Those pieces you designed for her were quite a sensation at the annual Belvedere Ball."

Sighing rudely to express his disinterest, Henri excused himself and wandered off.

Holly was relieved to have Jacques to herself. "I'm sure you know that Willow was very proud of the pieces you created. She often said you were a genius."

"Dear Willow was too kind and too generous!" He dabbed the corner of each eye with a royal blue handkerchief. "I have on my computer photos of several of the pieces she purchased over time from various estate sales. She asked me to reimagine these pieces as something more modern."

"Those photos would be amazing to have for my article. With such a unique fashion angle, I'm sure the article will be picked up for national, and probably international syndication!" Holly declared enthusiastically.

Allard smiled, pleased by the thought of gaining greater recognition for his work. "I will send you all these photos, just give me your text or email. I'm sure Willow would have been delighted to share how these old pieces became new."

"That would be wonderful," Holly exclaimed.

Her warmth and enthusiasm encouraged Allard to take a step closer, and whisper into her ear, "I must tell you a secret. I think our little Willow was perhaps a very naughty girl."

"How so?" Holly said with feigned shock.

"I have a friend in Paris—a private investigator, Roger Guilbert. He was hired by Willow's lawyer, Monsieur Finch, to spy on Willow and her lover Kozlov—the famous Russian violinist."

"How did Roger come to tell you that?"

"He read online that Willow had been murdered, and he called concerned that perhaps the husband asked this Finch to find out what his wife was doing with this man! Roger thought maybe the husband did not want to contact him directly...How you might say, 'get dirty hands'—oui?"

"Oui! How did you come to know Guilbert?"

"He has worked for both my company and for Henri. We both need security now and then. He knew, of course, of Henri's connection to Willow, and my connection to Henri. Paris is smaller than its reputation, mais oui? He's been most worried that the proof he provided of Willow's, what would you call it?..."

"Indiscretion?"

"Oui! This indiscretion may have led to her murder."

"Really?"

"A jealous husband can be most dangerous. Certainement?"

"That's what I've been told," Holly said with a smile, determined to appear unfazed by this brief but spectacular exchange.

E ddie followed James down into the reception hall, where he and his wife talked with William and stood by his side as he continued to greet and thank his neighbors for their attendance.

When, finally, James wandered over to the refreshments table, Eddie walked up and introduced himself. "Would you have time to see me tomorrow? I want to ask you a few questions about the late Mrs. Adams."

James slipped Eddie his card and said, "I should be in the office all day. Anything I can do to help, of course. Just call my secretary in the morning."

"Happy to, Mr. Finch."

"Are you making any progress in the case?"

"Right now, I've got more questions than answers. But you have to take it one day at a time."

As Eddie walked off, James once again thought of the phone calls he had made to Willow. He suspected that the topic would be raised when he and Eddie spoke.

Just as they stepped outside the church and began the walk back to their car, Oscar and Gloria heard a voice behind them, "Excuse me."

They both turned to find an older gentleman with unruly white hair and bright blue eyes.

"I'm Bob Ivan," he said, sticking out his hand.

Gloria, emotionally exhausted, looked down and said, "You're not with the press, are you?"

"No, not at all. I'm an attorney here in Marin. I was planning on calling you both tomorrow."

"What did you want to see us about?" Oscar asked impatiently.

"Your daughter came to me shortly after her marriage to William Adams. She had no will and asked that I prepare one for her." He handed them a business card. "Here is my phone number and address."

"But why would you want to talk to us?" Gloria asked.

"Your daughter never spoke to you about her will?" Bob asked with a look of complete surprise.

"Neither of us has any idea what you're talking about," Oscar said, hoping to be left alone.

"Well, that's certainly a surprise. We shouldn't go into all the details standing out here on the street, but Willow left both of you the bulk of her estate." Bob waited a few moments for the obvious shock of his words to sink in. "At your earliest convenience, I'd like you to come to my office so that we can review her bequest."

"I...beg your pardon?" Oscar said, appearing to have not understood what he was just told.

Bob leaned in. "With Willow's unexpected death, it will be some time before the will is settled in probate. But when that's done, you'll receive nearly two hundred million dollars. We'll discuss the details when we meet. Just call me at your earliest convenience."

The aging lawyer reached out once more to shake hands and express his condolences on their loss. "Such a tragedy. Your daughter was so young and so beautiful."

This time Gloria held Bob's hand as if it were a lifeline.

He gently patted the hand of the bereaved mother, smiled kindly at Oscar, then turned and walked off in the opposite direction.

Shaken by this unexpected news, Oscar and Gloria walked two blocks farther to their car. Once inside they were both too astounded to speak. They rode home in silence. Finally, after they walked back into the small home they once shared with their only child, they held each other and cried for a very long time.

CHAPTER THIRTY-FOUR

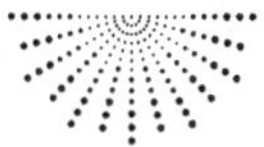

Sylvia and Holly were two of the last people to leave the church. Stunned by what they had learned, they walked in silence down Bayview Avenue toward Sylvia's car.

They came out of their fog when they encountered Eddie leaning against the front fender of his car. Studying text messages on his phone, he looked up as they approached. "Did either of you come up with anything of value?"

Simultaneously they answered, "You won't believe what I heard!"

Happy to see their enthusiasm, Eddie smiled. "Great! Where's someplace we can talk?"

"My place is two minutes from here," Sylvia offered.

"I'll drive you to your car, and you can lead the way."

"No need, my car is less than half a block away. Where's Rob?" Sylvia asked.

"Karin was having a meltdown over the kids, so he took off."

Five minutes later, Eddie and Holly sat down at Sylvia's kitchen table, while she busied herself making tea.

"I don't know about the two of you," Holly began, "but I struck gold."

"I think I did too," Sylvia added.

"I'm all ears," Eddie said, removing his pocket pad. "Holly, go for it."

"Jacques Allard told me several new pieces he made for Willow were from the jewelry she bought through an agent who attends estate sales. Here's the best part—I said I was writing an article about the new pieces that Willow wore to the Belvedere Ball, all of which he designed. Jacques offered to send me photos of the pieces, both before and after, that he stored in his computer. He'll be back in Paris in a couple of days."

"I'm betting that Pamela and Julia's pieces are going to be in that collection of photos," Sylvia said.

"I wouldn't wager a dime against that," Holly replied.

Sylvia brought over three cups of tea and some cookies, setting everything in the center of the table. "I think everybody at the reception had time to eat something, except us."

"I was shocked at the story Willow's mother told me," Sylvia declared. When she finished, Eddie said, "Sounds like their little Willow was a sociopath."

"That's what I told Sylvia a couple of days ago," Holly added quickly.

"But did this, or any other theft, serve as a motive for her murder?" Eddie asked.

"I saved my best piece of news for last. Eddie, did you get to talk to William's partner, James Finch?" Holly asked.

"Just briefly. I'm hoping to interview him at his office tomorrow, why?"

"Allard told me he knows a private investigator, who was hired by James Finch to spy on Willow when she visited Paris recently.

Apparently, she was having a tryst with Viktor Kozlov, which confirms your suspicion regarding Willow's involvement with him."

"That seemed fairly obvious given the number of phone calls between them. But more importantly, this puts Finch in the spotlight," Eddie said. "I wonder if Adams asked him to have Willow watched?"

"Allard didn't know. He told me it was the reason the Paris PI reached out to him after learning of Willow's murder. The man was wondering if Adams was the one who put Finch up to contacting him about Willow's rendezvous."

"My conversation with Gloria Bukowski confirmed Willow's penchant for stealing, at least from those she appeared to dislike," Sylvia said. "That included her parents and a half dozen or more girls in her high school class.

"Sounds like my list of potential suspects is growing longer by the day," Eddie said with a shake of his head.

"It's certainly not getting any shorter!" Holly added.

As he drove home, Eddie realized that his investigation was going in a variety of different directions, many of which, while interesting, could be blind alleys.

When he got home, Eddie wrote up all his case notes from the time that he learned of Willow's disappearance, and then added all of what Holly and Sylvia had uncovered after Willow's funeral service. When he was done, he called Rob.

"What are you doing for breakfast tomorrow morning?"

"Wheaties, milk, orange juice, and coffee. Why? Do you want to join me? Fair warning—Karin won't let donuts anywhere near the house! She's on a no-sugar kick. Claims the kids have been getting all hopped-up at birthday parties."

"I've got a different idea. Let me swing by your place, pick you up, and we can grab some take-out at Bridgeway Café and bring it up to your office. I need to borrow that twisted mind of yours for a short while. If that's alright with you, Dr. Watson."

"Sure, Sherlock. My twisted mind and I will meet you at seven-thirty."

"Deal."

Armed with a couple of breakfast biscuits filled with eggs and sausage, along with a healthy side of hash browns, Rob and Eddie turned the corner from Bridgeway onto Princess Street. The sidewalks were quiet now, but in two hours would begin to fill with tourists looking for souvenirs of Sausalito to take home.

Rob unlocked the door to his office and climbed the steep steps. Eddie followed, still groggy from a nearly sleepless night.

They spread out their food on Rob's desk, and Eddie placed a chair alongside.

Eddie pulled out his notebook on Willow's homicide. "I need you to read over these notes and give me a fresh perspective."

"Sure, no problem."

After the first few hits of Kona coffee, Eddie's focus began to sharpen.

Rob looked up when he finished and said, "I agree that Willow had to know the person who flagged her down on Tennessee Valley Road."

"She was not the type to pull over to help a driver with a flat tire."

"Agreed."

They sat silently for a time, imagining Willow's final moments, then Rob said, "This law partner of Adams, James Finch, needs a close look."

"Absolutely. I'm calling his secretary this morning to get on his calendar for later today."

Rob stroked his chin as he thought out loud. "Given the calls Finch made to Willow and the PI he apparently hired in Paris, it seems possible that Finch was blackmailing Willow. What doesn't fit is, why would he kill the golden goose? To keep her affair with Kozlov off the radar should have been worth millions to someone with Willow's money. But with her death, the value of that video diminishes by ninety plus percent."

"With what Holly learned from Allard after yesterday's service, it could cut both ways," Eddie suggested. "If it turns out that Adams put Finch up to hiring the French PI, that creates a series of questions regarding Adams. Finch's contacting Guilbert could have been done at Adams' behest."

"True," Rob conceded, "but I suspect you're thinking what I'm thinking—it's unlikely Adams would go down that path. Finch is his longtime partner, so using him as a go-between with the Parisian PI is certainly possible, but wow, that would be a huge risk for Adams to take if he was going to punish his bride for having an affair. And by punished, I mean murder. It would be like leaving a trail of blood that leads right to your doorstep."

"Plus, Rob, if you'd seen Adams when he had to identify Willow at the morgue, you'd know," Eddie said as he shook his head. "I realize I've said it before, but if that guy killed his wife, he's a fantastic actor. And if Adams knew he was playing second fiddle to Kozlov—pun intended—with his money, he would have instructed the house staff to pack up her things, and have his chauffeur drive her away, probably giving her another hundred million bucks for promising never to call him again."

"Who does that leave?" Rob asked. "I can't imagine it was one of the Peninsula society women Willow robbed. They're far more likely to give you the cold shoulder than a hammer to the head."

Eddie laughed. "I agree. Pamela Botherton doesn't fit the bill. I spent time with the woman; she might talk you to death, but she is hardly the type to be out in the woods on a Saturday morning doing wet work."

"In what I've read in your notes and heard from both Holly and Sylvia, Willow was likely involved or at least in contact with some pretty unsavory characters. I don't mean LeBon's boyfriend, Allard. I would guess he had no idea those jewels were stolen, or why would he be sending Holly photos of the pieces Willow brought him? But given Willow's passion for taking what did not belong to her, there's no telling what kind of dangerous characters she knew."

"Agreed," Eddie said with an approving smile.

"From what I can tell, Willow's actual life was a swamp of lies and misdirection. Arguably well-hidden underneath a polished surface."

"My only way forward is taking a close look at every individual in her life."

"You mean the usual suspects?"

"Exactly!"

For a time both friends stood shoulder to shoulder, hands in their pockets, by the big window behind Rob's desk. They looked out onto Princess Street just as the tourist shops were beginning to open.

"Eddie, what if Finch was paying the guy in Paris to spy on Willow—not for Adams, and not to blackmail her for money, but out of jealousy or to coerce her into becoming, or staying, his lover?"

"Wow. That's out of left field, Rob."

"Were her calls to or from Finch limited to regular business hours?"

"Hardly. Some were early, some late, some on weekends; although many were during regular business hours. We did note that Finch placed many more calls to Willow than she made to him."

"Finch was talking to people at the wedding, bragging is more like it, about how he was responsible for putting Adams and Willow together. Their relationship predates her meeting Adams, that's for certain."

"Interesting the risks that you'll see people take," Eddie said. "But you've got to figure no matter how long Finch has practiced law in San Francisco, a guy like Adams could put a serious dent in Finch's future if he were indeed having an affair with Willow."

"True. But Willow had a legion of guys who appeared willing to follow her wherever she led. That Kozlov character was obviously one."

"I don't doubt that a lot of smart men have done a lot of dumb things over the love of Ms. Wisp. Perhaps James Finch was one of them."

"Eddie, I can't say whether Finch was capable of killing her or not, but I watched him up close at that wedding, and he struck me as a pretty creepy guy."

"You might be onto something Rob. Finch is deserving of a very close look."

"I'm not sure if I've made your job easier or harder?"

"I've got Canning breathing down my neck for some real progress in this case. And I don't have to tell you that the press can be like holding off a pack of crazed wolves."

"They're just people doing their jobs, Detective Austin."

"That would be your point of view. Well, maybe Finch will be the break I've been hoping to get. I haven't had a good night's sleep since I first looked into Willow's cold, dead eyes."

As Eddie turned to leave, Rob said, "Wait! There is a way you can tell if spying on Kozlov and Willow was an idea initiated by Adams or Finch."

"What's that?" Eddie asked as he turned away from the door.

"Willow's Customs records show the date and time she returned from Paris after meeting with Kozlov."

"And?"

"I think you would find your answer in her cell phone records soon after her return. You said the normal pattern would be Finch making several calls, and she either not calling back or calling him just once. If suddenly that pattern changed and now she is returning his calls, or even initiating phone contact, then it seems logical Finch had something on Willow, and she was attempting to negotiate with him about that. It could be money, sexual favors, or both. If investigating Willow was something Finch did on behalf of Adams, why would he be leaning on her? He'd just drop the report in Adams' lap and leave it at that."

"Rob, I must be overworked to have missed that one. You're absolutely right. If Finch ordered the surveillance of her and knew she was cheating on Adams, then he'd have the upper hand. And she would be calling him."

"Absolutely!"

"You make a pretty good snoop," Eddie called out as he hurried down the stairs.

"It's called being a reporter," Rob shouted back.

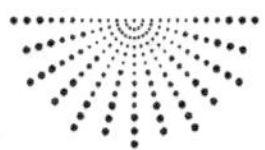

CHAPTER THIRTY-FIVE

Without hesitation, James, who had decided to work from home that day, suggested to Eddie that he come up to his house off Shady Lane in the Marin County town of Ross.

As he turned off Highway 101 and drove west onto Sir Francis Drake Boulevard, Eddie thought about his earlier conversation with Rob. Could Finch be the thread that unravels this mystery?

James greeted Eddie with a broad smile and ushered him beyond the entry foyer of the recently renovated Craftsman-style home, onto a comfortable side veranda that overlooked a shaded yard covered in lush green ivy, high above Ross Creek.

"Can I offer you something to drink, detective?" Finch asked.

"No, I'm great, but thanks. I have just a few questions, and I'll let you get back to the rest of your day."

Eddie, who had resolved to keep his comments non-threatening and straightforward, for the time being at least, ran through a set of easy questions:

How long had James known Willow?

What was his experience working with her as a client?

Did she speak of any enemies that she had or long-standing unresolved legal disputes with past friends or business associates?

How long had he known William and worked as a partner in the firm?

James made every effort to be exceedingly pleasant. He gave comfortable, wordy responses, filled with high praise for both Willow and William. James told, once again, of how he first introduced the couple on the night of the symphony's gala, and how delighted he had been to "watch as they grew in love."

"Yes, from what I have learned, they appear to have been a very happy couple," Eddie said, and then added, "but given their age difference, do you think she ever considered, well, having a relationship with a younger man?"

"Unimaginable," James snapped back without hesitation.

Having stepped across one of Eddie's tripwires with a blatant lie, Eddie confirmed his suspicion that Finch was a well-practiced liar.

"Willow was your client for several years. Any thoughts as to any enemies she may have made during the time you knew her?"

"Honestly, no. She was a remarkable woman. Very generous to all who knew her."

Eddie could have pressed on but resisted going further. Better to leave James with the impression that he had done a fantastic job in misleading him.

"Thank you for your time, Mr. Finch. I'll let you get back to your work. It's such a beautiful day I'm taking a half-day off and going home after lunch. My wife and I live in Sausalito, and we're planning an afternoon bike ride. We love going out to Baker Beach and up into the Headlands."

"Oh? So, you're a mountain biker?"

"Hard not to be with all the back roads, trails, and scenic overlooks we have in Marin."

"My wife and I both have mountain bikes. On the weekend Jade heads out riding, while I go off to play golf," he explained with a relaxed smile. "I always feel a little guilty because I know she's getting a much better workout than I am."

"Where does she like to go?"

"All over the county, but she likes the headlands best—usually going out through Mill Valley."

"My wife and I love that area too. We grew up in Marin, and we got into mountain biking when we were teens." Eddie paused, as if in thought. "In fact, I was thinking of getting her a new bike for her birthday, which is coming up in a couple of weeks. She's been using an old hand-me-down from her sister. What brand of bike does your wife like?"

"Well, if you've got a minute, I'll show you. We keep our bikes in the garage."

"Sure, I appreciate any suggestions you might have. I know my wife would love it if I got her a new bike."

This guy is trying so hard to make a good impression, Eddie thought. If I asked him to bake me a pie, he'd probably go straight off and turn on the oven.

The garage was a separate structure, located just steps away from the house. Like the main house, it had been redone from foundation to roof. After using an entry code to open the roll-up door, James waved Eddie inside.

Finch placed his hand on the seat of Jade's bike and said, "I think your wife would love a bike like this one."

"Wow, this is a beauty," Eddie said enthusiastically while hoping James wouldn't ask any detailed questions about the type of bike he was looking for, given the fact that neither he nor Sharon knew anything about mountain bikes. "I hate to impose, but would you have any idea what this bike cost?"

"I bought this one for my wife just a few months ago, from Caesar's Cyclery. It's a few minutes' drive from here on San Anselmo Avenue."

"Oh, yeah! I know the place."

"Let me run upstairs and take a look. The receipt is in a file in my desk. I'll have your answer in two minutes."

"That's very kind of you, sir."

"No trouble, Detective Austin. Happy to help."

Debbie Salem suggested that if Eddie got the opportunity, he should try to secure photos of any bike that Finch might own. If it wasn't for his spur of the moment idea to ask about a birthday gift for Sharon and sending James away to find the sales receipt, Eddie was prepared to begin a coughing fit, claiming an allergy, and sending James off to fetch him a glass of water.

Eddie quickly pulled out his cell phone, snapped several quick photos of James' front and rear bike tires, then did the same with Jade's two tires as well. He rotated each tire a third before clicking an additional photo.

Moments after slipping his phone back into his pocket, Eddie could hear James' footsteps on the gravel path that led from the main house to the garage.

"Sorry it took me so long."

"No need to apologize. Thank you for checking. Your wife's bike is a gem."

"Seventeen hundred dollars," James announced as if that amount was a pittance.

Eddie chuckled. "I'm afraid that's pretty steep on a detective's salary."

"You should go over there and mention that you were looking at a Diamondback Recoil Pro with an aluminum frame and twenty-seven gear combinations with Shimano shifter," James insisted. "If they have something comparable, you can probably get it for under a thousand dollars."

"Could you write that Diamondback model description on the back of my card? I'll get over there and never remember the entire name."

"Sure, no problem. Go over and check them out; they're a great bunch of guys."

"I'll do that."

James wrote down the model description of his wife's bike using his left hand, but the killer, as Max had explained, was assuredly right-handed.

Eddie hid his disappointment as he said, "Many thanks for your time and hospitality. It's been great meeting you."

Back in his car, Eddie headed straight to his department's crime lab. He knew there would be many more questions for James, starting with his numerous phone calls to Willow's cell and, most importantly, why he would hire a PI to spy on Willow. Finch was likely not the killer, but he might provide a path to the killer's doorstep.

And, what about Mrs. Finch? Rob might be correct that Mr. Finch was leaning on Willow for sexual favors. If that were the case, it's possible that Jade Finch knew about their relationship. Maybe that was the lucky break that Eddie hoped would fall his way.

CHAPTER THIRTY-SIX

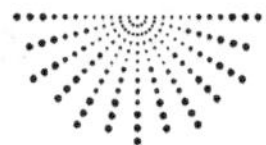

Hours after Eddie departed, Jade Finch returned home from a blissful day. She had a leisurely lunch with friends at Flores, the upscale Mexican Restaurant in Corte Madera's Town Center, steps away from the REI store she visited days before Willow's murder. After lunch, Jade made the short drive over to Nordstrom's at The Village for three hours of browsing in their Collectors department. There she rewarded herself with six thousand dollars in new fashions after what had been a very stressful week. In fact, this was the first day she had gone without thinking of Willow's murder.

Jade knew Willow was less than a minute away from her location along Tennessee Valley Road because of the GPS tracker she had placed on her car a week after observing Willow's rendezvous with her husband at the W Hotel. In her silent rage, she thought first of killing James, but Jade convinced herself that Willow had instigated the affair.

Willow's invitation to hike Tennessee Valley was an unexpected bit of good fortune that Jade could not pass up. If Willow kept to her plan to meet Holly and Sylvia at the trailhead, this was the moment she had to act.

Jade left home on her bike shortly past eight that Saturday and waited at the Starbucks in Tam Junction for Willow's car to announce that it was on the move. Once it had, Jade picked up her light blue REI backpack, tossed the remainder of her coffee in a trash bin, and completed the short ride to the pullout, where she waited for Willow.

Leaning her bike against a tree, well back and hidden from the road, Jade held onto the backpack, which contained the clear vinyl garment bag, the note from a "crazed fan," a bottle of Willow Wisp perfume, a nail, and a ball-peen hammer.

As she reached the road's edge, Jade uncapped a small container with a mixture of water, oil, and red dye and poured it down the side of her leg.

Quickly checking her phone's app, Jade saw that Willow was passing the small subdivision behind Tam Junction known to locals as Birdland. Her victim was less than a minute away. Jade smeared a little mud on her leg, above and around the mixture of fake blood. Pleased with her efforts, she anxiously looked down the quiet road; in less than a minute she spotted Willow's bright red Mercedes convertible with the top up to keep out the morning chill. Jade winced in pain and waved her arm in distress.

Willow could hardly believe her eyes. Oh, my God, that's Jade! Instantly, she went hard to the brakes and parked sixty feet beyond the pullout.

Willow practically leaped from her car.

"Jade, you poor dear! What are you doing here and what happened?"

"My plans for the wine country trip got canceled last night when one of our group came down with the flu. This was such a beautiful morning I decided to take advantage of it. I was taking a back path through the woods when my bike hit a rock. I went flying over the handlebars."

"Let me take a look at that cut," Willow cooed.

"Oh, it's not a big deal. It isn't all that deep—more like a really nasty scratch. The bad part is that I hit my head when I landed. Thank God I was wearing my helmet! I just don't think I can bike back home to Ross right now. James is out, and I can't get a signal on my cell. I'm not even sure if the bike is in good enough shape to get me home if I tried."

"Jade, don't be silly! I'll take both you and your bike back home. I think you've had enough adventure for one day."

As Willow walked over the wet leaves, she thought how little she liked the idea of putting Jade's filthy mountain bike in the trunk, or worse, on the back seat of her pristine car. But this was undoubtedly her moment to shine by assisting poor Jade, who limped gamely behind her.

Perhaps later, after getting Jade home and giving her time to shower and change, Willow could take her to brunch, and raise the topic of James' constant pursuit of her. It would be a bold act, but she was determined to put an end to Finch's unwanted advances.

Jade's stomach tightened, and she wondered if she could act now that the perfect moment had arrived. Her impulse to destroy the woman who had brazenly ensnared her husband and ruined her marriage, however, was overwhelming. All her planning and preparation could not be set aside. Jade knew she would never have a better opportunity. She willed herself to be free of the slightest hesitation.

As Willow bent down to take a better look at the supposedly damaged mountain bike, her killer slid the ball-peen hammer out of her bag and cocked her arm poised to strike.

Into that blow Jade placed all the great anger she felt toward Willow, a woman who had everything, and now needed her husband as well! The vibration that went from the point of impact traveled up Jade's arm and through her shoulder like an unexpected electric shock. Willow's knees buckled, and then, without a sound, she fell onto her side.

Jade nervously looked around. Quickly she pulled a pair of blue surgical gloves from her bag and put them on. Blessedly, there wasn't a soul in sight. Next, she removed the heavy clear plastic garment bag out of her backpack. With surgical scissors, she hurriedly cut through every stitch of Willow's clothing. The final items she removed were a white cotton top and powder blue panties. Jade stuffed Willow's clothes into the blue denim backpack, taking care to remove the only thing she found in Willow's pocket: the keys to her Mercedes.

She rolled Willow's nude body face down against the forest floor and removed the crazed fan note she had sealed in a small plastic lunch bag. She used a thin, two-inch nail and the ball-peen hammer to strike the note into the base of Willow's spine.

Jade felt sure that Willow had expired because her shallow breathing had stopped and her skin felt cold to the touch. Once more she rolled Jade over, this time into the garment bag. Hurriedly she picked bits of leaves off her body before zipping the bag shut.

As a finishing touch, she opened a bottle of Willow Wisp perfume and poured its contents over the plastic bag and onto the surrounding soil. Quickly, she piled leaves, dirt, and sticks on top of the shallow grave. Jade waited to cover the very top of the bag. She wanted one last look at the famous fashion model's perfect features. One last scoop of leaves, dirt, and twigs, and Willow vanished into her shallow grave.

Jade walked farther back into the woods. There, she opened the eighteen-ounce bottle of water she had left alongside a cotton rag, which she used to cleanse off her imaginary leg wound and the splatters of Willow's blood that sprayed upward onto her killer's hands and forearms.

Jade biked back to Tam Junction, unknowingly passing Holly and Sylvia, who in turn failed to notice Willow's car in their rush to reach the Tennessee Valley trailhead.

Behind the strip mall that faces California Highway 1, Jade walked to a trash bin and dumped her backpack. Mission accomplished, she collected herself and strolled back into Starbuck's to treat herself to a Midnight Mint Mocha Frappuccino. Reaching into the pocket of her red and white nylon biking jacket, Jade pulled out some cash to pay for her drink. It was then she felt Willow's car key.

The problem was not the key; she never intended to move the vehicle, and the key would be disposed of in any one of a thousand trash receptacles between Tam Junction and Ross Valley. The GPS tracking device she left attached to Willow's car was the problem. Jade had no idea if that device could be traced back to her, but she thought it far too high a risk to leave behind.

Jade's heart was racing as she rode furiously back down Tennessee Valley Road. How could she have been so careless? Jade quickly forgave herself. She was so focused on the murder and preparation of Willow's body that this one detail simply escaped her.

It took less than ten minutes to bike back to the site. Jade pulled out a spare pair of surgical gloves packed in her jacket and waited until the road was empty of traffic. Quickly she removed the GPS device, which was tucked up inside the rear passenger side wheel well.

Biking home, she made a quick detour to stop at one of the three dumpsters outside student housing at the San Francisco Theological Seminary in San Anselmo. There she opened a twist top oversized black garbage bag and tossed the GPS device inside. She biked another three blocks to another dumpster and disposed of Willow's car key in the same manner. Not for a single moment had she thought of removing and disposing of both her bicycle's tires.

James was in the city at his office, and Jade had the house to herself. She stripped off her blood-speckled clothes and put them in a large trash bag that she would dispose of in another dumpster one hour later. Standing under a hot shower, she washed whatever might be left of Willow's blood off herself and wondered how long it would take the police to find the body of the woman she despised.

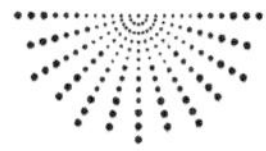

CHAPTER THIRTY-SEVEN

With each passing day since the murder, Jade grew more confident. Seeing everyone, including her husband, mystified by Willow's disappearance only added to her delight.

She regretted William's worry, and then his pain after the discovery of Willow's body. But Jade took comfort in the knowledge that she had unburdened her husband's partner of the woman he had married without careful consideration.

Jade was blissfully unaware of the visit Eddie made to her home or his interest in buying a mountain bike for his wife's birthday. James chose not to speak of Eddie's visit, convinced that it was routine and more confident than ever that any phone records revealing his frequent calls to Willow were attributable to attorney/client conversations.

As for calls to and from the Paris private investigator, if and when asked, James resolved to ascribe those to his overzealous concern that Willow was deceiving his longtime friend and law partner. He did not want to share such suspicions, however, without first confirming them through the use of Guilbert. Given the relatively brief time between his learning of Willow's promiscuous behavior and her death, James thought it best to leave William with the misimpression that his wife had been faithful. It was an easy enough lie for a man of his character and experience to tell convincingly.

As to any calls that went back and forth between he and Willow after her return from Paris, James would ascribe those to his failed attempts to get her to come clean to William regarding her affair with Kozlov.

Late on Wednesday afternoon, Eddie called Rob and asked if he and Holly were in the office.

"Yeah, Eddie. We're still here, working away. What's up?"

"Good! Stay there. I'll be over in twenty minutes. I have some news I want you both to hear. We're announcing a major break in the Willow Adams case tomorrow morning at ten."

Holly, who was usually anxious to head home and take one of her early evening walks, felt this was more than enough reason to stay late.

"Whatever Eddie's going to announce tomorrow, I'm glad we're getting it now before tomorrow's deadline for the Peninsula edition," Rob told Holly, while wondering if James Finch was indeed the killer.

Eddie arrived twenty minutes later and began by thanking Rob. "Your curiosity about James Finch was spot on."

"So he was the killer?" Rob asked excitedly.

"Nope. But you were very close. We're arresting his wife, Jade Finch, for the murder of Willow Adams."

"Jade!" Rob exclaimed. "How did you land on her?"

"A gift from the gods: mountain bike tire tracks very close to where we located Willow's body. An impression we made at the scene matched her front bicycle tire perfectly. After that, all the pieces fell into place. The ironic part of it is that I suspect she killed Willow for having an affair with her husband, when I'm quite sure it was her husband who was pressuring Willow into having sex with him," Eddie said, dazed by the irony of it all.

"Wow," Holly said in stunned disbelief. "James Finch better hope the jury sends his wife away for a very long time. If not, he might be the next one to get a hammer to the back of the head—which, I can honestly say, would be okay by me."

The following day after he returned to his Paris home, Allard sent Holly an email with a dozen photos of Willow's favorite jewels. As expected, the pictures accounted for Botherton's and Hassie's lost gems, along with the wedding rings of Oscar Bukowski's parents and several other missing items dating back to Willow's years at Marin Academy.

Kozlov recorded an album of violin solos he called "A Willow in the Wind," and went on an international tour promoting his work and speaking freely to journalists of his "much deep love of Willow."

In the weeks and months that followed, the sordid stories of James, Viktor, Jade, and Willow all unraveled in full view of an astonished public.

One shocking disclosure after another drove William Adams into an increasing state of isolation. The twice grief-stricken billionaire walled himself off from the continuing news coverage that detailed a deluge of "shocking revelations."

Three unauthorized biographies of Willow Wisp appeared within a year of her death and the subsequent trial and conviction of Jade Finch—the most popular of which, "A Scent of Deceit," put sales of LeBon's bestselling perfume into a death spiral.

By the time the scandals were all played out, William Adams

wondered how he could have been so foolish. The beautiful woman he had called his delicate flower was a fraud. And while he regretted her unfortunate end, he was pleased to be rid of his wicked wife.

THE END

NEXT UP!

THE PHANTOM PHOTOGRAPHER

(Book 3)

Michael Marks, the community-spirited volunteer photographer for the picture perfect town of Mill Valley, always has a smile on his face and a camera ready to capture his adopted hometown's many community events.

Not only is Michael one of Mill Valley's most popular citizens, he's also a source of wonder to his neighbors. How can this camera store clerk, who lives year-round in sweatshirt and sweatpants, afford to dine in the town's most expensive restaurants?

His sudden death puts Mill Valley's rumor mill into overdrive. Was he just a generous eccentric with a particular passion for pleasing others? Or, was there another side to Michael Marks: a side that only his victims ever have the chance to see?

HOW TO REACH MARTIN

Martin Brown is an author and journalist whose articles on health and relationships have appeared in *Redbook, Playboy,* and *Complete Woman* magazines.

He and his wife, novelist Josie Brown, live in the city of San Francisco, where their grown children and granddog also reside.

For more Murder in Marin mysteries visit:
murderinmarin.com

Or go here to quickly sign up for Martin's newsletter:
subscribepage.com/MartinBrownEletterSignUp

You can also find Martin at:

facebook.com/MartinBrownCA

twitter.com/MurderInMarin